GOING
UNDERGROUND

It's not about living in the
past,
it's about living with it...

GOING UNDERGROUND

By

Suzie Tullett

Mirador Publishing
www.miradorpublishing.com

First Published in Great Britain 2011 by Mirador Publishing

First edition: 2011

Any reference to real names and places are purely fictional and are constructs of the author. Any offence the references produce is unintentional and in no way reflect the reality of any locations or people involved.

A copy of this work is available through the British Library.

ISBN : 978-1-908200-22-8

Mirador Publishing
Mirador
Wearne Lane
Langport
Somerset
TA10 9HB

For Robert, Adam and Ben

You are my life.

CHAPTER ONE

FUNERAL PYRE

"There's a distinct musical theme to this funeral, isn't there?" whispered Tracey to Jonathan and as she took another look around at the other guests, she was beginning to wonder what she'd gotten herself into.

There was certainly a motley crew of mourners amongst the congregation, she noted, and mainly from the Mod scene, judging by the number of replicated Paul Weller haircuts in attendance. Although it wasn't a look that everyone could carry off, she couldn't fail to discern, especially when it came to men of a certain age.

"I take it they're all life long fans?" she asked, once again leaning into her husband. "Either that or they're all struggling to grow old gracefully." However, unfortunately for her, it seemed Jonathan didn't quite appreciate her concerns; *then again, how could he?* she asked herself, bearing in mind his eyes hadn't stopped facing forward since their arrival.

"Shush!" he insisted instead and wondering why he was getting his knickers into such a twist, she was, after all, only making an observation, she was forced to turn her attentions back to the actual service.

Not that Tracey thought things were much better when it came to the Vicar either – although to be fair to him, she could see he was at least *trying* to get on with things.

Poor chap, she couldn't help but muse, deciding he wasn't just a bit young for a man of the cloth, but also clearly new to the profession, considering his nervous disposition. Quite an affliction taking into account his range of duties, Tracey considered, at the same time having to concede that with all the commotion taking place courtesy of the deceased's mother, under the circumstances she'd have probably struggled to keep on track too.

"Why does she have to keep doing that?" she asked, genuinely troubled.

But much to her annoyance, Jonathan only demonstrated the same lack of shared solicitude on this particular matter as he had over all the dodgy coiffuring.

"It's very annoying..." she complained.

She supposed it could've been the sight of Malcolm's coffin laid out before her or the target flag that was smoothly draped over it, serving to provoke images of Malcolm's tragic and untimely demise. Yet whatever the reason and much to Tracey's continuing consternation, every time the Vicar got anywhere near to mentioning her son's name, Mrs. Riley would let out a long and unnerving wail. On top of that, his anxiety mixed with her rather loud lamenting meant the Vicar kept losing his place – which, in turn, meant he then had to start reading his carefully constructed notes all over again and so the cycle continued. Leaving Tracey no choice but to admit she'd never been to a service quite like it, what with stuttering Vicars and all that unnecessary bemoaning.

Yes, she'd seen stuff like this on the telly; a funeral on Coronation Street or Eastenders just wouldn't be the same without some sort of fiasco taking place to disrupt events. Nevertheless, to experience such happenings first hand was all new to her and the idea of life imitating art imitating life was leaving her feeling almost as nervous as the Vicar. After all, if Mrs. Riley really was going to come over all Peggy Mitchell like and suddenly throw herself face down onto the coffin, it wasn't as if in real life someone was going to shout *Cut!* was it, thus giving everyone the opportunity to then try a more sedate approach to their mourning. Although if someone didn't do something soon, Tracey was convinced there was a real possibility they were going to end up sitting there all day.

"Oooh!" she suddenly winced, at the same time taking a sharp intake of breath. Moreover, as Tuesday suddenly shifted position in her heavily pregnant belly she didn't just feel the resulting pain, included in her discomfort was an almighty surge of guilt.

It was as if her unborn baby was reminding her that she, herself, was about to become a mother just like Mrs. Riley. And this being the case shouldn't she, therefore, be more charitable and understanding in her thoughts? Furthermore, wouldn't she, too, be so out of control with grief if, *please God no,* she also had to bury her own child...?

It was a fate too disturbing for the mother-to-be to even contemplate and she automatically looked to Jonathan, taking hold of his hand, for some sort of reassurance.

"You okay?" he asked, giving her palm a gentle, comforting squeeze in return and despite this not being quite the word she would've used to describe her current state of mind, Tracey did appreciate the gesture, crossing her other fingers and nodding to the affirmative regardless.

But as she, once again, attempted to get back to the service, it wasn't as if she could now concentrate. Instead, she felt like she could have kicked herself, knowing full well she had to take at least some of the responsibility for the predicament she was now in. After all, if she hadn't gotten it into her head that her husband was harbouring some sort of mysterious past to begin with, she acknowledged, then she wouldn't even be at this funeral. She'd be safe and sound where she belonged, away from all this misery. Away from all these peculiar people that Jonathan had made clear he hadn't wanted to reacquaint himself with anyway.

On the other hand, that wasn't to say she was prepared to shoulder all of the blame either, she counter-argued. After all, if her husband hadn't been so insistent on keeping everything about his former life to himself from the start; if he'd only opened up to her a bit more over the years. Then there would have been no reason for her to be suspicious to begin with. There'd have been no deep, dark past just waiting to be discovered.

Just imagine how you'll feel if you don't go to his memorial, Jonathan? she recalled herself saying to him. *You need to go, it'll give you closure...*

Manipulation at its very best and looking back, such was her growing curiosity she'd known all along these words had been meant more for herself than they had for him and as she looked about the congregation once more, she couldn't help but wonder if the woman at the centre of all Jonathan's secrecy was somewhere amongst them.

Not that he'd ever admit there's a woman involved in any of this, Tracey begrudgingly thought to herself.

Oh no, it was the well fingered snap shot she'd found hidden deep inside his wallet that had told her that.

CHAPTER TWO

NEWS OF THE WORLD

"This is going to be One... Long... Funeral..!" a male voice from over in the next aisle suddenly somewhat miserably and rather loudly proclaimed. "And I'm bleedin' dying for a fag..."

However, be that as it may and shocked by such a blatant lack of respect, as Tracey looked over to see the voice belonged to a forty-something year old adult, she wondered how on earth a grown man could reach such an age without having yet mastered the art of whispering.

At least I only murmured my complaints, she told herself and whilst she readily admitted he might have only been saying what she and, no doubt, everyone else was thinking, she also had to ask if he really needed to make such an announcement about it?

Worse, he didn't even seem to notice her own or anyone else's dirty looks that were now flashing his way thanks to his rudeness. It seemed the only disapproving frown he was concerned with, was coming from the twenty foot effigy of Christ on the Cross staring down onto the whole congregation. Leaving Tracey unable to help but question if he was in some way mentally challenged, especially when she then saw him begin slowly leaning first over to his left, then to his right and back again, giving her the distinct impression he was actually checking to see if the idol's eyes really were following him.

Jesus! she thought to herself, momentarily forgetting where she was.

Although whatever problems she, herself, might have been having with the man's behaviour, she knew they had to be nothing compared to what the poor woman sitting next to him was going through. Obviously his partner in life, she presumed, judging by the way the woman was currently flushing red and having to smile politely and apologetically on his behalf – something Tracey insisted she would point blank refuse to do for Jonathan, should her own husband even remotely choose to behave that way...

All at once, however, her thoughts were interrupted when the church doors suddenly burst open and she found herself automatically turning along with everyone else, to see who would dare disturb the proceedings of a funeral.

Not that she should've been surprised by the arrival of a couple of late comers, she acknowledged. Latecomers who *also* seemed to think they were the bee's knees of the Mod world.

However, despite their get up, at least the female of the two had the courtesy to appear red-faced by the sea of disapproving frowns that greeted them. Unlike the male, Tracey noted, who didn't look at all fazed by the negative attention they were receiving; in fact, if anything, he seemed to be relishing in their grand entrance. Which again was hardly surprising, Tracey told herself, going off all the other odd balls that happened to be in attendance.

She watched them make their way along a row of less than accommodating mourners to the only free seats available and with quite an age gap between them, she found herself questioning the nature of their relationship.

Father/daughter? Uncle/Niece? she pondered and whilst she observed the male expertly continue to keep his cool, calm and collected exterior in check, she could see it was fair to say that for the young female, the Krypton Factor's obstacle course would probably have been easier.

"Sorry... excuse me... ouch!" Tracey heard her say over and over again, the poor girl trying her best not to trip over every set of feet in line as she attempted to get to their intended destination. Except when the two of them did finally manage to reach their seats, whereas it was clear the young woman, at last, felt able to heave a sigh of relief, for some reason it was now the guy's turn to tense up.

"Pepper," he said, formally acknowledging the man he obviously hadn't banked on finding himself sitting next to and as the two exchanged a civil but hostile nod, for Tracey it was more than clear that there was no love lost here.

Mmmm, she thought to herself, as she finally twisted back round to face forward.

I wonder what that's all that about then? she asked, curious.

CHAPTER THREE

TOO MUCH TOO YOUNG

The service now over with and at last back out in the fresh air, Pepper couldn't help but watch the rest of the congregation with interest, all keen to talk to Mrs. Riley before they joined their loved one on his final and sombre journey towards the crematorium.

You should've signed yourself up to a body farm like me, mate, he said to the deceased, having long decided all this pomp and ceremony wasn't just a waste of time, but a waste of good money too. *Yep, just stick me in a nice bit of woodland somewhere and be done with it,* he added. In fact, as far as he was concerned, leaving such a fine specimen of a body like his to medical science wouldn't just benefit humankind, it would also be gentler on the environment and didn't involve all that religious crap he'd just been subjected to on top of everything else.

Then again, he said, as he spotted Mickey P. loitering over by the headstones. *I suppose a send off like this can be much more fun...*

Having made a habit of appearing as if from nowhere, he decided it only fitting he should use the element of surprise on this occasion too. *After all, I wouldn't want to disappoint now, would I?* he said. And whereas a gravelled churchyard path underfoot might have been enough to signal the arrival of anyone else, he knew full well it would take a lot more than that to give notice of a light-footed commando type such as him. What's more, as he crept along at the same time careful to choose just the right moment, he waited until Mickey P. was about ready to savour the first intake of his proclaimed much needed nicotine fix – only then revealing himself to his target.

"Didn't think funerals were your thing, Michael?" he suddenly asked and making sure to employ the usual condescending tone he always used when it came to Mickey P., he was glad to see his arch enemy somewhat rattled by the unwarranted intrusion.

"Keeping tabs are yer?" he asked.

"Only on you Michael," Pepper replied. "Only on you."

He looked over to where the other mourners still gathered outside the church. "I see all the old gang's here," he said. "And all doing alright for themselves as well by the look of it."

Then he chuckled before returning his attention back to his old adversary. "All except you that is, eh?"

Smugly watching him throw his now ruined cigarette down to the ground and purposefully grind it out with his foot, Pepper knew Mickey P. wanted nothing more than to knock the smile off his face. Aware that if he played his cards right and pushed hard enough, that's exactly what he would do.

Which is why, he thought to himself. *It's time to up the ante.*

Thanks to their shared history, Pepper couldn't think of anything more pleasing than to have Mickey P. arrested for assault. After all, it wouldn't just get the man locked up for a very long time, brawling per se let alone on hallowed ground, would probably destroy his relationship with Andrea. Something which was more than an added bonus and the opportunities that might spring forth as a result, well Pepper could only imagine...

What's he doing here?" a woman's voice called out.

Damn! Pepper thought to himself – as usual, the voice signalling game over. *Talk of the bloody Devil!*

Not that Andrea's arrival came as any great surprise, he frustratingly admitted. Disappointingly, it was always the same when it came to these two. No matter where or when, the fun would be just about starting, Mickey P. would be almost ready to bite and then she'd turn up to save the day, just like some bleeding Fairy Godmother.

Well, not to save everyone's day, he woefully conceded. *Just Mickey P.'s.*

9

"Nice to see you too," he sarcastically interjected. Except the trouble was underneath it all, he knew he did actually mean it and as a result he couldn't help but let his eyes linger on hers for what was in all probability longer than strictly necessary – such was his admiration for the woman.

However, it soon became apparent that Andrea had taken this as him throwing down some sort of gauntlet, her returning glare just daring him to be the one who looked away first. And in trying to appear as confident as ever, this was a challenge Pepper knew he just couldn't refuse – even though he also knew Andrea could, indeed would, stand there all day in defence of one of her own if she had to.

But the last thing Pepper wanted was to lose face in front of Mickey P. and he told himself that if he concentrated hard enough, his face wouldn't, in fact, begin to redden under the weight of her stare. That if he focussed properly, he'd come out the other side the better man, with his pride still one hundred per cent in tact.

Nonetheless, as he fixed his gaze more than ready for the long haul, he quickly realised he should have known better, especially when his eyes suddenly and involuntarily began to divert.

Damn! he thought to himself for a second time.

Not that he was prepared to give Andrea and Mickey P. the chance to celebrate their victory and in sucking up his embarrassment, he was determined to ensure the upper hand was still his.

"Yeah well," he hastily excused, trying to give the impression he'd been in control of his eyeballs all along. "Some of us don't have the choice to stand here all day, do we... some of us have a job to get back to."

Moreover, as he began to saunter away, all the while determined to appear the epitome of self-control, he just couldn't resist making sure he definitely got the last word.

"Oh and about Friday, Michael", he called back. "Try not to be late this week, eh? There's a good boy."

CHAPTER FOUR

GHOSTS

"I still don't see what we're doing here," said Jonathan, as he somewhat less than enthusiastically swung his car into the pub car park. "We went to the service, surely that was enough as far as paying our respects go."

But having committed herself thus far, Tracey didn't see the point in not finishing what she'd started. Besides, just because the church service had turned into a bit of an ordeal, as far as she was concerned, that didn't necessarily mean the wake was going to pan out that way too.

"We're not stopping long," she easily lied, resolved to stay as long as it took. "Just a couple of drinks to show our faces..."

"But..."

"And then we'll be off."

She looked out of the passenger window and much to her surprise the building's exterior did actually look quite nice as far as venues went. What with its pretty, blossoming hanging baskets and nicely tended garden area off to the side. And with her spirits now beginning to lift thanks to what she'd seen, Tracey even began to think those die hard musical odd bods from the church just might have a modicum of taste after all.

"Come on then," she eagerly continued, releasing her seatbelt. "Let's go."

However, as she happily made her way to the entrance and pushed her rather reluctant husband through the pubs doors, as she did so she felt her confident smile suddenly and positively freeze.

Of course, she thought to herself, deflated, as she, once again, took into account the day's events so far. *I should have known something would be wrong somewhere.*

Not exactly the classiest of places and certainly not the kind of hostelry she would normally frequent, there was no getting away from the fact that this was obviously a pub for the hardened drinker. More to the point, as she looked about the place, the garish burgundy carpet on the floor was in the mother-to-be's mind, no doubt, hiding a multitude of spillages. Although looking at the dodgy, old guys propping up the bar, she wasn't about to postulate over what kind of spillages these might be.

Then there was the yellowy hue of the room's nicotine stained walls to take account of, a hue that was already starting to clash with the pink beer flushes forming on some of the mourners' faces. Something that caused her to question why the owners hadn't given the place a lick of paint since the introduction of the smoking ban; it had, after all, been in place for quite a while now.

Or maybe they have, she went on to counter consider. *Only to go and ruin it all over again, thanks to illegal, late night smoker lock ins!*

"Now can we go?" asked Jonathan, clearly hopeful thanks to her discomfort.

However, as attractive as it was to think that Jonathan might, indeed, have the right idea and that they should just do an about turn and go home, Tracey was not only determined to put a name to the face on the photo hidden in her husband's wallet, but to get the story behind the girl as well – which was why she decided to dismiss any notions of doing a runner completely.

Oh no, she thought to herself. *I'm not going anywhere.*

After all, whilst maintaining her social and hygienic standards was one thing, she knew it was quite another to miss out on what could be her one and only chance to do some digging. So if that meant being on the fringes of some secret, smoking sub-culture, then that's just where she had to be.

"Nope," she said, through gritted teeth and a false smile. "We're staying exactly where we are."

"Now you go and find us a seat," she then instructed, observing not just her husband's apparent disappointment, but also the ten deep queue at the bar. "It'll be quicker if I get the drinks."

"Yeah right," said a sulky and very much doubtful Jonathan.

Nonetheless, Tracey had long since learned that being pregnant certainly had its benefits, especially when it came to standing in line, or in her case, not. "Oh ye of little faith," she said, taking a large intake of breath in preparation of proving her point.

"Woman with Child!" she suddenly bellowed and in commanding such a depth to her voice, she was glad to see it not only seemed to shock her husband into paying attention, but also near enough silence the whole room. "Woman with child coming through!"

Of course, just as she expected, there was an automatic parting of the waves and, as people began standing aside to let her pass, it was an invitation Tracey was more than happy to accept – just not before turning to her husband and fixing him with a very satisfying, 'told you so' smile.

Jonathan watched his wife head off to the bar, before awkwardly looking around the room and taking a deep breath of his own. He knew he shouldn't have let Tracey talk him into coming here and admonished himself for not putting his foot down and having the inner strength to just say no.

Then again, he reasoned. If he had insisted more forcefully, Tracey's curiosity would've only been heightened even further. So talk about being in a no win situation...

He'd known all along that everything about today was going to be too close for comfort and his flight or fight reflexes were telling him to just bloody well get out of there. On the other hand, he also knew the jam he was in was entirely of his own making for not coming clean in the first place and he reproached himself once again, only this time for not having had the guts to tell the truth from the off set.

The trouble was, the longer he'd left it, the harder saying something had become. Until in the end he'd resigned himself to actually not saying anything at all. Even so, Tracey had proved herself anything but stupid over the years and it was as if she'd always known he was keeping schtum about something, leaving her to just bide her time to find out exactly what that *something* was.

Which is why I now have a wife who suddenly thinks she's a private investigator... he grumbled. *Although not a very good one at that, considering it's more than obvious what she's up to!*

Having originally planned to kibosh her mission altogether, Jonathan realised he'd underestimated just how persistent his wife could be when she wanted and as a result, having completely failed at that, he was now forced to resort to Plan B – seeking to get away with a simple case of damage limitation. And a quiet secluded corner in which he could conceal himself, one where he and Tracey could sip their orange juices unnoticed, was just the camouflage he needed. However, thanks to his wife's exceptionally loud vocal outburst, he recognised even finding one of those was no longer on the agenda. That thanks to her booming announcement, it seemed his cover had been blown even before he'd found it.

"Swifty!" a man's voice called out. "Swifty! Over here!"

It was a name Jonathan hadn't heard in years, yet his instincts mindlessly took over and he found himself automatically spinning round to locate where it was coming from.

Not quite the right reaction for someone who was trying to lie low, he quickly realised and Jonathan could've kicked himself for a second time; even more so, when he spotted that the voice actually belonged to Mickey P., with both him *and* Andrea now excitedly motioning him over.

However, under the circumstances the last thing he wanted to do was go and join them, especially with Tracey due to make an appearance at any given moment. But with nowhere to hide and the two of them already moving coats out of the way so he had somewhere to sit, what choice did he have but to accept their invitation?

Even if every fibre of his being was screaming at him not to.

CHAPTER FIVE

I'VE HAD ENOUGH

"Swifty Parkes..." said Mickey P.

"Yep... That would be me..."

"I can't believe you're actually here..." said Andrea.

No... Me neither... thought Jonathan, somewhat sarcastically.

Things had been decidedly difficult for him ever since he'd sat down. Not least because there seemed to be an air of expectation that he should be the one to say something of substance first. And whilst he fully appreciated why that might be the case, conjuring up the right words to start even the simplest of conversations was proving somewhat tricky. In fact, all he'd managed to come up with so far was a couple of uncomfortable smiles.

Still, chatting about where he was living now, what job he was doing or even a topic as safe as how lovely the weather had been of late just didn't feel appropriate. Then again, neither did talking about what had happened either. Although in sensing his hosts' anticipation that he was, indeed, going to bring it up some time soon, they clearly didn't share his view on the matter.

"So..." said Mickey P. "How long's it been?"

Leaving Jonathan with no choice but to respond with yet another uneasy smile.

He knew that when it came to anyone else, such a question would have been the perfect ice breaker; old friends who hadn't seen each other in a while quite often spent a few minutes trying to work this out. However, although it had been twenty-five years since they'd all last graced each other's company, a simple enough sum to get some sort of conversation going, when push came to shove, he had to admit Mickey P.'s question was actually quite pointless.

16

Pointless because Jonathan knew it wasn't just himself, but everyone present, who already knew the answer – twenty-five years ago being a time none of them were ever likely to forget.

Not that he altogether minded Mickey P.'s lack of tact. At any rate, *someone* had to come up with something to break the embarrassing silence that had enveloped them. Besides, he supposed some people just never changed. The problem was, Mickey P. had opened the door on a past that Jonathan had spent the last two and a half decades trying to keep shut and with Tracey lurking somewhere in the wings ready to pounce on every last available detail, he most certainly didn't want to talk about it now.

"We did mean to get in touch," broached Andrea. "But you know what it's like... the longer you leave something, the harder it is..."

Oh yes, thought Jonathan, praying to God that Tracey had somehow got held up at the bar. *I know all about that.*

He waved a dismissive hand. "It's okay. You don't have to explain."

"But I want to," she insisted and much to Jonathan's frustration as she prepared to continue on with her apologies regardless, unfortunately for him, he felt the big, black cloud already hanging over his head suddenly get a whole lot bigger.

*

"So this is where you've got to, Darling," said Tracey, pleased to see Jonathan actually sat in company, rather than tucked away in a corner all on his own somewhere as expected. And as such, as she approached the table she made sure to not only use her best telephone voice, but to also wear her friendliest of smiles, telling herself there was nothing wrong in wanting to create a good first impression.

Although it was just a shame not *everyone* had the decency to care about how well they were perceived, she was forced to acknowledge; her stomach all of a sudden sinking somewhat, as she recognised the first of her husband's hosts.

Please, no... she thought to herself, a look of disenchantment momentarily flickering across her face. *Not that disrespectful oaf in need of a cigarette.*

Only as she then resumed her well practised smile turning it onto the female seated next to him, rather disappointingly, she had no choice but to concede that her initial identification had, in fact, been correct.

"Come on then, Jonathan," she said. "Make room for a small one." Then, placing her two freshly bought glasses of orange juice down on the table, she ensured to maintain her gracious composure as best she could, as she squeezed both herself and her pregnant belly into the seat next to him.

You don't have to like these people, she told herself, all the while smiling politely. *You just have to interrogate them...*

Nicely, of course, she added, just as a reminder.

Or at least that would've been the plan had someone dared to speak.

"So..." she said, eventually coming to the conclusion it was about time someone broke the silence.

Not much of a preamble to get her investigations underway, she quickly realised, but being new to the detective game it was the best she could come up with. Unfortunately for her, however, even a gentle questioning wasn't going to be possible without some sort of formal introduction first, but as she eagerly waited for Jonathan to do the honours, none actually seemed to be forthcoming. And despite the fact that these two weren't usually the kind of people she would normally insist on sitting and chatting with, on this occasion it was a case of needs must and after a few moments of impatient yet polite silence, she finally nudged her husband into action.

"Well..." she said. "Aren't you going to introduce us?"

"Erm yes, sorry, of course...Tracey, this is Mickey P. and Andrea... Mickey P. and Andrea, this is Tracey, my wife."

"Pleased to meet you," said the mother-to-be, holding her hand out to first him and then to her and in deciding enough time had been wasted already, as her focus lingered somewhat on the latter, she delicately attempted to ascertain whether or not Andrea could, indeed, be the girl in Jonathan's photo.

Her blondish hair colouring certainly appeared similar enough, she noted, which told her she couldn't automatically rule her out. But then again, it was cut to a completely different shape. Not that that was much of a clue either, she acknowledged; after all, didn't most women go shorter as they got older?

Although I would've expected someone a bit more polished, she further considered. *Someone with a bit more flair and panache.* And as she thought back to all the effort she, herself, had gone to that morning, for goodness sake, even her own knickers were brand new, she realised exactly the kind of woman she'd been expecting to find.

Someone like me... she admitted – which this Andrea person most definitely was not.

In addition, neither was there any getting away from the uncomfortable atmosphere that weighed heavily around the table, Tracey noted, so there had to be some sort of history between this woman and Jonathan. Furthermore, ex-girlfriend meets current wife for the very first time would be quite a predicament under the most normal of circumstances, let alone when there was some sort of tangled chronicle in the mix.

Mmmm, she thought to herself. *Time to really start delving, me thinks.*

"So what have I missed?" she began, all innocence and smiles. "Reminiscing about the old days, no doubt?"

"Not really," Jonathan cut in. "In fact, we were just talking about Malcolm and the tragedy of it all. Weren't we Andrea? Mickey P?"

"Were we?" asked Mickey P., slow to catch on. "Oh right... yes we were, talking about Malcolm, that is."

It was enough to inform Tracey that her other half clearly had an idea as to what she was up to and she threw him an eyebrow in response.

So that's the game you're going to play is it? she silently asked and ready to take him on, she decided the best way forward from here was to simply stir things up a bit. To start challenging the one thing every single person in the room, bar herself, seemed to have in common – a love of all things 'Mod'.

"Well if you ask me," she said, pretending not to have noticed Mickey P.'s confusion. "It's no wonder he came to such a sticky end. Everyone knows those things are death traps, I mean just ask Jonathan. You've got a scooter in the garage, haven't you? One that you won't ride because they're so dangerous? Beats me why you bother hanging on to it."

"Maybe it's got some sort of sentimental attachment, eh, Jonathan?" asked Andrea.

A double edged question if ever Tracey had heard one and again, enough to tell her she was on the right track.

"I shouldn't think so," she said. "Jonathan doesn't do sentimental, do you, Jonathan? Not unless it's green and lives in a pot of some kind, eh?"

"He's a landscape gardener," she said, feeling the need to explain. "Just in case you didn't know..."

"Well Darling?" she said, once again, returning her attentions to her husband. "Do you...? Do sentimental I mean?"

Jonathan looked from one woman to the other, obviously feeling caught between a rock and hard place.

"I don't know. Possibly," he said. "Like you say, it depends what it is."

Again... Interesting, thought Tracey. Although aside of his conspicuous discomfort, she realised she should've known all along that that machine would have had something to do with something. Why else would he have kept it all these years?

"Anyway, we're not here to talk about me, are we?" continued Jonathan and despite Tracey knowing this was meant as some kind of hint, it wasn't one *she* was about to take on board, even if the other two were.

Especially not when she was on the brink of getting somewhere.

CHAPTER SIX

BOY ABOUT TOWN

"Mods! Modettes! How the hell are you?" a voice suddenly boomed out as if from nowhere, leaving Tracey somewhat frustrated by yet one more interruption to her investigations.

However, try as she might, it seemed her husband's shared history with Andrea and Mickey P. was a definite no-go area. All thanks to Jonathan's ability to stone wall her at every turn and the other two's loyalty in letting him get away with it. Plus here she was having to contend with another diversion, which was something she could've very much done without. And feeling like this was turning into a bit of a habit, she realised she'd no choice but to once again look round along with the others, to see who the voice actually belonged to.

Oh no, she thought, spotting the latecomers from the church fast approaching their table. *Please don't tell me Jonathan knows these two as well.* Unfortunately for her, there was no getting away from the fact that he clearly did and she had to endure the misfortune of her prayers being left unanswered.

"Swifty... My man!" the latecomer bellowed, making a bee line straight for her husband – and somewhat over zealously at that, Tracey noted; particularly when his words weren't just accompanied by a firmer than necessary handshake, but one that only just stopped short of a complete arm dislocation.

This chap obviously has something to prove, she observed, wondering if she should intervene on Jonathan's behalf. After all, she might have been irritated by her husband's success in slowing down her enquiries, but it wasn't as if she'd quite got to the stage of wishing him any physical harm just yet.

"Roger," Jonathan seemed to just about manage in return.

"Please," continued the latecomer. "Call me The Ace Face. Roger is so yesterday... don't you think?"

Only then did he release his grip.

The Ace Face! What kind of name is that? Tracey asked herself. Not that she had time to dwell on the subject, however. What with this rather strange man already taking hold of her hand and now bowing Walter Raleigh style to her Elizabeth I.

O...M...G...! she said to herself, her eyes widening in horror as he then did the unthinkable and kissed her fingers – a somewhat over the top gesture for both herself and the twenty first century, she couldn't help but think.

"The Ace Face at your service," he offered.

Then he just as quickly moved on to whom Tracey could only consider to be his next victim; mercifully giving her the opportunity to wipe her hand down the side of her dress – a necessary action that she just hoped no-one else had noticed.

"Now if my eyes don't deceive me..." The Ace Face sang. "The lovely Andrea..."

Tracey watched him pull her into a massive bear hug before he leant back slightly to take a good look at her.

"You haven't changed a bit." he said.

"What?" thought Tracey, incredulous. *"If she's the girl in the photo, then she's bloody well changed a lot!"*

She couldn't help but wonder why this man seemed to have to be so larger than life that it wasn't just cringe worthy, it was down right painful. Thinking it no wonder Jonathan had been so guarded about his past. After all, wouldn't anyone with friends like these? Maybe that was it, she considered. Maybe there hadn't been any skeletons in his closet at all; maybe his silence was just the result of sheer embarrassment. A theory Tracey was more than happy to give some credit, especially when The Ace Face then suddenly and animatedly began looking about himself, as if to say he'd lost something.

"Now where's my better half," he said, eager to do the introductions and grinning from ear to ear, as he proudly beckoned his companion over. "Everyone, this is Megan. Megan O'Melia, my girlfriend."

As Megan happily stepped forward, her hand out ready to greet everyone, Tracey found herself, once again, in shock. So much so, that she was forced to look to Jonathan for confirmation.

"Did he just say girlfriend?" she mouthed, although to be fair, her husband did seem just as surprised – as did Andrea and Mickey P., she duly noted, who seemed to have momentarily lost their tongues as well.

Quite understandable when seeing this woman at such a close range, assessed Tracey. In fact, the poor girl didn't just look young enough to be this chap's daughter as she'd previously concluded; in no more than her early twenties, she looked very much young enough, indeed. Not that it seemed to bother a man like The Ace Face, Tracey further clocked, whom, whilst in the process of slipping an arm around his girlfriend's waist, seemed to be quite enjoying the moment.

"Right," he said, using his free hand to raise his glass. "I'd like to propose a toast."

With nothing else for it, Tracey pulled herself together and alongside the others, she found herself following suit. It was, at any rate, only fitting that someone offer some sort of ode to Malcolm, she acknowledged; especially considering the supposed reason as to why they were all there in the first place was to commiserate the poor man's death.

"To Brighton!" The Ace Face said, instead.

"To Bri..." she and the rest of them began.

Mid sentence, Tracey looked to Jonathan once more for an explanation, just glad to see that once again, she wasn't the only one who didn't have a clue as to what this man was talking about.

And just as before, neither, it seemed, did Andrea or Mickey P.

"Lads..." said The Ace Face, clearly disappointed their collective toast had come to such a limp and premature ending. "You've got to come with me. It's what Malcolm would've wanted."

CHAPTER SEVEN

BEHIND BLUE EYES

"I'm really looking forward to today," enthused Tracey with a mouthful of toothpaste but not an ounce of guilt and even if her husband sulked until his bottom lip fell off, it wasn't as if she was going to change her mind any time soon.

As far as she was concerned, so what if Jonathan wasn't going to Brighton to scatter Malcolm's ashes with his long lost friends. It wasn't as if the deceased would know he wasn't actually there. And with regards to the other two, they weren't the ones expecting a baby in no more than a week now, were they? Not that Tracey felt she should've had to point a little issue like that out to her husband and besides, it was all his own fault they still had too much to do around here anyway. Like getting on with decorating the nursery for one; a job she'd been asking him to do for way too long now as it was.

"And whilst I'm thinking about it," she happily continued, mid spit and rinse. "Did you look at that list I gave you?"

She paused to glance at her husband through the bathroom mirror, awaiting at least some sort of response. But despite having finished showering ages ago, he continued to show no sign of movement at all. Instead, he chose to just stand there with his eyes closed, letting the hot, steamy water needlessly flow over him – along with her conversation, it seemed.

She efficiently rapped her toothbrush on the side of the sink, hoping to get her spouse's attention as well as get rid of its excess water. A successful action on both counts and she was pleased to see Jonathan finally open his eyes.

"The list..." she repeated. "...of names?"

26

"Sorry, I've been busy," he excused, at last switching off the shower and grabbing a bath towel to dry himself off with.

Sadly, this wasn't quite the response Tracey had been anticipating and she couldn't help but start to wonder if he really was just punishing her for putting her foot down? Or was there a genuine lack of interest with regards to their unborn baby at play? After all, at eight and a half months pregnant, who wouldn't think it was time they stopped referring to their unborn child as 'Tuesday'?

She thought back to that Tuesday night all those months ago, when her body temperature had yet again signalled ovulation and she'd yet again summoned Jonathan to the bedroom. *Not the most romantic of occasions*, she had to admit. *More a means to an end than anything else.* Still, that didn't explain why when she, as the mother-to-be, had been drawing up a list of potential baby names ever since, Jonathan, as the father-to-be, had been hell bent on keeping his enthusiasm tightly under wraps.

"I'll have a look later," he added. "I promise."

Not that Tracey could say she was one hundred per cent convinced by his pledge. But it did offer her just the excuse she needed to be able to push her concerns to one side – at least for now.

"Later," she said, half to herself and half to Jonathan, half joking and half serious. "That magic time when suddenly a whole host of baby related jobs will, at last, get done."

*

"Maybe she's right," said Jonathan. "I can't keep putting things off forever."

But whereas Tracey had been referring to all things baby related, he, himself, was talking about something entirely different; which was why, whilst she'd taken herself off shopping, leaving him under strict instructions to be ready, willing and able to start decorating the minute she got back with the paint, preparing the nursery for such a task was actually the last thing on his mind. And although now in the garage supposedly looking for paintbrushes, Jonathan found himself mooching about the place doing anything but.

Up until now, he'd managed to keep a reasonably tight lid on his cauldron of demons, letting its contents just quietly simmer away somewhere in the dark recesses of his mind. Suddenly, however, it was as if that big, black pot of his was starting to bubble over and he wasn't sure how long he'd be able to keep its lid in place. An understandable reaction after Malcolm's funeral, he told himself, considering in that one day he'd come face to face with everyone and everything he'd spent years trying to forget and all because his wife couldn't keep her bloody nose out.

"Cheers Tracey," he said, placing the blame for his feelings squarely on her shoulders.

He could just hear her now – *But why wouldn't you want to pay your last respects? Did you have a falling out or something? You must have had a falling out if you don't want to attend the poor man's funeral?*

On and on she'd gone until he'd finally conceded and agreed that she was right, they should go. So now and for the zillionth time, he was yet again telling himself it should have been him lying in that coffin and no-one else.

Oh, who was he kidding? he scorned, knowing underneath it all he had no-one to blame but himself. History was history – it could never be changed and neither could the way he felt about it.

So why, he had to ask, was he in such an emotional quandary over a frigging trip to Brighton?

It wasn't as if they were simply talking about three old friends revisiting the headiness of their youth here, was it? Reliving the good would also mean reliving the bad – something Jonathan didn't feel in any way ready to do.

Then again even if he did, there was still his impending fatherhood to think about as well and after everything he and Tracey had been through to get Tuesday in the first place, he couldn't very well risk leaving his wife to give birth on her own, now, could he? Not when it was so close. Plus early labours weren't exactly a rarity, therefore no-one was going to actually guarantee her waters wouldn't break during his absence and knowing his luck, he scoffed, that's exactly what would happen.

Still, none of this seemed to silence that nagging, inner voice that was growing inside of him. The one that kept telling him the very reasons as to why he shouldn't be going to Brighton, were, in fact, the very reasons as to why he should. The nagging voice that he wished would just keep quiet.

Frustrated, he suddenly grabbed at something, anything and violently threw it across the room. Not that this action made him feel any better, he acknowledged. Especially when he saw that he'd actually thrown a paintbrush and that it just happened to land next to the neglected Vespa sitting in the corner of the room.

Ironic to say the least, although at the same time he did have to concede the scooter was yet another obstacle that stood in the way of his taking a trip down memory lane.

Once his pride and joy, he would've had no problem racing up and down the streets of his hometown showing off his riding skills – now, however, it took every ounce of his courage just to sit on the damn thing.

Which was something else that that inner voice of his was suddenly suggesting he should try and do.

CHAPTER EIGHT

MARCH OF THE GHERKINS

"Friday is my most favourite day of the week," Pepper announced to his colleague, as he loitered in the office behind the enquiry desk.

Not a great revelation as revelations go, he realised, on account of everyone else liking Fridays too; it did, after all, signal the start of the weekend.

However, *everyone else* didn't have the added bonus of being able to assert their authority over their life long enemy, did they? he self-gloated. Of being able to accidentally misplace something as mundane looking as a bail register. So that a five minute job, a simple case of Mickey P. putting his mark on the dotted line before bidding a polite farewell, turned into at least an hour. Such was Pepper's power as a Police Officer and this week's hour, he happily noted, was fast approaching.

"Fifteen minutes and counting," he said, rubbing his hands together in eager anticipation as he registered 9.45am on the wall clock.

"Did I tell you I grew up with him?" he asked, finally taking a seat. Not that he was necessarily expecting an answer one way or the other, which he deemed just a good job considering he didn't actually get one. Although quite why his colleague had to bury his head so deep into his paperwork he wasn't really sure.

"I did you know," he continued, regardless. "And he's always been the same has our Michael. If it's shiny, expensive and more to the point if he doesn't even need it, then he'll nick it! Why he can't thieve drug money like normal people I'll never know."

He paused to check the time again; at 9.49 am he still had a bit of time to waste.

"Remember that song?" he went on. "It was in the charts years ago? That bloke sang it?"

And then he started to sing – badly.

Mind, as far as he was concerned it was of no consequence that he couldn't remember all the right words, or the song's proper tune for that matter. As long as he, himself, knew the point he was trying to make, which of course he did. Something else which was just a good job, he once again noted, seeing as his audience still wasn't all that attentive.

"He used to sing that to me you know..." he continued. "Today they'd call it bullying, but I suppose back then things were different..."

"Naturally *she'd* tell him off for it. She was always good like that was our Andrea... nice... you know... Still is in fact. Trouble is, she's still with him 'n all."

He let out a wistful sigh, not for the first time resigning himself to the prospect that he and she just might never be.

Then a bell suddenly rang out at the front desk immediately interrupting his thoughts and dragging him back to the here and now in the process.

"Hello, hello," he joked. "What's going on here then?"

He glanced at the wall clock once more, surprised to find it was still only 9.56 am.

"He's early!" he said, somewhat taken aback. "Mickey P.'s never early! I mean he might be a couple of minutes late sometimes, but he's never early."

He double checked the time against his wristwatch just to make sure.

"Must have wet the bed!" he remarked.

Then, as he got to his feet, he simply smartened himself up and set off with a confident swagger towards the door.

*

"Oh!" said Pepper, as he made his way out to the enquiry desk.

Ready to lord his supremacy over Mickey P., the last thing he expected was to be confronted by a complete stranger, let alone a rather upset one at that and as a result, he felt his trademark superior smile begin to droop somewhat.

"Me scooter's been nicked!" said the unknown male. "Me Lambretta!"

And you're clearly under the misguided impression that I'm in a position to help for some reason, Pepper thought to himself.

Not that he had any intentions of actually doing so, he secretly admitted. As far as he was concerned it was Friday and there was no way he was missing out on the one and only highlight of his week, simply because some alleged victim wanted to report an alleged crime.

"Right," he said, without giving away even the slightest hint of compassion. "If you just hang on there a minute I'll go and get someone to..."

"I was only in the shop two bloody minutes," the man interrupted – much to Pepper's annoyance. "And when I came out, some bloody bloke was riding it down the bloody street!"

Obviously a prized possession, considered Pepper. *Judging by your somewhat over the top response. But that's what you get for leaving the keys in the ignition sir, isn't it?*

It was just a shame he couldn't actually point the man's own stupidity out for real, he thought to himself. That would be far too unprofessional.

"Like I said," he instead began to repeat. "If you could just give me a moment or two, I'll be more than happy to get someone to assist you." But as he turned on his heels desperate to do just that, he frustratingly found the stranger to be equally as persistent.

"Beautiful machine," he cut in. "Runs like a dream. And the paint job... all shiny and expensive looking."

Pepper stopped in his tracks, all at once his attention now seriously pricked. "Shiny and expensive looking you say?"

He checked his watch again. At 10.02 am Mickey P. was late. Of course this could all just be a coincidence, he deliberated. Having not wet the bed at all, his absence might simply be down to a dodgy alarm clock. But Pepper knew from old just how much Mickey P. loved Lambrettas – especially the shiny and expensive ones.

He stepped back towards the enquiry desk with a smile and took out his pen, now more than ready to take down all the details.

After all, if his sixth sense was right, which it invariably was when it came to his long standing arch enemy, he told himself, it was becoming increasingly possible that this particular Friday might just turn out to be his best one yet.

CHAPTER NINE

GOING UNDERGROUND

The only sound breaking through the silence was the repetitive tick tocking of the kitchen clock – very annoying to say the least, particularly for a man who already knew he didn't exactly have time on his side.

Still, with Mickey P. and The Ace Face already out front waiting for him to join them, coming up with the right written words was proving just as problematic as the spoken and Jonathan continued to just sit and stare at the blank sheet of paper before him, struggling over what to say.

He knew the fact that he was still in two minds over the trip to Brighton to begin with wasn't exactly helping matters any. However, if he was to have any real peace of mind at all, he also recognised he had no choice but to finally face up to his past and at least *try* and deal with it. And surely Brighton, he thought to himself, would give him the best possible chance of doing that.

Nevertheless, there lay his dilemma. After all, hadn't Tracey had made her views on the subject more than very clear? As far as she was concerned, Jonathan was staying exactly where he was. So, with his bag already packed and his helmet dusted off, he just had to trust that once she knew the reasons behind his reticence all these years, she'd understand why he was about to go behind her back.

A scooter horn beeped outside, signalling its rider's growing impatience and with no time to write anything else, he simply put down the words: 'Sorry. Will explain everything when I get back' Then, as he hoped against all hope that that would be enough of an explanation until he did, indeed, return home, he put the note inside an envelope and gently kissed it, before placing it in the centre of the table.

He grabbed his rucksack and headed straight for the front door, finally letting himself out of the house.

"At last!" cried The Ace Face, relieved. "No more listening to him harping on about how good Lambrettas are, when anyone with any sense knows Vespas are by far the more superior machine."

Jonathan tried to raise a smile in response, determined not to let them see he wasn't really looking forward to the prospect of having to ride on either.

"Thought you'd changed your mind," Mickey P. called out.

However, as tempting as that was, Jonathan tried to at least appear steadfast in his resolve, as he locked the door behind him and began making his way down the garden path.

"Hang about here much longer," he quipped. "And I might just do that."

But he knew all the bravado in the world couldn't make up for the fact that he felt like he was about to risk his life as much as he was risking his marriage and as he took the pillion seat behind The Ace Face, he felt that very same feeling only intensify.

"Ready?" asked The Ace Face, donning his headgear and eagerly starting his engine.

"As I'll ever be," replied Jonathan, nervously ensuring his own helmet was securely fastened and his scarf well and truly tucked in.

Not that Mickey P.'s and The Ace Face's insistence on giving their departure a sense of occasion did anything to ease his sense of dread. In fact, their excitable beeping of horns and excessive revving of engines only served to make matters worse. And as they pulled away from the kerb, leaving a plume of two stroke oil smoke in their wake, Jonathan was just glad it was only his curtain twitching neighbours who could see the downright fear now written all over his face.

CHAPTER TEN

MAKING TIME

"I haven't seen him since the funeral," said Andrea, her denial almost enough to make Pepper laugh.

He hadn't just been in this game long enough to know when anyone was lying, he'd had enough dealings with Andrea to know exactly when she was lying too.

Although if he were to generously put Mickey P. to one side for the moment, as he glanced around the shit hole of an estate where she was living, he could to some degree appreciate her current lack of co-operation. Not exactly inhabited by the most law abiding of citizens, he could almost smell the criminality and what with its burnt out cars, gangs of youths and stray dogs wandering about the place, he could see why someone might choose to stand on their doorstep arguing the toss with the police, as opposed to being seen as helping them with their enquiries.

No, he thought to himself. *This certainly isn't the place for me – with or without this uniform.*

However, as far as he was concerned it wasn't the place for Andrea either; he just wished she could see that for herself.

"I've told you," she continued, Pepper's dreaming once again dashed. "We had a row and he upped and left."

He tried to sneak a look inside of the house behind her.

"Come on, Andrea," he replied, getting back to the task at hand. "You're gonna have to do better than that. Skipping bail's a serious business and he could get locked up for it."

He craned his neck to get an even better look, but she rather frustratingly went on to pull the door to and any potential clues he could have gleaned were ultimately blocked from view.

"Like I said," she further insisted. "He had too much to drink. We both argued and he stormed off. As to where he is now, your guess is as good as mine and no, I don't know when he's coming back!"

Pepper sighed, unable to hide his disappointment. Not only had he heard all this spiel before, she had her answers so off pat she could have been reading off a shopping list. So not for the first time when it came to this woman, he'd reached a stalemate.

"Well when you do see him," he said, at the same time unable to help but admire her loyalty, even if he did think it somewhat misplaced. "Tell him he's not going to laugh his way out of this one."

With nothing else for it, he began making his way back to his car, convinced he could feel her eyes burning a hole into the back of his head.

Probably making sure I'm definitely off, he told himself as he pondered over his next move.

Although I suppose I could always just wait here for Mickey P. to come home, he considered. *After all, he's bound to turn up sooner or later.*

On the other hand, taking into account both his current, somewhat dodgy location along with his personal safety, he decided that probably wasn't such a good idea, after all. Plus, as he'd already put a call out to his colleagues asking them to be on the lookout for a no good thief riding around on a Lambretta, he reasoned it would only be a waste of resources were he to drive around doing the same thing...

"Jesus Bloody Christ!" he suddenly called out, his thoughts all at once thrown into disarray as a car suddenly screamed into view. In sheer panic he felt himself immediately freezing to the spot, as the vehicle came to a screeching halt literally millimetres away from his torso. And, amidst what felt like a mini heart attack, with thoughts of an arrest for attempted murder now racing through his head, it was all he could do to pull himself together.

He very quickly, however, changed his mind again and thought better of bringing such dangerous driving to the attention of the actual driver. Watching her now fling open the car door and attempt to haul both herself and her humongous belly out from behind the steering wheel, as far as he was concerned hormonal women could be a force to be reckoned with. More to the point, as this woman wasn't just heavily pregnant but clearly about to drop, she was, no doubt, going to be more hormonal than most; which was why he chose to remain quiet on the matter instead, taking a moment or two to catch his breath.

Hang on a minute, he thought to himself. *Haven't I seen her somewhere before?*

Then, as she finally broke free of her vehicle and marched her way straight past him and on towards Andrea's front gate, he remembered.

Of course... It's Swifty's wife. They were both at the funeral together.

His policeman's nose began to twitch and he realised if he hung about long enough she might just provide him with the lead he'd been looking for. After all, in his experience whilst hormonal women had to be avoided at all cost, angry ones quite often said things they shouldn't and this woman seemed very, very angry indeed.

He bent down, pretending to fasten his shoelace. Corny, he knew, but sometimes the old ones definitely were the best.

"Please tell me you didn't know they were going to Brighton today either?!" she called out to Andrea.

"Yes!" said Pepper, secretly congratulating himself.

Not that getting the information he needed stopped him from feeling a bit sorry for Jonathan, being married as he was to someone who could make a question sound more like an order. Still, that wasn't his problem, was it? And more importantly, now neither was locating the whereabouts of Mickey P.

He watched Andrea usher her guest inside, knowing full well she'd be praying to God he hadn't overheard.

Not that anything's ever that simple anyway, he was forced to admit, realising he was going to have to do a bit more delving to find out exactly what Mickey P. was up to.

Although in hazarding what he considered a pretty good guess that it probably had something to do with Malcolm, he decided that Mrs. Riley would be his next port of call.

However, even then he knew he still had the little question of how he was actually going to get his hands on his arch enemy to think about, especially with him already being out of area.

CHAPTER ELEVEN

TIME FOR ACTION

Despite the fact that at Malcolm's wake everyone had swapped contact details and made numerous promises to keep in touch, Tracey hadn't for one minute believed that that would actually be the case. As far as she was concerned no-one she'd met there had been particularly useful to her investigations and it wasn't as if they were the kind of people she'd choose to mix with socially. Yet despite knowing all this and with no-where else to turn, here she was on Andrea's doorstep and not for the first time looking for answers.

"I can't believe he's done this," she fumed, as her hostess led her through to the kitchen.

However, once in there Tracey did begin to think it might have been a better idea to telephone first – unless the ambience of a Chinese launderette was now in vogue when it came to the supposed heart of the home, something which she very much doubted. Although as far as she could tell at least Andrea didn't seem to mind the numerous piles of just washed clothes sitting on what seemed to be every available flat surface. Her 'take me as you find me' philosophy in the end, not really coming as any great surprise.

And besides, Tracey told herself. *It's not as if you're here to compare notes on housewifery, is it?*

She forced herself back to the matter at hand, whilst looking for a free seat on which to park herself and unable to find one, she began pacing the length and breadth of the room instead.

"I just don't know what he thinks he's playing at..." she seethed. "Although I suppose you knew all along what was going on?"

"If you're talking about Brighton," said Andrea. "Then of course I knew."

Tracey watched her hastily retrieve a pile of clothes from one of the kitchen chairs and was, at last, finally able to plonk herself down. And having begun to feel a little bit dizzy herself, the mother-to-be could only imagine what all this unnecessary excitement was doing to Tuesday. Still, on the plus side, she drily conceded. If it did induce an early labour, at least there were plenty of clean towels on hand with which to get the job done.

"Well this," she exclaimed. "Is how I blooming well find out!"

She began to rummage in her handbag, eventually producing a rather screwed up envelope and throwing it down onto the table.

"Ouch..." Andrea sympathised.

"I know," said Tracey. "And when I get my hands on him, his life's not going to be worth living."

"Well at least you don't have to wait long then," replied Andrea, clearing the seat next to her. "They're gonna be there and back before you know it."

Nevertheless, for the mother-to-be that wasn't really the point.

"And if I go into labour in the meantime?" Tracey asked, viewing this as a genuine, not exactly unheard of, possibility. "Jonathan should be here just in case, ready to help me through it... Not gallivanting up and down the bloody country."

"As if that's going to happen," laughed Andrea. "From what you told me at the funeral, you're still not due for another week or so, are you?"

But as far as Tracey was concerned that wasn't pertinent either and all the reassurance in the world wasn't going to make the situation any better. One week or one day, it was all the same to her.

"Do you know how long it took us to get pregnant?" she asked. "Month after month of praying that yes, this time the test was going to show positive. Then when it finally happens, more to the point when we get to the home straight... what does Jonathan go and do?"

41

Her shoulders sank.

"I can't do this on my own, Andrea. I need him here."

She looked down and placed a protective hand over her belly.

"You know," she said. "Anyone would think he didn't want this baby."

"You could always phone him? Tell him to come home?" Andrea suggested.

"I tried," Tracey replied. "But he didn't answer."

"Then try again."

"I can't. I haven't got my mobile,"

"Well where is it?"

"In a million pieces all over the kitchen floor..." she explained. "When he didn't pick up I threw it against the wall. Not very clever of me as it turns out and certainly not very ladylike, but sometimes needs must. You know the feeling..."

"Here," said Andrea, reaching for her handbag. "Use mine."

"I can't," repeated Tracey, downcast. "I don't know his number..."

"Well who memorises numbers for Pete's sake?" she quickly defended. "I mean they're saved into the phone so it's not as if it's necessary..."

She started to feel a bit silly about it all and just sat there, wondering what to do next.

"You could ring Mickey P.'s phone? I could speak to Jonathan on that instead," she said.

"I can't," replied Andrea. "He hasn't taken it with him. Mind you, at least this time it was intentional. As per Roger's, sorry *The Ace Face's,* instructions... some sort of male re-bonding fest I think. No interruptions and all that."

Tracey raised an unimpressed eyebrow.

"I know, I know. I'm with you. But who are we to judge what goes on in a man's head?"

Tracey could've cried. However, unaccustomed to showing her innermost feelings to relative strangers to start with, she decided she had no choice but to try and come up with another solution.

"Well I suppose there's nothing else for it," she said, after a moment's contemplation. "I'll just have to go and get him. Bring him back."

"You can't do that!" exclaimed Andrea, visibly identifying all the risks that might entail. "I mean I'm all for direct action when it's called for, but what if your contractions start when you're half way down the M1?"

"So you do think Tuesday's going to make an early appearance then?" asked Tracey, contrary to what her host had implied only minutes earlier. "Which is all the more reason why I should go."

"I'm not saying that," Andrea defended. "Though you have to admit it is a possibility."

"Well what choice do I have then?" asked Tracey, determined. "I've already told you I'm not having this baby without him."

"Alright, alright," Andrea conceded. "But you're not going on your own, I'll have to come with you. Just let me make a couple of calls to sort the kids out first."

*

"You're joking aren't you?" Andrea bluntly asked, as she locked the door behind her. "That thing only just gets me to work of a morning. There's no way it's going to get us to Brighton and back. We'll have to go in yours. "

Except Tracey wasn't sure if she wanted someone else behind the wheel of her brand new saloon and had hoped the battered and bruised exterior of the old Fiesta she was now standing next to actually belied a rather solid and reliable engine.

Although a quick glance around the neighbourhood and she did find herself starting to re-assess the situation somewhat, realising there was a distinct possibility of someone else taking her own car out for a spin, even if Andrea didn't.

And at least mine's already fitted with a baby seat, she told herself. *Should the worst, indeed, come to the worst...*

"I suppose you'll be wanting these then," she said, reluctantly rooting in her handbag for the keys and tossing them over. "Just make sure you're careful. The last thing we need is to be involved in some sort of accident."

It was obvious Andrea had never driven something as brand new as this before, observed Tracey. Judging by the mixture of excitement and nerves the woman demonstrated as she climbed in. *Or as clean,* Tracey further mulled, having already noted the number of empty sweet wrappers and children's toys strewn all over the inside of the Fiesta – as well as the number of scuff marks on the upholstery, she added, and the amount of dust in the foot wells.

So why did her driver no longer seem keen to get going?

If anything, Tracey would've thought Andrea would be chomping at the bit to get the keys in the ignition. Instead, her initial anticipation seemed to be faltering somewhat.

"Well come on then," said Tracey. "What're we waiting for?"

"I haven't got a driving licence," Andrea eventually admitted, scrunching up her face as she awaited a response. "I've just never got around to sitting my test, although I do have a provisional..."

"And I'm not a bad driver," she hastily continued. "So I'm sure we'll be okay."

"I don't think so," replied Tracey, unable to even consider letting her touch the accelerator after that little announcement.

"Well if not me, then who?" asked Andrea. "It's not as if you're in any condition to drive all that way, is it?"

Tracey thought for a moment and having gotten herself into this mess, thanks to her insistence she and Jonathan attend Malcolm's funeral in the first place, she was just as determined to now get herself out of it.

And that, she told herself, didn't involve giving up at the first hurdle.

"We could always ask someone else to drive?" she optimistically suggested. "Someone else with their own car?"

Then, as she and her travel companion put on their thinking caps, the only question left was who that someone could be?

CHAPTER TWELVE

DRIVING IN MY CAR

"Did you know," asked Megan. "That the name 'Louise' actually means 'famous battle maid'?"

All very interesting, considered Tracey, at the same time wondering what on earth the girl was going on about. *But a simple 'yes' or 'no' will suffice.*

"And everyone knows that grief can make people do things they wouldn't normally do, don't they?" she continued.

Yep, now I'm completely lost, the mother-to-be couldn't help but tell herself – unable to quite connect the two statements in relation to each other, let alone with a request to drive both her and Andrea down to Brighton.

"And should one particular famous battle maid feel the grief stricken need, the last thing I want is my Ace Face in a position where he has no choice but to oblige, isn't it?"

"Right..." said Tracey and in realising this was all somehow part of Megan's decision making process, she found herself slowly nodding in agreement - despite not having a clue as to what it was that she was actually agreeing with.

In fact, none of what this young woman was saying was making any sense whatsoever and she began to wonder if this had been such a good idea after all.

She looked to Andrea for some assistance.

"So, does that mean you will drive us to Brighton then?" Andrea duly obliged.

"Yes," came Megan's simple reply. "Of course it does."

Tracey shook her head, by now completely baffled.

"Louise is Malc's girlfriend," whispered Andrea, by way of an explanation. "The plan is for her to meet up with the boys when it comes to them scattering his ashes."

Not that Tracey gave one iota who planned to be present, as long as by then Jonathan wasn't amongst them.

"You two load your bags up," Megan instructed, whilst pointing in the general direction of the garage. "I'll go and let mum and dad know where I'm off and then I'll grab my toothbrush."

Tracey watched her happily head off back inside the house, at the same time speculating over whether or not she'd inadvertently entered some sort of twilight zone – a feeling that only got worse when Andrea proceeded to lift the up and over garage doors, revealing what had been hidden within.

She looked from what she saw to Andrea and back again.

"You've got to be kidding?" she said. "Someone please tell me this isn't happening."

CHAPTER THIRTEEN

DOESN'T MAKE IT ALRIGHT

In spite of its shaky start, Pepper was really beginning to enjoy his day. And now back in the office behind the enquiry desk with his colleague, he wasn't just happily applying himself to his own stack of paperwork, he was determined to have the backlog signed, sealed and delivered by the end of his shift. More to the point, whereas as a rule he would literally have hated being tied to a desk, on this occasion he somewhat surprisingly even began to whistle whilst he worked.

At no time during his career as a Police Officer could he remember any operation putting him in such a good mood; especially one that warranted him pursing his lips and blowing out a tune. At least he thought it was a tune – not that he could name it.

"So where is it you're off to at such short notice then?" asked his colleague.

Up until then, Pepper had been under the impression his co-worker had for some reason lost his voice, although he could quite understand the curiosity. After all, such was his dedication to the job, time off was usually something that had to be forced upon him kicking and screaming. Not that that meant it was any of his colleague's business however, he told himself; a secret operation wouldn't be much of a secret, were it broadcast to the whole station.

"I'm hoping to catch up with a few old friends if you must know," he cagily replied.

"What? Like a re-union type thing?" his colleague continued to delve.

Pepper smiled to himself, a warm feeling spreading through his belly. He'd always suspected he was a major player on the team and his colleague's persistent probing into the whys and wherefores of his up and coming leave only served to confirm this. Yes, he was pleased to note it seemed he wasn't the only one to think the place couldn't run smoothly without him. *So no wonder you're being so inquisitive,* he revelled.

"I suppose," he replied, thinking a re-union was as good a description as any. "Something like that."

Then he told himself he'd better get a move on, if he didn't want to give Mickey P. too much of a head start.

CHAPTER FOURTEEN

TALES FROM THE RIVERBANK

A couple of scooters might never be described as a cavalcade but Jonathan could see The Ace Face and Mickey P. were enjoying the ride down the M1 as much as when they were taking part in the one hundred plus scooter processions of their youth – unlike himself, however, who wasn't having anywhere near as much fun.

In his now or never reasoning, he realised he hadn't given as much thought to the nitty gritty of their getting from north to south as he probably should have done. Particularly with one rather large lorry directly in front of them and another looming somewhere close behind and he didn't just feel very small and vulnerable as a result, he felt completely out of his depth. The unbelievable noise of the passing traffic and the wind blowing a gale around his ears only serving to compound his fears and he now wished more than anything that he'd actually listened to Tracey instead of going against her.

Why didn't you just do as she said and stay at home? he desperately reproached. In fact, he couldn't think of anything he wanted more than to be able to turn back the clock to do just that, telling himself even getting the nursery ready for Tuesday's arrival had to be preferable to this.

Notwithstanding, the safety offered by the up and coming service station was coming in a close second, he acknowledged. So much so, that when Mickey P. clicked on his indicator, signalling for The Ace Face to follow him down the slip road and onto the car park ahead, Jonathan couldn't help but praise the Lord.

"Just like old times, eh lads?" said The Ace Face, as they all de-helmeted and disembarked.

Although under the circumstances as far as Jonathan was concerned, the man couldn't have said anything more ridiculous if he'd tried.

"Well I wouldn't say that exactly," replied Mickey P., now stretching his legs and arching his back. "I don't remember my arse ever feeling quite this numb."

Jonathan watched the second of his friends begin to vigorously rub his bum in an attempt to get the blood flow circulating again, unable to help but question what on earth an anaesthetized backside had to do with anything.

Back in the day I wouldn't have been this scared shitless! he wanted to correct. *And a certain someone would've been cadging a lift on the back of me, instead of the other way round.*

"You think this is bad," laughed The Ace Face. "You want to try doing the Euro Rally in Perugia."

No I don't! corrected Jonathan. *I don't want to try anything of the sort.*

However, as he then observed The Ace Face now delve into his rucksack and rather disconcertingly pull out Malcolm's casket of ashes for all to see, his vehicular predicament and churning guts did suddenly seem less of a priority.

"What are you doing?" he asked.

"Well we don't want him feeling left out, do we? Not when it's *his* send off."

"But you can't..." Jonathan tried to say, only to now find he was talking to the back of The Ace Face's head, as it seemed he was already heading off in search of a cup of coffee.

Jonathan looked to Mickey P. hoping it wasn't just himself who found this all a bit strange; though the responding shrug of indifference was enough to tell him it probably was. That's if he discounted the passers by, who, in also clocking a dead man's urn in their midst, were suddenly giving him and his friends a very wide berth, indeed. Not that Jonathan could blame them for freaking out like that, but still, at least they had the luxury of being able to escape.

Unlike him and with nothing else for it, he was forced to apologetically swallow his embarrassment and reluctantly follow his travel companions inside.

"Yep," said The Ace Face, proudly continuing his earlier conversation about Perugia as they plonked themselves and Malcolm around a vacant table. "Five hundred scooters, riding en mass through the Greek mountains, bet there isn't a sight like it?"

Jonathan, slightly confused for a moment, started to say something before thinking better of it.

"Oh I don't know about that," joined in Mickey P. "We had a week in Butlins once. And there were some bloody sights there I can tell you."

"Hardly the same thing," replied The Ace Face – a bit too pompously for Jonathan's liking. Not, he further noted, that Mickey P. seemed to mind.

"Andrea collected them tokens out of the paper," he continued, regardless. "Whole thing only cost us about fifteen quid."

He went on to regale them with stories about glamorous grannies and joke about how furious Andrea had been when she accidentally won a knobbly knees competition and Jonathan could, at last, feel himself beginning to relax. *Now this really is like old times*, he told himself, even managing to raise a smile or two. *Mickey P. ever the joker keeping the rest of us entertained.*

Not that The Ace Face seemed very amused, Jonathan suddenly picked up on. Talk about a mood swing.

Nonetheless quite *why* he should now be looking so miserable, well that was anyone's guess.

CHAPTER FIFTEEN

MY WORLD

"I'm gonna have to get a grip of things," Pepper told himself, as he rummaged through his dirty laundry basket, making a mental note to at least *try* and get some sort of routine going when it came to the household chores. Not that he needed clean clothes very often, he realised, it would've just been nice to have them to hand on the very few occasions when he did.

"This one's not too bad is it?" he asked, sifting out and sniffing yet another pre-worn shirt. After all, he didn't want to have to wear something that ponged too much. Then, in dismissing all the creases as something that would simply drop out once the shirt was actually worn, he put it to one side ready to pack in his overnight bag.

He stopped what he was doing for a moment and feeling a bit guilty, turned to his audience. "Now I don't want you worrying whilst I'm away," he said, genuinely concerned. "Which is why I've arranged for Mrs. Matthews from next door to come round and check on you in the morning."

"And I promise to be there and back before you know it," he reassured. "So you've got no reason to fret. Do you hear me?"

He offered a bolstering smile to Harry his pet hamster, pleased to see him then offer one of his own in return. "There's a good boy," he said, before getting back to the task at hand.

"Didn't I tell you I'd get him one day?" he proudly crowed, at the same time examining another item of clothing. "And as I keep saying, magistrates don't take too kindly to breaching bail conditions. They're probably gonna lock him up and throw away the key after this..."

" I did tell you I saw him at the funeral, didn't I?"

He looked to Harry for a response only to find him now burying himself so deep into his bedding he was almost out of sight.

Pepper sighed to himself, fondly realising he'd been wrong to think Harry wouldn't mind being deserted for a couple of days. That no amount of consoling was going to make his furry, little friend understand this was something he just had to do. But it wouldn't be right to let a hamster prevent him from doing his job, now, would it? he found himself asking.

No, he finally dismissed, with an affectionate shake of his head. *That would just be plain silly.*

And putting his not so clean clothes inside his travel bag, he purposefully zipped it shut.

CHAPTER SIXTEEN

KEEP MOVING

Not only does it have to be said that the classic mini wasn't exactly built for comfort, thought Tracey. *But its creators certainly didn't have heavily pregnant women like me in mind when it came to its design process...* And although with a little help from the other two she'd just about managed to shoehorn herself into the back seat, she couldn't help but feel she'd been paying for British Leyland's lack of foresight ever since.

On top of that, it's not enough that I can feel every lump, bump and dip in the road, she continued to complain. *Thanks to one very careful owner and some rather over cautious driving, we haven't even topped thirty miles an hour since pulling out of the garage.* A rate that didn't just mean were they never going to catch up with Jonathan, The Ace Face and Mickey P., she calculated, but that their other halves were no doubt going to make it all the way down to Brighton and back again, before they'd even crossed over the Lancashire border.

Another quick glance out of the back window, however and she could at least console herself in the fact that she wasn't the only one struggling with their current lack of progress – it appeared the numerous people in the mile long tailback behind didn't appreciate their meandering along like elderly Sunday drivers either. Not that Megan seemed to care about this ever growing queue of impatience, Tracey noted, leaving her wondering if it might be an idea to intervene.

Of course, she didn't want to step on their Chief Navigator's toes and in coming to the conclusion that the job of chiding their driver along also fell within that particular position's remit, she discreetly tapped Andrea on the shoulder by way of a prompt.

"As lovely as this is," Andrea tentatively ventured, mercifully for the mother-to-be having taken the hint. "I don't really think the scenic route's such a good idea, do you, Megan?"

"Well having never driven on a motorway in my life," she replied. "I don't really think now's the right time for me to be starting..."

Definitely not the answer Tracey had been hoping for and she gave Andrea another prod, instructing her to try again.

"You'll be alright in the slow lane," Andrea patiently continued. "You just won't be as slow as this."

Patience, however, was something that Tracey, herself, was fast running out of and thanks to Megan's clear refusal to budge on the matter, she decided maybe she should take charge of the situation, after all.

She leaned forward in her seat accordingly, ready to take a more direct approach. "In case you haven't noticed," she calmly yet sternly pointed out. "One of us is expecting a baby in the next seven days. Now call me daft if you will, but we really do need to be there and back before the actual birth..."

Megan laughed. "Well I'd have thought that was obvious," she said.

"Ha ha ha," Tracey sarcastically joined in, wondering if this girl really was so stupid as to think she was joking here.

"Well put your bloody foot down then!" she firmly shouted in response.

However, the last thing Tracey expected was for Megan to do the exact opposite and all at once slam her foot down on the break as opposed to the accelerator. And feeling Tuesday suddenly hurled up into her chest cavity before immediately descending in what could only be described as an almighty internal thud, not even the mini's screeching tyres were quite enough to mask the sound of the crash, bangs and wallops coming from the queue behind.

"You want speed..." said Megan, politely yet somewhat icily, as she turned to her passengers. "Then I'll give you speed. But I'm still not going near any motorway."

Of course not one to be outdone, Tracey did her upmost to meet Megan's unruffled composure with a cool, calm and collected exterior of her own. Not that conveying the epitome of self control was an easy task, she was forced to acknowledge; especially when the seatbelt she'd been wearing hadn't done such a sterling job of keeping her in her seat.

"That's alright then," she simply said, through gritted teeth.

However, as Megan suddenly put the metal to the floor and she, in turn, discreetly hung on as if for dear life, it was through these very same clenched pearly whites that she began to question whether she was actually going to come out of this in one piece.

*

"Well I hope you're happy now!" said Tracey, as she and her travel companions sat hopelessly staring out of the windscreen and much to her annoyance, it seemed any ground that they had managed to cover in the last speedy, yet nerve racking, fifteen minutes was fast being rendered useless.

She let out an almighty sigh, realising that with nothing else for it, she'd no choice but to wait for the masses of steam now billowing from the motionless mini's engine to eventually subside.

"You can't blame me," defended Megan. "You're the one who insisted I drove quicker."

The trouble was, Tracey knew she was right.

Somewhat piqued, she looked out of the side window, tempted to stick her tongue out at all the passers by who insisted on slowing up to gawk at the three women now broken down at the side of the road. *And yet not one of you are prepared to stop and help us out, are you?* she silently protested.

"Well one thing's for sure," said Andrea, suddenly opening the passenger door. "We can't just sit around here all day."

"Where are you going?" asked Tracey, hoping to God she wasn't really suggesting they continue their journey on foot.

"Don't worry, leave it to me," she said, thankfully proceeding to pop the bonnet and start tinkering under the hood, instead of setting off down the road.

"Found it!" she eventually called out. "It looks like it's the fan belt!"

Tracey was suitably impressed, knowing full well that she, herself, wouldn't have known where to start when it came to trouble shooting a car engine. But then again, she re-considered, a degree of knowledge in car maintenance would be an obvious essential for anyone who chose to drive round in a battered, old Fiesta like Andrea did.

"It's snapped," Andrea continued, now efficiently making her way round to Megan's window. "You're gonna have to give me one of your stockings until we can get a new one."

Stockings! thought Tracey – even in her *pre*-pregnancy days she couldn't have imagined anything more uncomfortable or less practical. However, much to her dismay and, *Oh my God, please no,* embarrassment, Megan clearly didn't seem to find them a problem at all.

"No worries," she simply said, disembarking the vehicle to rather expertly and unashamedly unclip and unroll as instructed – the ensuing response leaving the mother-to-be feeling even more uneasy.

As if the first batch of passing cars hadn't been enough, her irritation quickly turned into discomfort thanks to the next lot of driver's. This particular consignment not just feeling the need to slow down for a good gawping, but to also provide Megan with some sort of musical accompaniment, in the form of beeping horns and wolf whistles.

Give me a decent pair of tights any day, she thought to herself, at the same time shielding her eyes until the offending nylon was handed over.

"You can have it back when we get it fixed," said the impromptu car mechanic, with a smile.

Tracey watched her head off back under the bonnet to set about making her temporary repair, finding herself curious as to just how she'd known Megan was wearing stockings to begin with.

"How could she tell the difference anyway?" she asked, truly perplexed. "Between your stockings and a simple pair of tights?"

"I think it's in the quality of the weave," explained Megan, all matter of fact.

"I see..." said Tracey, even though she didn't.

But rather than dwell on the subject, she decided to just wait for Andrea to finish doing whatever it was she was doing to sort their car problem out, telling herself the only real concern here was in the hope that it was going to be enough to actually get them to a garage.

CHAPTER SEVENTEEN

IT'S HARD

The relief Jonathan was feeling now they'd left the hysteria of the motorway behind was immense.

As a young lad, he'd never realised just how much larger and faster other vehicles were compared to a scooter; or thought about the dangers they represented when such vehicles came way too close for comfort or zoomed by at break neck speed.

Today, however, he hadn't been able to get his mind off anything but – the hectic motorway lanes only reflecting the chaotic panic taking place in his head. To the point that when they happened upon a blue POLICE ACCIDENT sign sitting on the hard shoulder, he actually thought his mind was going to explode, thanks to the merging sounds of screeching tyres, blood curdling screams and wailing sirens, all clamouring to be heard at the same time. He could just see the mangled metal of the wreckage, dazed survivors helplessly watching on as paramedics tried and failed to save the most injured of the crash victims... so for him, their sudden detour couldn't have come a moment too soon.

"This has got to beat us sitting in a long queue for hour after hour," said The Ace Face. "Eh, Jonathan?"

"You're telling me," he replied, wondering if the decision to take an unexpected diversion had, in fact, been solely for his benefit.

After all, it wasn't as if they'd really have been stuck at the back end of a long line of traffic, was it? As frighteningly small as these scooters might seem to him now, even he knew there was no better mode of transport when it came to nipping between the rows of stationary vehicles. Not that Jonathan was about to complain or point that out; he was just grateful to get away from the frenzied nature of the motorway, no matter what the reasoning.

Besides, it wasn't as if it was The Ace Face's idea to leave all the hustle and bustle behind anyway, he realised. As lead rider, it had been Mickey P.'s decision to take them up the slip road. However, Jonathan didn't really care about the whys and wherefores of his decision making processes either; now riding down the more sedate A428 towards Bedford, it was just nice to feel some of his earlier stresses finally begin to leave his body.

As he took in his surroundings, it struck him how this backdrop couldn't have contrasted more with the urban, industrial landscape he was used to. Passing through villages such as Brafield on the Green, Castle Asby and Yardley Hastings, even their names sounded more upmarket. *And expensive,* he added. And although he knew it could never be described as a bad part of town where he, himself, hailed from, in fact, it was one of the better and more scenic suburbs, he couldn't really compare it with 'the good life' that seemed to be on offer here.

He admired the passing quirky cottages, ivy clad manor houses and lavender filled gardens, at the same time unable to help but think of Tracey. She'd always said she wanted to live in the quintessential village, no doubt the reason why she insisted on watching all those 'new life in the country' type programmes on the telly, he laughed to himself. Although in their case, it would probably take a jackpot lottery win for them to afford the massive country house that she envisaged them one day living in and even then, that would be after the tennis courts and pool house had been crossed off her long list of requirements.

That wasn't to say she'd ever complained about what they did have, Jonathan was also pleased to acknowledge. She was always saying it's not where a person starts that counts, but where they finish. Then again, he reasoned, compared to some people, she didn't really have much cause to grumble anyway, now, did she?

Unlike Andrea, he told himself. After all, it wasn't as if Mickey P. could ever be described as a good provider, was it?

At least not in the material sense, Jonathan was then forced to admit, suddenly aware that for all his old mate's failings, at least Mickey P.'s relationship with Andrea was open and honest. Andrea knew everything there was to know about her other half, warts and all. Unlike Tracey, he was saddened to say, who in comparison knew nothing.

Feeling guilty, Jonathan made himself a promise. When he got home he wasn't only going to come clean about his past, he was going to do his damnedest to make things up to his wife – maybe even starting with the archetypal village of Tracey's dreams. And even if they could only stretch to a two up two down little cottage, at any rate it would be a start.

Not, he realised, that repairing the damage he'd caused was going to be quite as easy as that. He just had to keep his fingers crossed that she'd still be there when he did get back to let him at least try.

CHAPTER EIGHTEEN

DOWN IN THE TUBE STATION AT MIDNIGHT

As he made his way down the M1, the constant Boom! Boom! Boom! that came from his car radio was starting to give Pepper a headache.

"If this is what the kids of today are listening to," he said, with a disheartened sigh. "Then it's not surprising so many of them are going off the rails."

He began to wonder whether or not such music really could, in some scientific way, negatively affect young people's brains – rendering them clueless as to not just their persistent anti-social behaviour, but to its impact on those around them. After all, in his experience no matter what sanctions were doled out, nothing seemed to stop them just going off and committing the exact same kinds of offences all over and over again...

"Nah," he decided, coming to the conclusion that such a theory was simply down and out rubbish. "They're just little shits."

However, enough was still enough as far as the dreadful music was concerned and keeping one hand on the steering wheel, he used the other to find something more soothing to listen to – something he considered more up his street, something a bit more classy.

Not usually a Radio Four man, it was hearing the words 'criminal' and 'punishment' both in the same sentence that actually caught his attention and he immediately thought it worth tuning in. "Now that's more like it," he said, linking what he, himself, had just been mulling over to what was obviously a discussion on how best to deal with petty criminals.

"So if prison isn't necessarily the best form of penalty, Professor Richmond..." said the broadcaster.

"Professor eh," remarked Pepper, suitably impressed. "Obviously an expert."

"...then how do you think these offenders should be dealt with?"

"That's easy," said Pepper, eager to join in. "Bring back hanging, that's what I say."

"Well as everyone is aware," explained Professor Richmond. "The prisons are full to capacity. So in today's society it's not just about what is or is not the best form of punishment. There are other factors that we need to consider."

"Exactly!" asserted Pepper, in whole hearted agreement. "Hang the buggers. Problem solved."

"One solution to many of these issues," continued Professor Richmond. "Is a greater use of the Community Service Order."

"Bollocks!" said Pepper, not just suddenly affronted by such a suggestion, but almost coughing and spluttering at the very idea of it. "What a load of codswallop!"

"And I'm sorry Professor What Ever Your Name Is," he carried on. "But you obviously haven't got a clue what you're talking about."

"Thus, not only would this ease the prison population," suggested the Broadcaster. "It would enable these law breakers to give something back to the communities from which they have taken."

"That's right," agreed the Professor.

"I don't think so," counter argued Pepper. "They're not worth the paper they're bloody written on... Something I should know."

Insulted by the direction in which the discussion was going, he decided to snap the car radio off altogether.

"Bloody do gooders," he huffed. "Bloody countries full of 'em... You want to try doing my job mate, then you'd soon change your mind!"

He shook his head, unable to help but wonder what the world was coming to as he returned his attention to the road ahead.

"Oh what now?" he asked, as if the radio programme hadn't been enough.

Seeing all the break lights in front now beginning to glow red, the last thing he wanted was to be stuck in a traffic jam for hours; especially when in his experience, it was more often than not for no good reason at all.

"Probably a hot air balloon up there somewhere," he supposed. "Or something else that the front runners have slowed down to gawk at."

"Or some matrix still flashing thirty because the powers that be have simply forgotten to turn it off."

Reluctantly, he began to bring his car to a complete standstill alongside everyone else's. However, in spotting an up and coming slip road he saw no reason at all as to why he couldn't just use the hard shoulder as a lane in its own right; enabling him to sneak off the motorway and therefore, leave the potentially long standing queue behind. After all, isn't that what the Police did in an emergency? Pepper asked himself. What's more, just because he was on leave and happened to be in his own personal vehicle, that didn't mean he wasn't carrying out work related duties, did it?

He moved over to the left, crossing the solid white line accordingly, unable to help but congratulate himself on his initiative. And besides, it wasn't as if he couldn't simply rejoin the motorway at the next junction down, was it?

CHAPTER NINETEEN

SAVE IT FOR LATER

Jonathan had, at last, begun to settle into his journey and with no other vehicles in sight he was even beginning to think riding on the back of a scooter wasn't so bad after all. *As long as we stay on roads like this,* he told himself, content to continue soaking up the scenery in this more laid back environment.

"What the...?" he suddenly yelled out, all at once unexpectedly and somewhat abruptly finding himself jolted to the back of his seat.

Paralysed with fear, he realised he'd spoken too soon, as it seemed The Ace Face had decided to put the tarmac to the test and without warning, had dropped his gears and twisted his accelerator accordingly. Leaving Jonathan with no choice but to hurtle along as fast as the scooter would allow – much to his panic stricken fury.

"You fucking idiot!" he screamed. "What do you think you're playing at?"

However, despite his terror The Ace Face still showed no signs of slowing down; in fact, if anything, Jonathan could feel his speed seemingly picking up.

"What's up with you?" The Ace Face laughed, clearly more than happy to ignore Jonathan's plight. "We used to do this all the time."

"Well that was fucking back then, now slow down! You're gonna get us bloody well killed!"

Disappointed, The Ace Face reluctantly did as he was told and brought his scooter to a slow standstill – and not a moment too soon for Jonathan, who immediately jumped off at the first opportunity, at the same time loudly voicing a string of expletives that still didn't feel sufficient enough to reflect the depth of his feelings.

"I don't fucking believe you!" he fumed, struggling to free himself of his helmet. "How could you to do that to me?"

Finally, he managed to release the clasp on his headgear and undo the strap, only to then throw it down to the ground with such force that it simply bounced back up again, nearly hitting him straight in the face in the process.

"I was only..." The Ace Face tried to defend.

Jonathan fiercely put his hands up to silence his lead rider – in no uncertain terms warning him not to say another word. With his adrenalin still pumping, the last thing he wanted was to listen to a load of excuses and it was taking every ounce of his self control as it was to stop himself actually punching The Ace Face's lights out.

"Of all the stupid, stupid things..." he said. "And after everything that happened..."

Indeed, he was still heatedly pacing up and down by the time Mickey P. had finally caught up with them.

"You better just get out of my sight," Jonathan ordered.

"But..."

"No, I mean it Roger. Just go!"

The Ace Face hesitantly did as he was told, not that Jonathan's anger seemed to be going anywhere any time soon as a result and as he watched him go, not that he was quite sure what to do with it.

He took off his rucksack and dropped it to the ground, before plonking himself down on the roadside next to it and burying his head in his knees. And after a moment or two he could feel Mickey P. somewhat awkwardly joining him. *No doubt ready to act the peacemaker or come up with some crap that's supposed to make me feel better,* he told himself, not really in any mood to listen.

"Whatever you're about to say," he said. "Save it. I don't want to hear it."

"Well maybe you need to," replied Mickey P.

Jonathan let out a short, sharp burst of mock laughter. "So this is when you tell me I shouldn't be blaming myself is it? That none of it was my fault? Well if I wasn't responsible then go on, tell me. Who the bloody hell was?"

However, as he began pulling at the stray tufts of grass by his feet, he knew he wasn't being particularly fair. Mickey P. could never understand what it was like to have to live with something like that and hopefully for his old friend's sake, that's exactly how things would stay. Then again, who on earth could appreciate what it was like to walk in his shoes? Nobody, that's who, he asserted, which was one of the reasons why he never talked about it.

"What's it like?" he asked, eventually breaking the ensuing silence. "Being a dad, I mean?"

He could see Mickey P. was somewhat surprised by the question.

"Alright I suppose," he replied. "I've never really thought about it."

"I have," said Jonathan, flatly.

Nevertheless, if he were being totally honest he would've admitted it wasn't the day to day stuff like changing nappies and coping with night feeds that weighed on his mind; he would've confessed it was the never ending commitment that automatically came with being a parent that worried him. In fact, his shoulders felt so burdened with responsibility already, he really wasn't sure they could withstand the added strain that becoming a father would entail.

Not that he really felt able to discuss any of this with Mickey P. anyway. Having never been one for deep and meaningful conversations when they were lads, it was obvious he was still the same old, happy go lucky chap he'd always been. So Jonathan decided it was probably better to change the subject altogether, telling himself there was no point in the both of them being miserable.

Besides, it wasn't Mickey P.'s fault The Ace Face had decided to play the fool like he had, so why should he pay the price?

"Nice wheels," he said instead, nodding towards the Lambretta.

"Cheers," came the proud reply.

"Must've cost you a packet."

"Not really."

"What do you mean? Not really?" Jonathan asked. He may have been out of the Mod scene for quite some time, but even he knew these days machines like that didn't exactly come cheap.

"Yeah well, you know me," said Mickey P. "Always on the look out for a bargain."

"You're not saying that it's nicked, are you?" asked Jonathan, quickly realising there was no point waiting for an answer even if Mickey P. had been prepared to give one. "I mean it's one thing you helping yourself to the 'Pic n Mix' at Woollies when we were kids, mate. But helping yourself to someone else's scooter, God knows how many years on... well that's something else."

He shook his head, wondering if his day could get any worse and not for the first time was forced to ask what he'd gotten himself into. And realising it was all a big mistake he got to his feet and picked up his rucksack.

"Where are you going?" asked Mickey P., surprised.

"Home!" came his stark reply.

"Oh don't be such a soft shite, Swifty. It's me, Mickey P. It's what I do remember. What did you expect for God's sake?"

"Oh, I don't know," said Jonathan, once again full of sarcasm. "That you might have actually grown up by now... just a little bit."

He clocked The Ace Face making his return, cans of coke and packets of crisps in hand – a peace offering that seemed just as absurd as the ridiculousness of the situation.

"And I suppose you knew all about this?" he accused.

"Knew about what?"

"That that..." explained Jonathan, pointing to the red Lambretta. "Is stolen."

"Borrowed, if you don't mind," interjected Mickey P., all at once offended – not that his preferred choice of diction made any difference whatsoever.

The Ace Face shrugged indifferently. "News to me," he said.

Seeing the two of them standing there, genuinely wondering what all the fuss was about, Jonathan was left feeling equally as bemused.

"So let me get this straight," he said. "I've risked what semblance of normality I had at home, for a thieving so and so... and a bloke with a death wish? And I could quite possibly be missing the birth of my own child, for what turns out to be a couple of morons?"

"Absolutely incredible," he said, shaking his head and unable to believe his own stupidity, he simply turned his back on them and began to walk away.

CHAPTER TWENTY

ALL I KNEW

"We could have been in and out of here over thirty minutes ago had that mechanic not been paying you more attention than the car," complained Tracey, as, at last, job done Andrea got back into the mini.

"Don't be daft," Andrea replied. "He was just complimenting me on my handiwork, that's all."

"That's what they call it now, is it?" laughed Megan, starting up the engine. "Handiwork?"

Tracey rolled her eyes, unable to see what was so funny. "If we could just get going now," she instructed. "We have enough ground to make up as it is." And that being said, she wondered if now might be a good time to bring up the option of taking the motorway again, only to find her words thwarted before they were even out.

"The answer's still no, before you ask," jumped in Megan, eyeing Tracey through her rear view mirror – a refusal that Tracey found just as exacerbating as before.

"And I still don't see why not," she hit back.

She sighed somewhat, as she tried to console herself in the knowledge that at least they were now back on the open road and at any rate, going in the right direction. Although being cramped into such a small space wasn't exactly making it easy. However, as she began fidgeting in an attempt to get comfy, she finally had to admit that being squashed and uncomfortable was actually nothing compared to what was really bothering her – her real problem laying in the fact that she felt utterly powerless and at everyone else's mercy.

It was quite an alien experience for someone so used to being in control and an experience that she didn't much like.

If I'd have known things were going to pan out like this, she told herself. *I'd have blooming well just let Andrea get on and do the driving...* In fact, by now as far as she was concerned, with or without a proper licence, anything had to be better than this.

She thought back to the long journeys she'd taken with her family as a child, remembering how her mum used to encourage her to go to sleep because the time would pass quicker, causing her to wonder if that might work on this occasion too. Not that Tracey actually believed this in the literal sense anymore, but to be able to drop off and not wake up until they reached their intended destination certainly still had its appeal. Even so, as she shut her eyes to try and do just that, she quickly realised it was going to be a task easier said than done and once again, not just because she was a heavily pregnant woman who happened to be squeezed into an exceptionally small space.

"So come on then, Andrea," said Megan. "Tell me what The Ace Face was like when he was as young as me? I bet he looked soooo scrummy in his school uniform, not that I, myself, am quite as young as that, of course. But you know what I mean."

For Pete's sake, thought Tracey. *Who cares?*

In listening to her, she couldn't quite work out which was worse – Megan's choice of subject or the sickly, cutesy pie tone she'd suddenly adopted at the mere mention of her other half's name. And quite unnecessarily so, at that, she couldn't help but think. After all, it wasn't as if she was talking about an adorable little kitten here, was it? She was, in fact, referring to a once moody and hormonal teenage boy who, no doubt, had had the spots to prove it.

"Well he certainly stood out," came Andrea's reply – a somewhat carefully constructed response, if ever Tracey had heard one.

Mmmmm, she thought to herself. *Interesting... So that's your way of saying his trousers were always too short and his shirts a mucky shade of grey, is it? And that his feet were always wet thanks to a combination of the Great British weather and the holes in his shoes.*

Well no wonder he over compensates now he's all grown up, she considered, especially in view of his rather strange behaviour at Malcolm's funeral.

"Although I do know he was always top of his class," Megan proudly continued. "He told me that himself."

"Right..." replied Andrea, again very much non-committal. "I certainly remember him enjoying all the practical stuff."

Tracey put her decoding skills to good use once more. *So the word 'Academic' didn't actually appear in The Ace Face's dictionary, did it not? Never mind any of his school reports... Although ten out of ten to you Andrea, for being able to think on your feet like that.*

She forgot about her earlier desire to get some shut eye and eagerly awaited Megan's next question – not only keen to hear how Andrea would handle it, but to see how she, herself, could translate it.

"And what about girlfriends?" asked Megan, right on cue. "Bet there was loads of those?"

Ah, thought Tracey. *Now we're getting to the crux of it.*

However, at the same time she was rather surprised by her driver's need to make this kind of enquiry. Particularly when like most people she knew, she, herself, had always assumed in an age gap relationship like theirs, as the older of the two it would've been The Ace Face who'd get all insecure – not Megan. That in the end, having to keep pulling the choke on an old banger was bound to lose its appeal at some point or another; especially with all those younger models about the place, all happily revving their engines, more than able to keep up. Yes, Tracey found herself very surprised to learn that these insecurities could cut both ways, such an idea having never even entered her head before.

Maybe it's because with age comes experience, and with experience comes confidence, she pondered. *And everyone knows confidence can be quite the aphrodisiac when it comes to attracting potential mates. I mean, how else do all those ugly politicians end up with such gorgeous women on their arms?*

Then there was today's cosmetic surgery endorsing society to take into consideration, she further deemed. A society where it's far easier for a more mature individual to actually look younger, than it is for a younger person to carry themselves off as more mature.

Not that Tracey was prepared to think too hard on the matter – she was having way too much fun just listening to Andrea make The Ace Face's excuses. And from what had been said so far, in answer to Megan's latest question, he certainly wasn't going to turn out to be the babe magnet the poor girl was clearly anticipating he once was.

"Well..." said Andrea, thoughtful. "There was this one girl..."

"Oooh, go on," said Megan, clearly excited. "Start from the beginning."

No, thought Tracey. *Please don't. Telling long, drawn out and boring, old tales about the man's non existent love life isn't part of the game.*

"Well it all started when Swifty and Melanie wanted to..."

"Excuse me?" interrupted Tracey, all at once sitting to attention. "What's Jonathan got to do with the price of fish?"

She found herself suddenly interested and with her thought processes doing a one hundred and eighty degree turn, she wondered why her own other half was being mentioned in the same sentence as an unknown female.

"And who's Melanie?" she asked, her curiosity by now more than pricked.

As she lunged herself forward in order to get closer to all the juicy Lucy details, she couldn't help but speculate if they were, in fact, talking about the very girl that was pictured in Jonathan's secret photo. Eager yet nervous, she realised she could be just seconds away from finding out what her husband had been keeping to himself all these years.

So sod messing about with Megan's questions, she told herself. *Now it's time to get some answers of your own.*

"Well come on then," she said, keen for Andrea to get on with it. "Spill the beans."

Any further information, however, didn't seem to be forthcoming and much to her annoyance, Tracey was left wondering if she'd only imagined the awkward glances both her travel companions suddenly seemed to exchange.

Conversely, their accompanying silence did confirm that there was definitely something they preferred to keep to themselves. Not that Tracey's pride would allow her to delve any further; or, in fact, let them have what she saw as the upper hand.

"Not that it matters, of course," she said, taking a superior tone as she snootily sat back in her seat again. "If this Melanie person was really that important to Jonathan, I think I'd have heard about her before now, don't you?"

CHAPTER TWENTY-ONE

IT'S UP TO YOU

With no idea of how far the nearest bus depot or train station was, no mobile reception and no payphone in sight, Jonathan just kept walking. And as he ambled along, calculating at this rate he'd be back up north in about a month's time with his feet full of blisters, he couldn't help but wonder if he'd been a bit rash in the choice he'd made. At least if he'd stayed with Mickey P. and The Ace Face, he told himself, he'd have definitely had transport home – even if that did entail having to suffer the both of them in the meantime.

Moreover, he had to admit it wasn't just the practicalities of his decision to jump ship that were cause for concern, there was also the fact that he'd deserted both Tracey and Tuesday and all for nothing as it now turned out. In addition, what had initially seemed to symbolize some sort of rite of passage, a means of coming to terms with his past, he now realised was really just three blokes on two scooters travelling down the country, in order to do a favour for bloke number four.

Of course, on top of that there was Malcolm, his girlfriend Louise and Mrs. Riley for him to consider – yet three more names he could add to the list of people he'd let down thanks to his not seeing this whole sorry saga through. But at least as far as they were concerned, he could console himself in the knowledge that the other two were, no doubt, continuing on without him; so it wasn't as if Malc wasn't going to get his choice of final resting place at all, now, was it?

He decided the only thing for it was to try and cadge a lift from the next passing vehicle. However, instead of hearing the noise of a car engine coming up behind like he'd anticipated, he eventually recognised the rapid *ying*

ying ying sound that could only be attributed to a couple of classic scooters.

"I don't believe this," he said, stopping in his tracks as his two ex-travel companions pulled up along side. Do these two never get the message?

"It's a long way up North," said The Ace Face.

"Yeah well," replied Jonathan. "I'm a big boy, I'm sure I'll manage."

"You spoke to Tracey yet?" asked Mickey P.

"Nope," he replied, not that it was really any of his business. "No reception."

"Yeah, mine's flat on the orange as well," confirmed The Ace Face.

Flat on the what? thought Jonathan, despairingly and for someone who used to be such a nice guy, he couldn't help but wonder exactly when it was this man had turned into such a downright prat.

He looked up and down the road in the hope of spotting a vehicle whose driver might be willing to rescue him, but unfortunately there wasn't one in sight.

"Come on Swifty," coaxed Mickey P. "You don't have to do this. Brighton won't be the same without you."

Jonathan began to waiver, asking himself if he was just using Mickey P.'s stolen scooter and The Ace Face's over the top behaviour as an excuse to run away – again. After all, was it really fair for him to complain because one of them hadn't changed at all in the intervening years since he last saw him, yet at the same time become increasingly irritated by the other because he had?

Besides, even if he did go home and beg Tracey's forgiveness, he knew there were no guarantees she'd actually be there to listen – especially when if he were in her shoes, he had to admit he probably would have upped and left the minute he found the surprise note.

"Well?" asked Mickey P. "You coming or what?"

Not for the first time, Jonathan felt caught between the Devil and the deep blue sea. When it came down to brass tacks, however, he had to ask himself which was worse?

Having to spend another twenty-four hours in the company of these two idiots? Or spending the next twenty-four hours multiplied by God knows how long, with his thumb stuck out in the hope of hitching a ride?

"Shove up," he eventually ordered, stepping forward to re-take his pillion seat.

"But no more funny business," he warned. "You got it?"

"Plain sailing from now on," replied The Ace Face. "I promise."

Although as Jonathan put on his helmet and made sure his scarf was once again safely tucked inside his jacket, he still couldn't be entirely sure that that would, in fact, be the case.

CHAPTER TWENTY-TWO

TOWN CALLED MALICE

"Look at that," said The Ace Face, surprised but pleased to spot a crew of other scooterists now heading towards them.

Jonathan happily looked into the distance to see what was so interesting, glad The Ace Face had heeded his warning to ride more safely.

"Oh yeah," he replied, equally as enthusiastic.

Then recognition suddenly hit him smack, bang in the face and in that one single moment, he went from feeling the most content he'd felt all day, to very ill at ease, indeed.

It was the arachnid emblazoned flag attached to the front rider's Lambretta that he first picked up on. And in remembering it was the emblem of the Scorpion Scooter Rebels, the Hell's Angels of the scooter world no less, he recalled how scooter clubs the length and breadth of the country used to fear this mob turning up at their rallies – such was the devastation they left in their wake.

"Oh shit!" he said, aware that if his day hadn't been bad enough already, there was a good chance it was about to get a whole lot worse.

Although that was in the old days, Jonathan tried to re-assure himself. *And for all anyone knows, they could've given up on their trouble making antics a long time ago.*

However, he realised that that was just wishful thinking when he was very quickly proven wrong, leaving him with no choice but to helplessly watch on as the on-comers decided now was the time to live up to their long held reputation. More to the point, it only took one commanding signal from their leader before the whole gang started whooping and cheering in excitement and much to Jonathan's distress, expertly manoeuvring themselves across and into the travelling trio's path.

"Jesus Christ!" he blasphemed, telling himself he should have just gone home when he'd had the chance. Although judging by the response of his travel companions, it was more than obvious he wasn't the only one to think the three of them were in clear and present danger.

"What're we gonna do?" shrieked Mickey P., hastily bringing his scooter alongside The Ace Face's.

"We're gonna fucking die, that's what!" shouted Jonathan, knowing that even if they, themselves, were to cross lanes, the Scorpion Scooter Rebels would only follow suit and so it would just continue.

He was forced to just watch as his aggressors got nearer and nearer, evidently more than enjoying their part in this terrifying game of chicken; all the while showing no signs of slowing down, or more importantly, moving back into their own lane. So much so that the panic that had been rising in his belly was now starting to reach fever pitch and he could actually feel the colour draining from his face with every passing second.

Still getting closer and closer, Jonathan tried a desperate attempt at waving them over, whilst The Ace Face and Mickey P. frantically beeped their horns.

"Get back! Get back!" he shouted, a somewhat pointless exercise, he realised, considering this only seemed to excite them all the more.

In fact, it was clear that no amount of hysteria was ever going to stop these madmen and as his life began flashing before his very eyes along with the faces of the people he'd loved both past and present, Jonathan had to acknowledge he and his friends faced a stark and terrifying choice.

"We can either crash and burn into a mass of mentally deranged scooterists," he called out. "Or crash and burn into the hedgerow?"

"The hedgerow!" both The Ace Face and Mickey P. simultaneously screamed back and with only seconds to spare, they just about managed to hit their brakes and swerve over to the left, before the Scorpion Scooter Rebels came crashing into them.

"Aaaaargh!" screamed Jonathan, suddenly finding himself thrown up into the air.

However, as quickly as he went up, he began to come back down and as he made a somewhat swift decent, the greenery seemed to race up towards his face.

Everything went black.

CHAPTER TWENTY-THREE

RUNAROUND

Not only was Tracey still smarting over the fact that she hadn't been able to get the low down on this up until now unheard of Melanie person, it pained her to know she was still being taken all around the houses in her attempt to get to Brighton.

In the goodness knows how many hours she, Andrea and Megan had been on the open road, they seemed to have weaved to the east, then to the west and back again. Furthermore, having been treat to the rather forgettable sights of Lancashire, West Yorkshire, South Yorkshire, Derbyshire, Nottinghamshire and Leicestershire along the way, as Tracey spotted yet another 'Welcome to...' sign, it seemed the car was now crossing the border into the next county – which, she sardonically noted, was still nowhere near their intended destination.

"What joy," she said, wondering just what delights Northamptonshire could possibly have to offer.

She was convinced that the other two were now viewing this trip as some sort of jolly, having completely forgotten it was meant to be a mercy dash in a certain someone's hour of need. Not that there was any point in complaining, she realised and having tried and failed at that numerous times already, she just had to keep reminding herself that as long as they kept heading in the right general direction, they were bound to come across the south coast at some point or other.

On the other hand, as the car suddenly began slowing to a steady standstill she was also quick to recognize that even that consolation prize might now be in jeopardy.

"I don't believe it," she groaned from the back seat, an unexpected road block and its accompanying diversion being one of the last things she needed right now. "Only this morning everything seemed so simple..."

"Well I don't know what you're worried about," said Andrea. "All we have to do is go where it tells us."

Tracey glanced in the direction of the yellow detour arrows and it wasn't as if she could say she felt particularly reassured by her navigator's air of confidence. Seeing them point down what looked like some little used 'B' road, they were clearly going to be led into the middle of God knows where and taking into account how the journey had evolved so far, it was pretty obvious at least to her, what was going to happen next.

"Well if you ask me," she said. "If we go down there, we're going to end up even more lost than we are now."

"Who said we're lost?" asked Megan, offended. "Besides, if we do get into difficulty, although that's not to say we will, we've always got this."

Tracey watched her reach over and into the glove compartment. *Please don't tell me that's what I think it is,* she thought to herself, immediately ready to loose the plot if her driver suddenly produced an example of the latest in satellite navigation systems – a system that, aside of its inability to fix dodgy fan belts, would have saved them a lot of time and trouble.

"Oh," she said, suddenly and somewhat contradictorily disappointed.

After all, as frustrating as it would've been for her to know they'd had such technology to hand all along and simply hadn't, thus far, made good use of it, at least there would've been *some* light at the end of the tunnel. However, with Megan producing a bog standard road atlas to plonk in Andrea's lap instead, she now had to face the prospect of the second half of this outing being just as trying as the first.

"Well that's it then," she continued, defeatist. "We may as well just turn around and go home now!"

"Thanks a bunch," protested Andrea. "I'll have you know my map reading skills are second to none."

Nonetheless, even as the chief navigator began efficiently flicking through the pages determined to get them where they needed to be, the mother-to-be still couldn't exactly say she was convinced.

*

Tracey had never seen herself as being part of the 'I told you so' brigade. However, after another thirty minutes or so of what seemed like aimless driving into the back and beyond, she couldn't help but think that on this occasion such a group membership was, indeed, warranted.

"Didn't I tell you?" she said.

She leaned forward in order to get her point across more effectively and in the process just happened to notice how Andrea had actually positioned the road atlas. And as such, the very reason as to why they didn't have a clue where they were heading was instantly revealed.

"Andrea," she ventured. "Why are you reading the map book upside down?"

"What do you mean?" Andrea replied. "That's how I'm supposed to read it."

"No, it's not..."

"Yes, it is. Someone told me that's how it should be."

"Who?"

"I don't know. Just someone. I can't remember."

Exacerbated, Tracey once again flung herself back in her seat. *It was all supposed to be so simple...* she told herself. *We jump in the car, we catch up with Jonathan, we bring him home... That was the plan. But now look at us...!"*

It wasn't long before she learned she wasn't the only one getting fed up thanks to their lack of progress and, much to her discomfort, it seemed Tuesday had had enough by now too.

"Oooh," she winced, as her unborn child suddenly decided it was a good time to change position.

However, for the mother-to-be this new arrangement also seemed to include the use of her bladder as some sort of pillow and before she knew it her water works suddenly felt like they were fit to burst. Of course, not only did Tracey not want to ruin the car's nice clean upholstery, but neither did she want to have to sit in a wet patch for what was obviously going to be the foreseeable future and she found herself leaning forward once more, only this time to talk to her driver.

"Megan," she said, starting to fidget somewhat in a desperate attempt to keep the flood gates shut. "I don't mean to alarm you, but I think we really do need to stop and ask for directions."

The trouble was, when she then looked out of the window in the hope of spotting someone they could accost, it was clear that Andrea's map reading had taken them a bit too far off the beaten track. And crossing her legs as tightly as humanly possible, not only could Tracey not see another soul in sight, it wasn't as if she could see anything that remotely resembled a public toilet either.

CHAPTER TWENTY-FOUR

FAITH IN SOMETHING BIGGER

Jonathan only vaguely heard the Scorpion Scooter Rebels' rowdy en mass u-turn and traditional, celebratory ride by in honour of their victory. Hence, they were well into the distance by the time he came to sufficiently enough to finally get back on his feet. And whereas once of a day he would have been tempted to just jump straight back onto his own two wheels and go chasing after them, on top of the fact that he'd be seriously outnumbered if he did, Jonathan knew all too well he was no longer the hero he once was.

However, heroics aside, that still didn't explain why he didn't even feel angry enough to make the threat and all considered, as he checked himself over and dusted himself down, he was surprised at exactly how calm and together he did feel. *Surely I should be at least throwing up in the bushes?* he asked himself. *Or at any rate, be some sort of quivering wreck?*

He tried to put the strange serenity he was feeling down to the possibility of concussion, but even so, the complete lack of intensity to his feelings was still that bit disconcerting.

As it was, when he looked to the other two to see how they were faring under the circumstances, he noted it was Mickey P. who looked a bit green around the gills and The Ace Face who seemed to be having a bit of a nervous breakdown.

"My baby! My baby!" he was crying over and over again, all the while cradling and cuddling his now contorted scooter.

Jonathan rushed over to assist. However, rather than any damage to the vehicle, he found himself more concerned with the nasty, bleeding wound that The Ace Face had sustained to his hand. Then again, at the same time he also had to admit that dealing with a grown man in tears wasn't particularly his forte and the best he could muster by way of comfort was a somewhat awkward, yet manly pat on the back.

"Come on, Ace," he tried to reassure, whilst giving the Vespa a quick once over.

"It's not as bad as it looks," he pointed out. "Just a couple of bent mirrors and we can easily sort them."

Much to his relief The Ace Face suddenly fell silent and lifted his head as if to confirm Jonathan's diagnosis. Except instead of making things better it only seemed to make matters worse and once again Jonathan was left trying to console his friend, as he started his boo-ing and cradling all over again.

Jonathan then looked to Mickey P. in the hope that he could do better. But with him now sitting on the ground with his head firmly tucked between his knees in an attempt to tackle his nausea, it was obvious he was going to be neither use nor ornament when it came to helping anyone.

"Oh no!" shrieked The Ace Face, once again grabbing Jonathan's attention, only this time he seemed to be talking about his rucksack – or as Jonathan couldn't help but notice, what was actually left of it.

"I bought that especially for this trip," he tearfully continued, suddenly jumping up and heading for the bushes. "The shop assistant said it was the top of its range and could withstand even the harshest of treatments, that it was a quality item worth its quality price tag..."

Although as Jonathan watched him submerge himself in the shrubbery, he quickly realised it wasn't so much the bag he was bothered about, but what had been in it.

"Shit!" he said, the need to locate the whereabouts of their deceased friend becoming something of a priority for him too. And as he dashed over to assist, his eyes and arms now frantically joining in the search for Malcolm, the severity of this latest development hit him straight in the face.

How on earth were they going to tell Mrs. Riley that they'd failed in their task? he asked himself. And all because a rucksack couldn't live up to its reputation. That they'd lost the remains of her one and only son? Or, and possibly just as bad, that his final resting place was not, after all, the end of Brighton Pier as requested, but instead on the way to Bedford, at some random point along the side of the A428?

CHAPTER TWENTY-FIVE

HOUSE OF THE RISING SUN

Pepper may have found having to take an unexpected detour off the M1 more than a little annoying at the time, but as he continued to drive through the Northamptonshire countryside he could feel his earlier frustrations begin to dissipate.

In fact, now imagining himself as some sort of real life Inspector Morse, going above and beyond the call of duty in his quest to capture the good for nothing Mickey P., it no longer felt an inconvenience at all. And despite realising anyone with any geography knowledge would know the east of Northampton is closer to Cambridge than it is to Oxford, he was more than happy to dismiss such factual information on the grounds of it being subject to artistic license.

"This is the life, eh Sergeant?" he said, to an empty passenger seat – at the same time deciding a bit of Classic FM was needed, in order for him to really get into character. But as he turned his car radio back on, pressing this button and that button in an attempt to locate the correct station, it wasn't long before he realised taking his eyes off the road probably hadn't been such a good idea, after all.

"What the...?" he suddenly said, all at once bolting upright.

The car swerved somewhat as a couple of scooters bearing three riders between them noisily zoomed passed at break neck speed and well aware of what Morse, himself, would do under such circumstances, it wasn't something Pepper was about to let them get away with either.

"And if you think I am," he decidedly warned. "Well you've got another thing coming."

He put his foot down on the accelerator accordingly, determined to give them a piece of his mind.

"Hang on a minute," he said, at last, able to scrutinize the offenders more closely as he began to catch up. "Isn't that a Lambretta?"

His aggravation fast began to turn into excitement as he realised just what that could mean.

"And a shiny, red Lambretta at that, if I'm not mistaken..." he gleefully made out. "Just like the one Mickey P. made off with."

"Gotcha!" he triumphantly exclaimed, pleased to acknowledge that his keen observational skills had saved the day yet again.

"You can run," he said, finding himself coming over all American. "But you definitely can't hide!" Not that he could quite fathom why his Inspector Morse had suddenly turned into the Dukes of Hazzard's Sheriff, even if it was a rather good impression at that.

As Pepper continued his pursuit along the road towards Bedford, he decided it was probably better to now pull back a bit. After all, not only were scooters ideal vehicles with which to nip down little side streets and alleyways, whereas cars in his experience had a tendency to get stuck, as they got nearer to the town the last thing he wanted was for Mickey P. to spot him. Plus, bearing in mind the consequences of his arch rival being in a position to make good his escape, Pepper didn't want to find himself back at square one – only worse. Worse because if Mickey P. were to realise he was on to him, he might just disappear altogether.

He watched as the two scooters pulled up outside a pub.

"The Rising Sun... not a bad little boozer if you ask me," he noted, as he took in its exterior. However, knowing he wasn't there to critique the establishment and still not wanting to get too close, rather than pulling up alongside he looked around for an alternative space in which he could park his car.

"A useful little spot for any undercover agent," he told himself, as he espied a conveniently large enough gap just outside the Fancy Dress shop opposite.

He reversed in and discreetly disembarked, all the while pretending to be interested in the clown outfit currently displayed in the shop window – whilst at the same time congratulating himself on his ingenuity. In any case, not everyone had the ability to think about monitoring their target's reflection in the glass pane, he considered, whilst ensuring that they, themselves, continued to remain undetected.

Alas, he was quick to learn that even this simple action wasn't without its problems though and just as he was deciding how best to make his move, a lorry driver chose that very same moment in which to pass by, momentarily obscuring his view in the process. *Damn!* he swore, as in the same split second his quarry had just as quickly vanished and he was left in a bit of a panic, as he anxiously glanced up and down the street in the hope of relocating them.

However, sadly for Pepper, this was all to no avail and he reassured himself with the conclusion that they could only have entered the ale house. Still, rather than go in all guns blazing, he briefly contemplated whether or not to contact the local nick for back up, just in case things went awry. There were, after all, three of them compared to his one – but then again, he re-considered, why share the credit of capturing an offender at large if he didn't very well have to?

He determinedly crossed the road, shoulders square and back straight. Nevertheless, this confident sense of purpose wasn't enough to stop him popping his head around The Rising Sun's door to get the lay of the land first. "Nothing wrong with making sure everything is, in fact, safe," he told himself, quickly scanning the bar area for any signs of trouble and only upon seeing that all was, indeed, well, was he finally happy to step inside.

However, it took a more detailed examination of his surroundings before he caught sight of what he was looking for and finally spotting three helmets sitting on a table over in the tap room he couldn't have felt more self assured if he'd tried. Except as he swaggered on through, in eager anticipation of arresting his arch rival Mickey P., he didn't just feel the arrogant smile on his face suddenly freeze, he felt what he now realised to be his somewhat misplaced confidence, all at once evaporate.

CHAPTER TWENTY-SIX

TURNING BLUE

For Jonathan, the prospect of having to scoop up a dead man's ashes was almost as bad as losing them altogether, so the relief he felt when he did manage to spot something in the undergrowth only one hundred per cent intensified, thanks to the fact that Malcolm's urn was, praise the Lord, still in one piece.

He respectfully stood aside to allow The Ace Face the honourable task of retrieving it. Albeit, in underestimating the extent of the injury to his travel companion's bleeding hand and it wasn't long before he essentially wished he hadn't. The Ace Face's damaged prehensile subsequently and unexpectedly failed to take the casket's weight and before Jonathan knew it, Malcolm's remains were once again on their way back to hitting the ground. And this time, there was absolutely no doubt in his mind that the urn would, indeed, smash into smithereens if he, himself, didn't do something about it.

"Nooo!" he yelled, as everything around him suddenly seemed to move in slow motion and as he lunged forward in a heart stopping, goal keeper like, penalty save, he only just managed to catch it before it landed on the floor.

"You need to get that seen to mate," he exhaled, his relief almost tangible as he took a moment, before getting back to his feet.

"What a mess..." he said of their predicament, looking from the mangled scooter to The Ace Face to Mickey P.

Saying that, at least Mickey P.'s pallor had returned to a more healthy shade of pink, he was glad to note, signalling enough of a recovery for him to be able to at least take some interest in what was going on.

"We need to get him to hospital," he said, although quite how they were going to do that was something of a dilemma.

On the one hand, with Mickey P. in charge of the Lambretta and The Ace Face clearly unable to take responsibility for the Vespa, Jonathan knew he would've had to have been an idiot not to realise what that meant. However, on the other hand, he was also aware he hadn't been behind the handle bars of a scooter for nigh on twenty-five years; not that now was the best instance in which to be thinking about that time of his life.

He thought back to the heartfelt promise he'd made to Melanie all those years ago and suddenly felt the colour begin to drain from his own face. *No, now's definitely not the time,* he re-iterated; particularly as it seemed he was going to have to break his word and do the exact opposite of what he'd previously vowed.

Still, there was the option of flagging down the next motorist that came along to consider, he grasped, hopeful. But with The Ace Face's hand still oozing blood the way it was and no guarantee that a Good Samaritan was going to pass by any time soon, he had to admit it was fair to say that probably wasn't the best course of action.

Which is why you're just gonna have to get on and do it, he reluctantly told himself, at the same time trying his utmost to ignore the fact that he desperately didn't want to.

So come on, Jonathan, he instructed. *What are you waiting for?*

CHAPTER TWENTY-SEVEN

ONE STEP BEYOND

Much to each and every customer's surprise, Tracey suddenly burst through the doors of the greasy spoon cafe and began hastily scanning the room for the 'Ladies'.

"Toilets?" she called out, unable to locate them as quickly as she would've liked. Then, as numerous people all at once pointed in their direction, she made a mad dash towards them, as fast as her pregnant belly would allow.

Upon entering, she threw herself into the nearest cubicle, dropped her trolleys and sank into the porcelain. At last able to empty her screaming bladder, in what she could only describe as a moment of pure bliss. "Now that's what I call relief," she said, happy to enjoy the mother of all wees.

However, with that more immediate problem now out of the way, as she then went on to wash her hands, she could feel all the other issues surrounding this trip start to, once again, push themselves forward. Like this Melanie woman and her exact identity? she questioned. Naturally, Tracey assumed she was, indeed, the girl in Jonathan's photo, but as far as the mother-to-be was concerned that still didn't explain why she'd been such a secret all these years. Or offer any enlightenment with regards to anything else that Jonathan might be keeping from her for that matter.

She moved over to the hand dryer, unable to help but sigh as she stared at her own reflection in the mirror. "You do know you've only got yourself to blame for all of this, don't you?" she asked herself. "And if you hadn't insisted on turning private investigator not only wouldn't you have attended Malcolm's funeral, you wouldn't even know any of these people existed... So you certainly wouldn't be trapped in a car with them. And you're husband most definitely wouldn't have run off to Brighton!"

She imagined herself back at home where she belonged, sitting with her feet up on her lovely sofa, sipping on an equally lovely cup of coffee – decaf, of course.

"But where are you instead?" she continued. "You're stuck in the middle of nowhere, on what is rapidly turning into a wild goose chase."

However, despite rueing the day she happened to set off this ridiculous chain of events, she decided there wasn't any point in scolding herself too much. What was done was done and surely her number one priority now was to simply track Jonathan down so they could concentrate on Tuesday's birth. Which meant all the other stuff, including the question of why he'd pretended she was the one and only love of his life when she clearly wasn't, would just have to be dealt with later.

"Yep," she confirmed. "That sounds like a plan to me!" And with that, she set off in search of Andrea and Megan.

"That's better," she said, feeling all the more relaxed both physically and even mentally as she joined them at their table.

"You know, I once heard," said Andrea, somewhat randomly. "That when you're absolutely bursting for a wee like you just were, the feeling you get when you do manage to find a loo, is supposed to be the next best thing to an orgasm!"

"Who told you that?" laughed an incredulous Megan, clearly not quite able to believe it.

"No doubt the same person who taught her to read a map," said Tracey, impassive.

She looked about herself, for the first time noticing just how 'greasy' this greasy spoon was and although grateful to the others for having placed an order on her behalf, with a cup of dishwater masquerading as a hot drink before her, she couldn't help but grimace. Was it a mug of tea, coffee or, indeed, vegetable stock that she was expected to put to her lips? Well whatever it was, she told herself. It just wasn't going to happen.

"Although I must admit that wee did just feel pretty damn good," she said instead.

"Told you!" said Andrea, as if to say case proven.

"Yeah well, I'm sure we've got better things to talk about," said an enthusiastic Megan. "Like when..."

"Oh no," interrupted Tracey, knowing full well what was coming next. As far as she was concerned, she'd made her decision not to probe the past and the last thing she wanted was yet another snippet of information changing her mind again.

"If you're going to keep harping on with questions about The Ace Face," she carried on. "I'm going straight back out that door and throwing myself under the first vehicle that passes!"

"And so will I!" exclaimed Andrea – and considering the degree of creativity she'd already had to utilize thanks to Megan's last round of enquiries, it was an assertion Tracey found more than understandable.

When it came to his more youthful years The Ace Face had clearly been stretching the truth somewhat and she could see Andrea's having to negotiate her way through fact and fiction without so much as tainting his girlfriend's starry eyed view, was becoming increasingly difficult. *Although any man who chooses to call himself The Ace Face in the first place,* she further considered. *Should never have been believed to start with.*

Not that she was really in any position to criticize Megan too much, Tracey also realised. Loathe as she was to admit it, in view of the fact that neither of them seemed to know much at all about their partner's past lives, the two of them did have something in common.

"Well we can talk about Jonathan instead if you want," Megan offered – a suggestion that only a week ago Tracey knew she would have more than jumped at.

But as tempting as it was to take advantage of the situation, having been presented with an opportunity to get all the answers she needed like that, in the end Tracey decided to maintain her resolve and stick to her plan. "It's okay," she said. "I think it's best we leave the both of them out of our conversations, don't you?"

"Besides," she found herself somewhat paradoxically going on. "If there really were any skeletons in Jonathan's closet, like I've said, I'm sure he would have told me. And just because you've mentioned some old girlfriend, I mean what man hasn't got an ex-girlfriend or two..."

"What're you talking about?" Andrea suddenly blurted, in an unexpected interruption. "Melanie isn't an ex..."

As soon as the words were out Tracey could see that she immediately regretted them, in much the same way as she now regretted her own.

But if she isn't an ex, the mother-to-be was forced to ask herself, confused. *Then who the bloody hell is she?*

She began to feel sicker than she had throughout the whole of her pregnancy. "Go on then," she said. "You've started, so you may as well finish."

With Andrea reluctant to say anything else and no answer immediately forthcoming, Tracey felt her frustrations suddenly rise to the surface. "Tell me," she insisted, grabbing at Andrea's hand and knocking her tea/coffee/vegetable stock over in the process. "If she wasn't a girlfriend, then what was she...?"

CHAPTER TWENTY-EIGHT

I CAN'T EXPLAIN

Jonathan sat in a stunned silence, not quite sure if riding up front had been too much for him or not.

On balance, being forced off the road by a gang of thugs wasn't exactly the best way to be re-introduced to the joys of scootering. But then again, apart from the odd wobble here and there he had managed to make it safely to the hospital, which he had to admit, was quite an achievement. However, in spite of these mixed feelings, at least he knew if he were to suddenly develop a nervous twitch, have some sort of funny turn or even pass out due to the shock of it all, an accident and emergency department was, without doubt, the best place to be.

He looked over at the other two to see how they were faring, only to find himself surprised by The Ace Face's definite lack of animation. He had thought he'd be the kind of guy to wear an injured hand like that with pride; that like some over exaggerating 'war hero', he'd have been bursting at the seams to tell anyone who'd listen about how they'd come under attack from enemy forces and only just lived to tell the tale.

Instead though, he too just sat there quiet – although if Jonathan didn't know any better he could've sworn he looked like he was sulking. Not that he could see any reason as to why that would be the case and in deciding to give him the benefit of the doubt, he dismissed any such notion.

After all, these places can have that effect, he told himself, simply putting The Ace Face's muteness down to the fact that he just didn't like hospitals. *And let's face it,* he continued. *The smell of disinfectant, antiseptic, blood and death all rolled into one is enough to silence even the bravest of men.* Which wasn't exactly a reassuring train of thought considering his own previous experience of hospitals, he realised. So much so, that he suddenly felt a sense of nausea of his own beginning to set in.

"I can't believe I just did that," he all at once announced, in an attempt to focus on the more positive aspects of his situation rather than any of the bad. "I can't believe that after all this time I've actually taken charge of a scooter." Moreover, as it began to dawn on him *just* how much of an accomplishment that was, were it not for the fact that he probably was going to have to continue riding up front, he might have even suggested a drink or two to celebrate.

He did hope for some sort of congratulatory response from the others, but with The Ace Face clearly out of verbal action and Mickey P. too busy reading the various posters dotted about the walls, none was actually forthcoming.

He let out a disappointed sigh, as he watched Mickey P. turn his attention to the pamphlets on the table in front of them and in seeing him pick up a leaflet on some illness or other to peruse, he remembered how there was only so much a person could read when it came to the symptoms of allergic reactions and the need to dispose of needles stroke any unused medications both safely and correctly. Needless to say, he wasn't surprised to find the reading material Mickey P. had chosen failing to hold his attention for very long – as evidenced in how he went on to impatiently throw it back down again with a bit of a groan of his own.

"They'll come and get him when they're good and ready," said Jonathan, indicating to the voiceless one of their group.

"Yeah, I suppose you're right," replied Mickey P., clearly fed up of the wait. "You haven't got a paper or sommat, have you?"

Jonathan shook his head. "Afraid not, mate," he replied.

"What about you?" Mickey P. then asked The Ace Face, at the same time grabbing his tattered and torn rucksack without even so much as a please or thank you.

It was childlike behaviour that Jonathan thought rather rude, especially when he then went on to have a good rummage through, not just pulling out the newspaper he'd wanted but a small packet of neatly wrapped, brightly coloured tissue paper into the bargain.

"What's this?" he asked, curiously holding it up for all to see.

On the other hand, Jonathan thought to himself. *Taking things that don't belong to him is obviously second nature.*

On the plus side, however, Jonathan was pleased to note such a lack of manners did seem to jolt The Ace Face out of his sulk like trance. To the point that he almost made Jonathan jump when he suddenly lunged forward, using his one good hand to snatch whatever it was back. The trouble was, in his refusal to let Mickey P. have a look for himself, Mickey P.'s inquisitiveness only got worse and Jonathan was then forced to watch on as the two of them began tussling like kids, in the battle of the package.

"Alright! Alright!" The Ace Face, at last, conceded. "But I'm opening it."

He began gently and very carefully unwrapping the tissue paper. "This," he explained. "Is a gift from one Ace Face to another."

Jonathan observed him proudly reveal one of the tackiest gold rings, bearing what was probably one of the biggest imitation diamonds he had ever seen and he had to admit he couldn't quite share his friend's enthusiasm.

"It's the one Sting wore in Quadrophenia," he further detailed. "You know, the film."

"Der!" said Mickey P. – a sentiment with which Jonathan could only concur.

After all, like any good Mod back in the late seventies and early eighties, he'd watched it so many times he'd practically memorized the script word for word. Except in thinking back he couldn't quite remember any significance to Sting's ring at all – or anyone else's for that matter. *Still, I could be wrong,* he then thought to himself. *My memory's no where near what it used to be.*

He realised the double entendre in how he'd described the pop star come actor's jewellery and although he knew it was somewhat immature of him, he still couldn't help but giggle.

"What do you think, Swifty?" asked The Ace Face – leaving Jonathan struggling to maintain a straight phizog, despite the man's eagerness to get his opinion.

"What? About Sting's ring?" he asked. "I think it's impressive."

He could see his audience didn't have a clue as to what was so funny and as he tried and failed to keep himself from tittering, he simply told himself he had to get his kicks from somewhere.

"Well give us a look then!" said Mickey P., obviously keen to take a closer inspection, although Jonathan would've put money on his interest being purely financial.

"Something as unique as Sting's ring would sell for a fortune on e-bay," he said, both innocently and true to form.

Jonathan couldn't help but take this as more innuendo regardless of the speaker's intentions and as a result, he was sent into a fit of howling laughter. However, the more the other two looked to him for an explanation, the more he couldn't stop.

"Not likely!" The Ace Face retorted and from what Jonathan could see, deciding it best to just try and ignore him and his laughter. "With your track record it'll be the last I see of it!"

As Jonathan watched him hastily tuck what was clearly a prized possession deep inside his inside jacket pocket, never to see the light of day again, he realised it was time to take a hold of himself, for fear of causing offence. Saying that, he still couldn't help but let out the odd little chuckle, even as Mickey P. went back to his original plan of reading the newspaper.

"Check this out!" Mickey P. suddenly blurted, excitedly holding up an inside two page spread for Jonathan to have a look at. "Can you believe it? There's a rally on tonight and 'The Jim Jams are playing! Not only are they supposed to be the best Modfather tribute band on the circuit, it looks like they've got DJ's and everything!"

"Very nice," he replied and as he scanned the article for himself, his thoughts finally moved away from double entendres and innuendo in favour of recalling the fonder memories of his youth.

"The Jim Jams," scoffed The Ace Face. "Seen 'em loads of times. In fact, me and Jim, he's the lead singer, we're like that!" He crossed his fingers to emphasize the closeness of their relationship. "Not that you're suggesting we should go, are you?"

"Why shouldn't we?" asked Jonathan – after the day he had had, the thought of having a couple of hours to let his hair down a bit didn't seem such a bad idea. Not only that, having just done the one thing he never thought he would ever again do, he couldn't think of a more appropriate way to mark the occasion.

"Unless a gig like that's ticket only," he said, disappointed.

"Well even if it is," Mickey P. put forward. "If him and this Jim bloke really are like that..." He replicated The Ace Face's metacarpal gesture to prove his point. "Us not having the right pass isn't exactly gonna be a problem, is it?"

"Well I don't know about that!" spluttered The Ace Face. "Unlike some, I don't like to take advantage. And anyway, we do have Malcolm to think about as well."

"Well we'd obviously take him with us," said Jonathan, for once more than happy to align himself with Mickey P.'s reasoning.

"But we said we'd have him at the pier by dinner time tomorrow," argued The Ace Face, obviously still intent on dragging his feet.

"And we will," asserted Mickey P. "M1, M25, M23, A23... we'll easy be there by twelve noon... No problem."

"And what better way to give him a proper send off," agreed Jonathan."Than taking him to his last proper scooter rally..."

It was obvious The Ace Face wasn't buying it.

"Oh come on Ace," Jonathan wheedled. "It's not as if it's gonna do any harm, is it?"

CHAPTER TWENTY-NINE

THE SEEKER

Expecting to find himself face-to-face with Mickey P., Jonathan and who he assumed would be The Ace Face, Pepper instead found himself confronting three complete strangers. A trio made up of who just had to be the most uncompromisingly aggressive looking blokes he had ever had the displeasure to come across. However, as if that wasn't bad enough, one of them then rose to his feet, clearly annoyed at what had turned out to be an unwarranted interruption and all Pepper could do was gulp, as he watched him just get taller and taller.

Oh dear, he thought to himself, in something of an understatement – quickly realising his mistake lay in the fact that he'd paid more attention to the red Lambretta, when he should have been focusing on its actual rider.

The man giant suddenly began to growl and although Pepper couldn't decipher a single word of what it was he was trying to say, he could tell by the way the man was now bearing down on him that the ogre wasn't happy. So much so, that if he thought he'd been nervous before, it was nothing compared to how he was now feeling.

"S... sorry," he stuttered. "I thought you were s... someone else. A case of mistaken identity..." The trouble was the more Pepper tried to speak, the more his words just wouldn't come out properly and before he knew it, just like the man giant only seconds before, he was uttering a whole jumble of incomprehensible syllables.

Much to his relief, however, this did, in turn, lead to the man's complete and utter confusion and as he looked to his cronies to see if they had any inkling as to just what was, in fact, being said, it gave Pepper just the opportunity he needed to hastily make good his own escape.

"I'll leave you to discuss it then," he just about managed before hastily scurrying back out into the bar area, all the while fully intending to just get the hell out of there.

But having not seen the Landlady at all on the way in, such was his focus on catching Mickey P., he certainly couldn't miss the over-dressed, middle-aged, red-head now. And nor could he miss what was clearly an amused glint in her eye.

"Shit!" he muttered, realising she'd just witnessed the whole embarrassing affair and although he knew he wasn't what anyone could call worldly wise when it came to members of the opposite sex, he was certainly savvy enough to know it wasn't the done thing to wimp out in front of them. Which is why he then tried to make his subsequent about turn from over by the exit round to the bar area appear the most naturally flowing movement in the world. Knowing if he were to save any face at all, he'd have to stop and have at least one drink before running away altogether.

"Bitter, please," he said, ensuring to bring his voice down a couple of octaves as he chose what he considered to be a manly drink, for a manly man. However, as she then began somewhat overtly and rather suggestively pulling on the beer pump, leaving him not quite sure where to look in the process, he did wish he'd clarified it was just a half that he'd wanted instead of the pint she was now pouring.

"I've not seen you around here before," she purred, forcing Pepper to reluctantly make eye contact.

"Erm, no," he replied, doing his utmost to maintain a cool, calm and collected exterior regardless of what was going on inside. "Just visiting."

"Business?" she asked, still pumping away. "Or pleasure?"

"Business!" he quickly jumped in, wishing she'd just stop already when it came to all that thrusting. "Definitely business!"

"What a shame," she continued, holding his gaze for what Pepper considered uncomfortably longer than necessary. "Thought you might have wanted to book in for the night..."

He prayed to God that that wasn't the invitation it most certainly sounded like, finding himself getting a bit hot under the collar and as she plonked his drink down in front of him, he had no choice but to loosen his neckline accordingly.

"And why w... would you think that?" he stammered, his voice all at once demonstrating a squeak-like quality.

She pointed to a poster on the wall to his left.

"Oh, I see..." he replied, unashamedly powerless to hide his relief. "You thought I was here for..." He took a closer look at the advertisement. "For this scooter rally... thingy."

"Well, yes," he continued, thinking on his feet. "That's exactly what I'm here for. The scooter rally."

"I heard it's going to be a good do," she informed him. "So if you do fancy staying over for a bit of fun tonight...?"

He ignored her now provocatively raised eyebrows.

"And I'm sure if you ask nicely," she carried on. "Our Maximus here will only be too happy to let you tag along with him."

Pepper realised there was only one man a name like that could possibly belong to and as he felt someone approach to his right, he closed his eyes just hoping against all hope that on this occasion he would, in fact, be proven wrong. However, as he then re-opened them and turned his head, it was clear that wasn't to be the case and he once again found himself staring into the chest of the bloke he'd only minutes before tried to flee.

Beam me up Scotty, he silently pleaded and now also noticing the empty beer bottle in this rather large bloke's hand, as he glanced up at the expectant look in his eye, he couldn't help but wonder what on earth he'd gotten himself into.

Or rather, what somebody else has gotten me into, he very quickly corrected. *And believe you me, Mickey P., when I do get my hands on you, you're gonna really, really pay for it. And that's a promise!*

CHAPTER THIRTY

WALLS COME TUMBLING DOWN

"But Jonathan doesn't have a sister," said Tracey, unable to understand why Andrea would even say something like that. "You're obviously making it up for some reason... on account of me having never heard of any siblings let alone met any of them."

"Technically, maybe you're right," explained Andrea, at the same time making absolutely no sense to Tracey whatsoever – after all, either her husband was an only child or he wasn't.

"And what's that supposed to mean?" she asked.

"It means..." replied Andrea.

She was clearly uncomfortable at having to be the one to clarify all of this, but as far as Tracey was concerned, the woman had started so she could bloody well finish.

"That Melanie, Jonathan's flesh and blood, isn't with us anymore," Andrea continued. "Because she's dead..."

It was information that the mother-to-be struggled to digest. However, as she took a moment to allow Andrea's words to actually sink in, she suddenly found her thought processes all at once diverted, thanks to what felt like a sudden hard blow to her stomach. "Ouch!" she flinched, doubling over, whilst at the same time instinctively cradling her belly.

"Jesus!" said Andrea, to Megan. "I knew I should've just kept my bleeding mouth shut. You better get the car started. I think she's gone into labour."

"What do you mean, I've gone into labour?" worried Tracey. "You said it wouldn't happen for another week."

"I said it *probably* wouldn't happen," Andrea corrected. "But that was before all this stuff about Melanie came up."

Andrea and Megan tried to help her to her feet, but such was the shock of what she'd just heard, Tracey realised she wasn't just experiencing the onset of child birth. Unfortunately, she'd apparently lost the use of her legs as well and as the other two attempted to haul her up, she was forced to suffer the public humiliation of being half carried, half dragged out of the building. Furthermore, she then had to endure the embarrassment of being lugged all the way across the greasy spoon's car park and she found herself just wishing they'd had the foresight to leave their vehicle at least that little bit closer to the entrance.

"Why didn't he tell me...?" she wailed, her feet scraping along the floor.

"We can talk about that later," replied Andrea, puffing and panting amidst all the effort. "You just concentrate on the baby for now."

Then Tracey found there was the difficult issue of actually getting herself inside the car to contend with. Not an easy task, she recognised; not when she was experiencing a numbness of the lower limbs.

"Come on, Tracey," said Andrea. "Can't you at least try and help us out here."

"I would be only too willing if I wasn't paralysed from the waist down," she retorted, now on the receiving end of a lot of uncomfortable pushing and shoving.

"Shit!" said Andrea, suddenly realising they'd forgotten something. "We haven't paid the bill!"

"Sod the bloody bill!" yowled Tracey, as she was, at last, prized into the back seat. "Can't we just get going?"

"No," said Megan, aghast and starting up the engine. "We certainly can not. That would be breaking the law, wouldn't it?"

Breaking the bloody law, thought Tracey, under the circumstances wondering which planet this girl was actually on. *If I wasn't in so much pain I'd be breaking your bloody neck!*

Then again and much to her relief, at least one of her travel companions had the decency to recognise the urgency of her situation and as quickly as Andrea had raced towards the cafe and barged inside to settle up, she was thankfully just as speedily charging back out again.

"Go! Go! Go!" she shouted, at the same time throwing herself into the front passenger seat.

"You do know which direction we're supposed to be going in, don't you?" asked Tracey, by now beginning to panic somewhat as Megan hit the accelerator and swung out onto the main road.

"Shit, no," said Andrea, once again grabbing the map book and frantically searching through its pages.

"But I don't want to give birth inside a caaaaar...!" cried Tracey, the tears now really beginning to flow.

"Don't worry, we're not going to let that happen. Are we, Megan?" Andrea consoled, offering a comforting hand to the mother-to-be by way of re-assurance.

With another contraction beginning to rise in her belly, Tracey all at once seized it with a vice like grip.

"Ouch!" Andrea complained. "That hurts!"

Nevertheless, considering her own anguish Tracey was in too much pain to even notice the loss of blood flow to her comforter's fingers; or the fact that her navigator now had to examine the map one handed.

"Oh My God!" the mother-to-be desperately cried out instead, her contraction now starting to reach its agonizing crescendo. "We are going to get there in time, aren't we?"

CHAPTER THIRTY-ONE

I'M ONE

"A stroke of luck you managing to come by this polish like that, eh?" said Jonathan, make shift duster and tin in hand.

"Wasn't it just?" Mickey P. replied.

However, even aside of his mate's tell-tale grin, Jonathan had already guessed he'd probably stolen it from one of the hospital store rooms. Although on this occasion he did decide he could forgive his friend this one transgression, in view of it all being in a good cause. Not that the end always justifies the means, he further acknowledged, but in the bigger scheme of things he didn't suppose a single canister of shine spray was something the National Health Service would exactly miss.

"Pretty much as good as new, wouldn't you say?" Jonathan carried on, re-adjusting the last of the Vespa's mirrors before stepping back to admire their on-the-spot repair job.

"I'd say so," agreed Mickey P. "Definitely as good as new."

The hospital doors slid open and Jonathan looked up to see The Ace Face, at last, exiting to join them.

"And all we need now is a round of applause by way of a thanks for all our efforts," he said, ready to show its owner what they'd achieved. "And then we're good to go."

He eagerly waited for that all important response, yet it seemed The Ace Face was struggling to come up with the same degree of enthusiasm. In fact, much to Jonathan's chagrin, it appeared the best he could muster was a rather disappointing, half-hearted smile.

"Cheers lads," he said – a rather luke warm response if Jonathan had ever heard one, especially considering all the work he and Mickey P. had just gone to.

"Surely you can do better than that?" he said, thinking at least a bit of appreciation wouldn't have gone amiss.

"No, it looks great. I mean it," The Ace Face feebly replied. "Honestly."

Jonathan looked at the casualty's heavily bandaged hand, telling himself that this definite lack of interest was probably down to one of two things. Either the poor man was still in agony thanks to the extent of his injury, he decided; or the doctors had pumped him so full of drugs to get rid of the pain, that they'd actually dulled all his other senses in the process.

Of course, he knew neither of these things bode particularly well for a good time at the scooter rally; an event that he, himself, was really looking forward to. One of the reasons why, in having managed to forget all his own woes for now, he thought it was only right he help The Ace Face put his misery to one side as well.

He excitedly jumped behind the Vespa's handlebars, in an attempt to lift the patient's spirits. "Now we can't say this isn't like old times, can we?" he asked and making sure to leave plenty of room behind, he remembered how The Ace Face, or Roger as he was known back then, had been the gang's official pillion passenger. "Me up front, you posing at the back."

"Yeah well, your memory must be playing up a bit, mate," he damply replied. "I think you'll find you were the one doing all the posturing – not me."

Jonathan couldn't help but wonder if that remark really had meant to have sounded as cutting as it had come across, all his attempts to cheer up the walking wounded clearly not working.

"Yeah sorry, mate," he said, in the end choosing not to push the matter. Instead, telling himself that just because The Ace Face was *currently* in no mood to demonstrate the level of delight he'd been expecting, that didn't mean he wasn't going to chill out at some point along the line and actually start enjoying himself again.

"You ready?" he asked, helping The Ace Face fasten his helmet clasp before donning his own headgear, whilst at the same time making sure their scarves were well and truly tucked in. Not that he got as much as a please or thank you for this assistance either, he noted and somewhat annoyingly, he was forced to watch the Ace Face take his seat with something of a sulk on.

"So let the fun commence," scoffed Jonathan, hoping his pillion passenger would at least recognise the hint of sarcasm to his voice and maybe do something about his bad humour.

Although if he did pick up on it, he certainly wasn't letting on.

"Well fuck you!" Jonathan thought to himself as he started up the scooter engine. *"You ungrateful Bastard!"*

Hell bent on having a good time even if The Ace Face was as equally determined not to, he began revving up the Vespa somewhat more than was strictly necessary – both simultaneously and purposefully encouraging Mickey P. to do the same with the Lambretta.

Furthermore, when he did eventually decide to pull away from the pavement, Jonathan resolutely made a point of not looking back – mentally, physically or otherwise.

CHAPTER THIRTY-TWO

NIGHT BOAT TO CAIRO

"Look out!" screamed Tracey and as if the pain she was experiencing wasn't enough to contend with, she was suddenly forced to tightly grip her seat as well as her belly.

However, it wasn't so much the emergency stop that she found a problem; thanks to her condition she knew the mini would be screeching to an abrupt halt outside the hospital at some point anyway. Rather, as her face seemed to head straight for the car windscreen and her life started flashing before her very eyes, as far as she was concerned, it was three riders on two scooters who were responsible for her current predicament. All because they'd decided now would be a good time to inconsiderately pull out, without even having the decency to look first.

With Megan having to take sudden and evasive action, thus, preventing an even worse crisis than the one she was already in, Tracey knew it was something for which she would have gladly gone chasing after them – were she not in the throes of labour, of course.

"Morons!" she shouted after them, instead and although not quite the dressing-down she would've liked to have given, under the circumstances it was the best she could do. Still, despite her near death experience and let's not forget Andrea's dodgy map reading skills, she acknowledged, at least they'd actually succeeded in making it to the hospital in time – which she couldn't help but think was quite an achievement in itself. That being so, she now realised it was just a case of getting herself out of the car and into the building and going off experiences so far, she knew this probably wasn't going to be easy.

True to form, as Andrea and Megan jumped out to assist, it didn't matter how much huffing and puffing and heaving and ho-ing the three of them did between them, try as she might, the mother-to-be still couldn't seem to make herself budge.

"I am trying," she insisted, sensing the other two's growing frustration.

"Then try a bit harder," gasped Andrea.

"Yes, please do," pleaded Megan.

Unfortunately for Tracey, however, she could see their combined efforts starting to attract the attention of others and with quite a crowd now beginning to gather it wasn't long before some individual observers even stepped forward to help. This meant, with a number of people now huffing and puffing and heaving and ho-ing she couldn't help but feel like she was taking part in a modern day version of Alexei Tolstoy's 'The Enormous Turnip' – with herself playing the part of the giant vegetable, very much to her embarrassment.

"This is so humiliating...!" she cried, both desperate and mortified at the same time. "What did I ever do to deserve this, Jonathan?"

CHAPTER THIRTY-THREE

ITCHYCOO PARK

Jonathan felt freer than he'd felt in years. The exhilaration of two wheels on an open road was all coming back to him and it was as if the burden he'd been carrying all this time had suddenly been lifted – only to be replaced with a magnificent high. Moreover, such was the thrill of re-living this experience it was almost as if he was a young lad again; a young lad with no responsibilities, no worries and only himself to think about.

He pulled up at the approaching T-junction, telling himself that things couldn't get any better. Although when he looked to his left, he quickly realised that that wasn't strictly the case and if he played his cards right, the fun was only just getting started.

"Jesus Christ!" he said, his smile suddenly turning into a massive grin. "Have you seen this?" Not that The Ace Face was ready to share in his excitement just yet, he noted. But by now Jonathan had to admit he was past caring anyway.

He could see what had to be over a hundred scooters coming towards him – a mass of classic scooters, personalized scooters, countless Vespas and Lambrettas, some of them works of art in their own right, all heading in his direction. And as they began to sail past, apart from the odd Zip and Kymco that he noticed had sadly managed to invade the ranks, not only did Jonathan find the sight absolutely fantastic, he thought the accumulated noise from all the engines was in danger of rendering him a bit deaf.

He thought back to the time when he, himself, would have been amongst them; up until now, having never allowed himself to actually think about the Mod scene, or more to the point, just how much he, in fact, missed it. Hence, as memories of the music, the fun and the comradeship it had once given him came flooding back, he found himself very much wanting to be a part of it again.

So much so, that when some of the riders began beeping their horns in an open invitation for Jonathan, The Ace Face and Mickey P. to take part in their procession, it was an offer he found difficult to resist.

"Shall we?" he asked, just itching to join them.

"I don't see why not," replied Mickey P. "I'm up for it if you are."

Jonathan didn't see any point in getting The Ace Face's opinion on the matter. He'd already made it very clear that in his somewhat miserable view, they shouldn't even be going to the rally in the first place – somewhere that this lot were, in Jonathan's mind at least, no doubt heading. *And besides,* he thought to himself. *Even if you did ask for his take on things, do you really want to listen to any more of his whinging whatever decision he came to?*

He revved his engine, waiting for the smallest of gaps to appear in the masses so he and Mickey P. could pull out and as some of the other scooter riders slowed down to make this task that bit easier, for Jonathan it wasn't just a simple case of them considerately making room. It really did feel like they were welcoming him home.

"Nice wheels," a rider called out, speeding up to compliment Jonathan on the Vespa.

"Cheers mate," he proudly replied, not seeing any need to point out the fact that it wasn't, indeed, his.

"Fantastic machine," said another - this one slowing down to offer his accolade, having caught a glimpse of it in his mirrors.

And so it went until they finally reached the Northamptonshire field where the rally was taking place, however, even there Jonathan could see the Vespa continuing to attract more attention than many of the other scooters around. Understandably so, he acknowledged, considering the amount of love and attention The Ace Face had obviously lavished on it over the years – and that was on top of what had to have been a very large amount of cash.

Not that that stopped Jonathan from thinking he deserved at least a little bit of the credit himself. After all, were it not for his repair job, the compliments definitely wouldn't have come quite so thick and fast, now, would they? He just thought it a shame The Ace Face was still in no mood to recognise such assistance and as far as Jonathan was now concerned, an injured hand was no longer a sufficient enough excuse for a grown man to sit there with his bottom lip sticking out.

"Loving the scoot!" yet another enthusiastic voice called out.

Jonathan turned to see who it belonged to and judging by the clipboard the man was carrying, he could only assume it was one of the event organisers.

"Good chance of winning 'Best in Show' with that," the man enthusiastically continued. "I take it I can sign you up for the competition?"

"Too right you can," jumped in Mickey P., caught up in the moment – unlike Jonathan, however, who, although not completely averse to the idea, wasn't quite so sure considering he wasn't really the machine's rightful owner.

Besides, he didn't really think he had a chance of winning in any case. Especially when during a quick glance about at the next wave of scooters coming in, he managed to spot a couple of even more stylish examples than the Vespa. What with their intricately, hand-painted pictorial themes, he could see there was definitely some stiff competition around. Not that he fully understood the link between a Lambretta and portraits of the Kray Twins, he admitted. But scooters masquerading as works of art were bound to be recruited into the same 'Best in Show' category – and, no doubt, because of their craftsmanship bound to score higher.

Then again, what did it matter to him if the Vespa didn't place? And in also noting that The Ace Face wasn't exactly chomping at the bit to claim ownership of his own two wheels, *probably because he was too busy maintaining his strop to be bothered,* thought Jonathan, he couldn't see why he, himself, should be particularly worried about it either.

I suppose entering would be a bit of a laugh, he told himself. *Which is the whole point of us being here in the first place.*

And it's not as if I'd be hurting anyone, is it? he mulled, by now completely dismissing his earlier concerns.

"Go on then, where do I sign?" he suddenly asked, smiling.

CHAPTER THIRTY-FOUR

JAMES BOND

Pepper positioned himself in the marquee ready to pounce the minute his prey dared to show himself, thinking what a stroke of genius it was the way he'd found the Fancy Dress shop like that. What's more, thanks to one helpful Fancy Dress shop assistant, he wasn't just convinced he'd been provided with what was, no doubt, the perfect undercover disguise for the occasion, but also that the purple, two tone, nylon suit and badly fitting wig actually looked good on him.

The latter, as far as Pepper could tell, being something with which numerous other rally attendees seemed to concur. After all, why else would he be receiving so much attention from passers by, if they didn't?

"There's no way Mickey P.'s gonna recognize me in this get up," he proudly asserted, happy to delight in what he considered yet another admiring glance.

Not that he knew for sure Mickey P. was going to actually turn up, he admitted. But if he, himself, had been forced to take a detour off the motorway, he reasoned, it was odds on his arch rival would have had to do the same. In addition, if he, himself, had learned about this rally as a result, then he could hazard a pretty good guess that Mickey P. would have heard about it too.

"And with an event such as this in the offering," he said. "There's no way he'll be able to resist putting in an appearance... Now it's just a case of watching and waiting."

He looked around, first taking in the clusters of Scooter Boys dotted about the place. A rather scruffy bunch, what with their trademark padded, green U.S. Flight jackets and sleeveless denims, he decided, which left him wondering if they were as aggressive in their nature as they appeared in their attire. "Of course they are," he said, cynically telling himself such people didn't actually deserve his interest. Then somewhat condescendingly dismissing them altogether, he turned his attentions to the makeshift dance floor.

There, with their feet twisting, turning and gliding in what appeared to be one swift, circular movement, Pepper couldn't help but find himself impressed by the Northern Soul-ers. Albeit, he couldn't for the life of him figure out how they were doing it, even if it was for the want of trying. And as he continued to give it a go regardless, with his own two feet doing anything other than what they were supposed to, he soon found himself getting a little bit frustrated.

"Not that you've travelled all this way for dance lessons anyway," he reminded himself, choosing to just let them get on with it whilst he focused his efforts on locating the dastardly Mickey P.

Having long been aware of his arch enemy's sub-cultural leanings, Pepper knew if he was going to find him anywhere, he'd find him somewhere amongst the Mods. The problem was, it seemed picking Mickey P. out of this massive contingency was going to take a little bit longer than he'd initially thought. What with the marquee now steadily filling up and this group typically hell bent on appearing cool and sophisticated in their tailored suits and khaki green parkas, in this environment and with so many of them around, to him they all looked the bloody same.

Then again, Pepper wasn't going to let a little hiccup like that get in the way of things and as his observational skills once again swung into action, so did his determination to get the job done.

The DJ suddenly called out over the mic, interrupting Pepper's cool concentration in the process.

"And for all you fans out there..." he said, excitedly introducing his next track. "Here's 'James Bond,' by The Selecter.

Not that Pepper minded this specific noteworthy distraction and as the music kicked in, he immediately began to feel at one with the song's title character. "Now this is more like it," he said, tapping his feet to the beat accordingly. "After all, I am an undercover agent myself."

As he once again began surveying his surroundings, he realised it was fair to say that like the real James Bond, he was definitely attracting many a wide eyed stare from the women in his vicinity. However, despite knowing his newly found status in the physical attraction stakes was, in part, down to his purple suit and new head of hair, again like the real 007, it wasn't as if he could just ignore these sexual advances... Oh no, on this occasion, he was going to face them head on.

Obviously the best way to do that, he told himself, was to wink, click his tongue and simultaneously point his index finger at near enough every female who happened to glance his way. Moreover, as he got into the swing of things, he even found himself plucking up the courage to roar like a tiger at one particular woman; although he could see his animal magnetism was clearly too much for the rather fetching blonde to bear and no doubt the very reason as to why she subsequently turned on her heels...

Much to his disappointment, though, making like a tiger wasn't something he really got the chance to perfect; his roar quickly turning into more of a kittenish 'miaow' when he suddenly spotted the arrival of some of Maximus' unsavoury cronies.

As he watched them start to force their way across the dance floor, pushing and shoving anyone and everyone out of the way to clear a path for not just their leader, but also for the young female on their leader's arm, his confidence started to evaporate somewhat as he nervously realised they were making a beeline straight for him.

He swallowed hard, trying to pull himself together whilst asking himself what the real James Bond would do under these circumstances. Of course, he knew full well the answer didn't include jeopardising his assignment for the sake of a couple of bad guys; in fact, if anything, he acknowledged, he'd be more likely to embed himself amongst them in order to get nearer to his target. Thus,

Pepper was forced to admit that for the sake of his own mission, he was going to have to follow suit.

"You know you can do this," he told himself, at the same time squaring his shoulders, resolved to appear the epitome of composure as the gang members made their final approach.

Very much to his relief, it was an action that seemed to pay off. Nevertheless, even though Maximus' grunts definitely sounded less aggressive, this still didn't mean they were any more decipherable.

Whilst he could tell the man was clearly attempting some sort of gentlemanly introduction with regards to the woman adorning his arm, Pepper still couldn't understand a single word of what was actually being said. For all he knew, the gang leader could have been introducing his girlfriend, daughter, second cousin three times removed or even worse, heaven forbid, a combination of all three. Not that he was about to ask for clarification on the matter, of course – he did, after all, value his own life too much.

"Pleased to meet you," he simply and politely replied, instead.

He could see Maximus was besotted. On the other hand, quite how far these feelings were reciprocated was something else Pepper struggled to interpret; especially when in return, the girlfriend/daughter/second cousin three times removed was herself checking out the mating potential of every guy in long trousers – an action from which it seemed even he, himself, wasn't safe, very much to his further unease.

But whilst Pepper wasn't necessarily surprised by such unwanted attention, as far as he was concerned women had, after all, been throwing themselves at him all evening, he did think it best to ignore her exaggerated eye lash fluttering and lip puckering for fear of upsetting the giant of a man by her side. The giant of a man who was now thrusting an empty beer bottle his way for a second time that day, once again, expecting him to just automatically replenish it as a matter of course.

Desperate to just get on with the task at hand Pepper looked from the gang leader, to the ever expanding crowds around him and back again.

"This is going to be one long night," he found himself thinking, wondering what on earth else this evening could possibly throw at him.

CHAPTER THIRTY-FIVE

SHOUT TO THE TOP

"Wait for me..." a sulky, yet still very much expecting Tracey called out, as the hospital doors slid open, at last, allowing her to exit.

She felt wretched. Just happy to be with child in the first place and as it now turned out much to her regret, she'd never before taken the time to even consider the intricacies of childbirth and thanks to this lack of appreciation, she couldn't believe what she'd just been subjected to. That said, as if the bright lights, medical contraptions and complex monitoring equipment hadn't been enough to send her running for the hills, putting her off having babies for life, it was when the latex gloves had come out and the words 'medical examination' were mentioned, that things simply became too much.

"And for what?" she pitifully asked herself. "For a bloody false alarm, that's what..."

She made a stab at being optimistic about the whole thing, telling herself that Tuesday was probably better in than out anyway; especially with another week still to go before her pregnancy reached its full term. On top of that, even if she was still very much with child, now back out in the fresh air, at least she could feel some veneer of colour returning to her cheeks. Furthermore, on an equally positive note and if nothing else, she had finally managed to regain the use of her legs... "Something Andrea and Megan seem to be taking advantage of," she resentfully observed, her sanguinity disappearing just as quickly as it had arrived.

"It's not my fault," she petulantly and rather loudly whined. "It must have been the shock of everything."

Much to her relief this seemed to be enough to make the other two finally stop in their tracks, at last, giving her the chance to catch up.

"Shock!" hissed Megan – not even trying to appreciate where she, herself, as the mother-to-be was coming from, Tracey noted. "Don't talk to me about shock! I could be scarred for life now because of what you just put me through!"

The audacity of the woman, thought Tracey, unable to quite believe what she was hearing. *Anyone would think she was the one who'd been forced to endure all that intrusive prodding and poking.*

"Yes well," she counter argued. "Under the circumstances a bit of support wouldn't have gone amiss."

"Tracey, I was more than happy to support you..." Megan replied. "I would've just preferred to have done it from outside in the corridor, thank you very much. But oh no, every time I got anywhere near to the door handle you had to go and cry *Don't leeeave meee!* like some kind of wailing phantom!"

"It's not everyday you find out your husband's been hiding a dead sister in his closet, you know! So is it any wonder I was a bit upset?"

"And it's not everyday you find yourself having to watch one woman stick her fingers up another woman's..."

"Enough!" Andrea suddenly intervened. "Of course the doctors are going to want to do their checks. I'm just surprised the two of you are making such a song and dance out of it!"

"Excuse me..." said Tracey, shocked by such a wanton lack of understanding for the trauma she'd just been through.

"Excuse me, nothing... My two kids don't even bicker like this."

Tracey suddenly felt hurt. It was exactly because Andrea did have two children that she'd expected a little more compassion. Not that her now wounded disposition seemed to gain her any sympathy in any way; in fact, she was surprised to find her disconsolate demeanour only serving to make things worse.

"And whilst I'm at it," Andrea continued. "Can I just say, we've all found aspects of this journey hard to deal with in one way or another. It's just a shame not all of us have the capacity to realise that!"

"What do you mean?" asked Tracey. But as Andrea let out an exasperated sigh, turning her back on both women to head off in search of the car, it was clear she wasn't going to get an answer any time soon.

She watched her disappear into the distance, once again, wishing more than ever that she hadn't started all of this. That she hadn't gone to Malcolm's funeral; that she hadn't come running after her lying 'son of a so and so' of a husband; that she hadn't found out her husband was a lying 'so and so' to begin with; and finally, that she hadn't just had to endure the mother of all false labours...

"Well if that was the practice run," she eventually said. "I dread to think what the real thing's going to be like."

"Tell me about it," Megan simply replied.

However, as the two of them then began following in Andrea's footsteps, the mother-to-be knew if she was being totally honest, she would've admitted it wasn't so much thoughts of another labour that were now playing on her mind, as something else. She'd have owned up to being more concerned with Andrea's outburst and just exactly what it was she'd been getting at, when she'd said they'd *all* found this trip difficult in some way.

Had Andrea's frustrations really been the result of petty squabbling? she asked herself. Or had they stemmed from something else? Guilt for bluntly revealing Melanie's true identity in the way that she had, maybe... or guilt for what Tracey had just gone through... guilt for betraying Jonathan, even...

Still, whatever their cause, in Tracey's eyes, such feelings of culpability on Andrea's part were certainly misplaced.

As far as she was concerned, the only person truly to blame for all of this mess was, in fact, her husband. And maybe the time hadn't just come to stuff his whereabouts, his whys and his wherefores? For her, it seemed the time had come to just stuff him, with no maybe about it!

CHAPTER THIRTY-SIX

THERE'S A GHOST IN MY HOUSE

Whilst the loud music, electric atmosphere and musical, celebratory merriment of the occasion were exactly as Jonathan remembered, he was also forced to recognize that some things were very different. Like the fact that once upon a time he would've been more than happy to confidently strut his stuff out on the dance floor; unlike today, when he didn't just feel a tad self conscious, he secretly felt a bit of a prat. On top of that, no longer having the benefit of youth on his side, he had to admit he didn't have the stamina to keep up anymore either – whether he did, in fact, want to or not.

However, it seemed to him that not everyone was struggling like he was and having long since mastered Sting's moves in Quadrophenia to perfection, Jonathan could see The Ace Face was out to impress. Granted, as his old friend effortlessly utilized the space around his feet to its full potential, he did look quite the dancing artiste. Although in Jonathan's eyes he would've looked a whole lot better had he not had a dead man's urn tucked under his arm, as well as an inconsiderate mate in the form of Mickey P. by his side, who childishly kept insisting on pogo-ing into him.

"Time for a break I think, don't you?" Jonathan breathlessly and sweatily suggested, deciding enough was enough as he indicated to a gap in the marquee wall. And just glad to see the other two happily nodding their agreement, he headed off outside into the much needed fresh air.

"That feels good," he said, taking a moment to relish in the welcoming, almost chilly breeze that greeted him, grateful as he was for the opportunity to, at last, be able to both cool down and replenish his energy stocks.

"This is great, isn't it?" enthused Mickey P. as he lit himself a cigarette. "Although I have to say, I could do with a beer."

As Jonathan watched him take a swig from his less appealing bottle of mineral water, it was a reminder that that was yet something else which had changed since his last visit to a scooter rally. "Tell me about it," he replied.

He thought back to his younger days, remembering how he wouldn't have been able to conceive of having a good night out without downing as much alcohol as his system would allow – slurred speech and falling over being par for the course. Unlike these days, however, when thanks to the consequences of his getting older, his body could no longer cope with the side effects of consuming too much beer.

Not that he'd had the chance to test the alcoholic waters of late, Jonathan also and somewhat resentfully acknowledged; not since his wife had imposed a ban on all things moonshine. Then again, as her carte blanche prohibition had come into play some eight and a half months ago, were he to suddenly breach her ruling now, it was pretty obvious even to him that the morning after the night before would probably include one hell of a hangover. The prospect of which, again thanks to his age, didn't bear thinking about.

Of course, no-one would necessarily believe his sobriety under the circumstances, he considered. After all, one of his group had been carrying a casket of ashes around with him all evening. Furthermore, even though Jonathan had to admit that along with Mickey P. he'd actively encouraged the bringing along of their deceased friend, what he hadn't banked on, he realised, was The Ace Face's determination to show a coffer of burnt remains such a thoroughly good time. Which unfortunately for him meant his concerns weren't going to be alleviated any time soon, thanks to Malcolm's somewhat over zealous guardian's sudden suggestion that the dead had literally decided to join them.

"He's here with us, you know," said The Ace Face, full of absolute sincerity. "I mean actually here... as we speak."

Then much to Jonathan's surprise, he gave the urn a little pat, as if to only confirm this.

Jonathan didn't know what to say in response and he, instead, found himself wondering if the man before him should have had his head examined back at the hospital, as well as his hand. Though that's not to say a brain scan would've made him take The Ace Face's claims any more seriously, he further contemplated. Rather, he couldn't believe anyone would actually fall for all that 'eebie jeebie' nonsense, whatever the state of their skull.

"I bloody hope not..." said Mickey P., at the same time giving Jonathan a subtle wink.

"Because if he is," he continued, pausing for maximum effect and much to The Ace Face's anticipation. "It means we'll be chucking someone else's bloody ashes off Brighton Pier tomorrow.

Jonathan creased up with laughter, relieved to find he wasn't the only sceptic in the house, with The Ace Face's subsequent refusal to see the funny side of things only making his giggles worse.

"Oh come on..." Jonathan eventually said, at last trying to pull himself together. "You're not telling me you really believe in all that stuff, are you?"

"Yes... I mean, no..." The Ace Face excused. "I was just saying..."

"Well then," said Jonathan, still chuckling.

As his giggles continued, it suddenly dawned on him that he didn't actually need to be intoxicated to enjoy a good night out with the lads, after all. And in enjoying the moment, he even wondered if it might be time to get back on the dance floor, all of a sudden more than willing to prove his mettle.

"I propose a toast!" he announced – for once more than happy to raise a bottle of water as opposed to a glass of anything stronger. "To absent friends..."

He took a sip of his drink and the other two followed suit, at the same time realising he couldn't have chosen a worse turn of phrase if he'd tried. All thanks to his brain deciding now would be a good time to play a game of word association – 'absent friends' turning into 'absent without leave' and 'absent without leave' just as quickly turning into 'absent fathers'.

"Talking about people that aren't with us..." said Mickey P., although Jonathan wished he wouldn't. "Do you think Malcolm's mystery woman will still put in an appearance tomorrow?"

"She better had do," Jonathan gloomily replied, his mood becoming increasingly shrouded in guilt. "I'm in deep shit because of those two."

"I don't think so," said The Ace Face, defending his urn. "You're up to your neck in it 'cos you deserted your pregnant wife, mate. It's not as if you can go blaming a dead man and his innocent girlfriend for that!"

"Girlfriend...?" a seductive, female voice suddenly interrupted, as if from no-where. "And whose girlfriend would that be, then?"

CHAPTER THIRTY-SEVEN

ALL OR NOTHING

Tracey hadn't felt able to say much at all since getting back in the car to set off on the next leg of their journey. Now that she'd had time to absorb the seriousness of Andrea's surprise revelation, her mind was awash with nothing but yet more unanswered questions. Questions that she knew only Jonathan could answer – like why he'd been keeping secrets in the first place? Furthermore, she realised the fact that he hadn't been able to trust her with this information to begin with, had only served to shake her trust in him.

Even Megan's up until now annoyingly careful and methodical approach to driving didn't matter any more, she mulled. Not in the bigger scheme of things. In fact, such was the way Tracey was feeling, she knew if she, herself, had been the one in charge behind the wheel she'd have simply turned the car around by now and driven them all straight back home.

But having already dragged the other two half way down the country, it didn't seem fair to suddenly tell them it had all been for nothing. So, instead, she was left silently reflecting over the state of her relationship with her husband and having earlier made her mind up that it was no longer worth continuing with, she now wasn't quite so sure as to whether that was, indeed, the right decision.

Her thoughts swung like a heavy pendulum first one way and then the other; especially as she didn't just have herself to think about amidst all this sorry mess, she knew she had Tuesday to take into consideration as well.

I mean do you really want your child to grow up a single parent statistic? she asked. *To have only a part-timer for a father?*

Well that certainly wasn't something she'd planned on, she maintained. However, if Jonathan could keep something as important as his sister and her death to himself, she couldn't help but question what other skeletons he might have lurking in his closet.

She wondered if anything about their life together had, in fact, been real; or had he just been going through the motions all these years? It would certainly explain why he liked to shut himself off from the world, she thought to herself, spending more hours in the garden shed than she ever deemed was necessary. It would even explain his lack of interest when it came to all things Tuesday and their starting a family. And it would definitely account for the fact that Andrea and Megan, two women whom she'd only just met, seemed to know more about her husband than she did...

Of course, Tracey knew he left the toothpaste lid off its tube when he brushed his teeth and never put the loo seat down when he'd finished in the bathroom; that he took two sugars in his tea and liked to sleep on his stomach; and even that he had an unusual aversion to all things frilly, in particular red ribbons – she also knew stuff like that was just trivia compared to the things she didn't know.

Like him having a dead sister, for one.

Andrea and Megan even refer to him with a different name, for goodness sake! she began to silently rant.

Not that she had the slightest idea as to why they called him 'Swifty' in the first place, she was forced to admit. Particularly as it bore absolutely no resemblance to his actual surname which, as far as she was aware, monikers usually did.

Swift – Parkes! Swift - Parkes! Nope, nothing like each other at all, she scoffed.

Moreover, as far as she knew, it most certainly didn't come from him displaying any great, literary talent.

The only similarity between my husband and 'The' Jonathan Swift, she bitterly noted. *Being the fact that he's suddenly decided now would be a good time to go off on a Gulliver's Travel of his own!*

Her inner pendulum started to swing again and she found herself wondering why she was making such a fuss over a name. In fact, she asked herself, why was she making a to-do over any of it? Surely she knew enough about her other half by now to realise there'd be a perfectly plausible explanation for his apparent secrecy?

In an attempt to dismiss any doubts she was having, she consoled herself in the knowledge that there wasn't a relationship on the planet that wasn't flawed in some way or another.

And let's face it, she further comforted. *I only have to look at the two women in front of me for confirmation of that!*

After all, from what she remembered being said on the day of Malcolm's funeral, it seemed Mickey P. preferred to pleasure Her Majesty with his company than he did his own wife and kids. Not that Andrea chose to see it that way, Tracey uncharitably considered. In her case absence definitely made the heart grow fonder.

His numerous spells in prison operating like some sort of marriage guidance scheme, rather than a form of punishment, she belittled.

Oh yes, her Jonathan might have kept a few details regarding his past to himself, but at least he hadn't forced her to endure the humiliation of queuing up outside some prison gates once a month, just so she could see him. To be then searched by strangers and have her every move closely monitored and every word intently listened to, just in case they were planning some great escape. In fact, the mere notion that her own partner in life would put her through such an ordeal was quite unimaginable and she shuddered at the shame and embarrassment Andrea must have had to go through all these years.

Then there was Roger, The Ace Face, or whatever it was he chose to call himself these days, Tracey continued. A man who probably changed his name on more occasions than he cared to change his socks. And next time it would, no doubt, be to something even more ludicrous, she contended. So poor Megan would still have to suffer the consequential discomfort at formal introductions.

She found herself wondering what name Megan would take if the two of them did, heaven forbid, ever choose to tie the knot. Surely she'd keep her own surname instead of calling herself Megan Ace? Or worse, Megan Face? Still, Tracey did have to concede that despite the fact that the young woman was fed more crap than the proverbial flowers within, everything in their garden did at least appear rosy.

Nevertheless, in Tracey's view at least Jonathan had chosen to simply keep his mouth shut, as opposed to turning himself into some sort of Billy Liar like The Ace Face had done, on account of his having made up a whole history that simply didn't exist...

Oh, who're you trying to fool? Tracey sighed, at the same time telling herself she was just being unnecessarily mean.

Indeed, with her pendulum, once again, on the move, she knew she was in no position to criticize other people or, more to the point, mock their relationships. That no matter how much comparing and excusing she did, the facts of the matter would still remain the same, regardless.

Firstly, she began to sum up, despite Jonathan being somewhat vague when it came to talking about his past, to all intents and purposes she had thought she'd known him. Thanks to Andrea's startling divulgence, however, it seemed this was no longer quite the case. In fact, if anything, it was more than possible that she didn't know her husband at all.

Secondly and even worse, Tracey continued, was the knock on effect of point number one. That her husband was no longer trustworthy; which also meant Jonathan could be goodness knows where getting up to all sorts of goodness knows what... and all behind her back. And as he'd been very good at hiding the truth from her thus far, she acknowledged, there was also a good chance she'd probably never even know about it.

Not exactly a pleasant position to find herself in after years and years of marriage, she admitted. But with her mind now increasingly running away with itself, it all became a bit too scary for her to contemplate and she was forced to, once again, tell herself that she was just being paranoid.

Things are never quite as bad as they seem, she insisted, in a bid to take control of the situation. *Just because Jonathan hasn't told me about his sister, it doesn't mean he's lying about everything.*

And it certainly doesn't mean he's up to no good, she re-iterated. *Does it?*

CHAPTER THIRTY-EIGHT

POISON IVY

All at once, Jim from the Jim Jams raced onto the stage singing the beginnings of an upbeat Paul Weller classic and with him and the rest of the band, at last, making their appearance, Jonathan couldn't help but be affected by the resulting, yet fantastic surge of excitement – all thanks to the packed audience's reaction, as it immediately recognized the song lyrics.

It let out one, big, unanimous cheer in response, showing both its approval and appreciation of the song choice and within seconds it was as if everyone in the whole marquee was singing along, completely drowning out the front man's voice as they picked up the mantle.

"Wow! This is unbelievable...!" Jonathan elatedly called out, above the chorus.

However, as ecstatic as Jonathan felt in that moment and as much as he wanted to be a part of this exceptional enthusiasm, as he tried to join in with the sing along, he found himself just getting the words all muddled up. A part of him, he realised, suddenly feeling more out of the loop, than in.

Not that this was all his own fault as such, he was forced to acknowledge. He did, after all, along with everyone else, know the song word for word. Oh no, it seemed his libretto confusion was very much thanks to the young woman who'd appeared as if from nowhere outside of the tent; the very same young woman whom for some reason, he noted, had refused to leave his side ever since.

From that point onwards she'd made it very clear that she only had eyes for him and although Jonathan couldn't quite understand the raison d'être behind her interest, he was both flattered and frightened at the same time. Flattered because women didn't usually pay him that kind of attention, he admitted. And frightened because he didn't know how to deal with it. So now, due to the cramped floor space that seemed to have given her just the excuse she'd been looking for, Jonathan found she wasn't just up close and personal, rather, she was stuck to his side like a limpet.

And an overtly sexual limpet at that, he somewhat nervously observed. Her slow and inviting moves as she rubbed against him not just making it difficult for him to take part in the sing song, but much to his embarrassment, for anyone in the vicinity to actually ascertain which tune she was, in fact, dancing to.

However, despite finding himself a tad embarrassed by this mollusc-like, provocative display and musical mis-timing, if Jonathan was being totally honest he had to admit he wasn't finding it a wholly negative experience either. There was something of a pain/pleasure thing going on for him – even though as a married man, he knew the pleasure side of the coin certainly wasn't something he should've been enjoying.

He nudged Mickey P. in the hope of getting some assistance, but unfortunately for him, it seemed none was forthcoming.

"What happened to Swifty the Ladies' Man?" he simply called out instead and much to Jonathan's frustration, he seemed, if anything, to find his predicament somewhat more than amusing.

Not that The Ace Face's response was any more helpful, Jonathan couldn't fail to notice. *He* just shrugged and offered a dry smile – a dry smile that seemed to display anything but sympathy. So much so, that Jonathan even began to suspect The Ace Face was actually relishing his discomfort. And even though he couldn't think of any underlying rationale as to why that might be the case, as far as he was concerned, The Ace Face's actions were actually more unsettling, than those of limpet girl.

CHAPTER THIRTY-NINE

DREAMS OF CHILDREN

Pepper was beginning to think being an undercover agent might not be his forte, after all. Which was somewhat disappointing to say the least, he complained; especially when getting a fix on his target located somewhere in the crowds was proving nigh on impossible.

Furthermore, thanks to his having to try and fit in with a bunch of criminal Neanderthals, he had to admit he didn't just feel out of his depth, he felt downright bloody scared. Then again, looking at his watch and realising Maximus' girlfriend/daughter/second cousin three times removed was taking an unusually long time on her trip to the loo, he also had to acknowledge his fears were hardly surprising.

And the longer she chooses to stay away, he thought to himself, increasingly worried. *The more agitated this bleedin' monster is gonna bloody well get.*

Unsurprisingly, to make matters worse, the gang leader's anxiety soon included the return of his need to growl and shake his head at anyone and everyone who looked his way. And thanks to the covert officer's professional need to monitor the situation, he subsequently found himself on the receiving end of more violent displays than any of the giant's other victims put together. However, ranking number one on this particular occasion wasn't a position Pepper was particularly at ease with, so for the sake of his own stress levels if no-one else's, he recognised that at some stage he was going to have to come up with an excuse to distance himself.

Not that he found plucking up the inner strength to make his move exactly easy under the circumstances and he decided the situation called for a few deep breathing exercises first .

Or should I say deep breathing exercises along with a few swigs of beer for Dutch courage, he suitably corrected, before putting a three quarters full bottle of beer to his lips and downing the whole of its contents in one.

"I think I'll, er... go for a bit of a wander," he, at last, said and although glad to have finally built up the nerve to actually make the break, he just hoped the responding growl and head shake was only Maximus' way of consenting.

"I'll just go then, shall I?" he nervously continued, taking a somewhat apprehensive step away from the gang leader, just in case.

Then, realising it probably wasn't one of his better ideas to give Maximus the opportunity to make himself clear with regards to his position, he decided now was the time to just bite the bullet. At the same time undertaking a sharp turn accordingly, all at once running off into the safety of the marquee masses.

All in the name of resuming his hunt for Mickey P., of course, he told himself and as he looked around, he shook himself down and determinedly squared his shoulders, deciding that now was the time to start his search in earnest.

CHAPTER FORTY

SUMMER NIGHTS

"Look! There's another one!" squealed Megan in delight and much to Tracey's indifference she, yet again, tooted the car horn – such, it seemed, was her driver's inability to control her excitement.

"Mmmm," the mother-to-be replied, not even trying to hide the fact that she couldn't have cared one way or the other.

Besides, she could see for herself what appeared to be an unusually high number of scooters on the road. So the last thing she needed was Megan's persistence in pointing each and every single one of them out and for Tracey this wasn't just starting to get a bit tiresome, it was getting more than a smidgen annoying to boot.

As was the amount of unnecessary Road Runner, beep beeping going on and it seemed for every show of approval Megan just *had* to demonstrate with regards to all these two wheeled vehicles, in turn, it seemed these two wheeled vehicle riders were equally as keen to show their admiration for the quality of her mini.

Although I suspect the lot of you wouldn't be quite so appreciative, thought the mother-to be, of the scooterists. *If you were the one's stuck here in the back of it, instead of me.*

"There must be some sort of event going on," joined in Andrea – leaving Tracey wondering who was worse; Megan for her over the top enthusiasm or Andrea for stating the obvious?

"Either that," she said, flatly. "Or we're entering the scooter capital of Great Britain, which I very much doubt somehow, don't you?"

Not that her travel companions appeared to give one iota about her lack of interest, she duly noted. Instead, it seemed she was now going to have to suffer the misfortune of having to endure yet another trip down memory lane. Something she wasn't sure she could actually stomach after some of their earlier disclosures – disclosures that she was now doing her damndest not to think about.

"Oh, it does take me back," said a wistful Andrea, leaving Tracey no choice but to let out a despondent sigh. "The jam packed ride outs, making fools of ourselves on the dance floor... And that's not to mention the drinking that went on. All before heading back into the next muddy field to camp for the night."

"Yep, them were the days, eh?" Tracey sarcastically replied, not that she'd ever actually done any camping. Moreover, in being honest, she quite frankly couldn't think of anything worse.

Apart from having to put up with this lot, she thought to herself, as yet one more scooterist came onto the horizon. And *surprise, surprise, not!* this one also insisted on doing a great Looney Tunes character impression, before finishing with a big thumbs up as he passed by, again much like his predecessors.

"Shall we follow them?" asked Megan – clearly under the misguided impression, thought Tracey, that this would, in some way, be quite a daring move for them to make.

"Nah," replied Andrea, still in reminiscent mode. "I don't think so. Wouldn't be the same without Mickey..."

"Besides," she continued, all at once back in the here and now. "We do have Tracey to think about. And it's not as if scooter rallies are exactly conducive to the needs of heavily pregnant women, is it?"

Tracey's ears suddenly pricked. *Excuse me...* she couldn't help but think. *What do you mean? Aren't exactly conducive!*

Despite knowing full well such words were, to all intents and purposes, said with the best of intentions, it nevertheless didn't give them the right to talk about her like she wasn't even there, thank you very much. Heavily pregnant or not, as far as she was concerned, she still had the ability to speak for herself.

And the ability to have a good time, for that matter, she asserted.

"It's probably better we think about sorting a room for the night," Andrea continued. "It is getting a bit late."

"I suppose," sighed Megan, clearly disappointed.

"Well *I* think we should follow them," Tracey suddenly piped up, just glad to see she'd caused enough of a stir to make Megan bring the car to a hasty standstill.

"Really?" she asked, excitedly turning to the mother-to-be.

"Really?" Andrea asked, unsure.

"After the day I've had, I could do with a laugh," Tracey adamantly replied. "And anyway, it'll give me the chance to see what all the fuss is about, won't it."

She watched Megan turn to Andrea with a broad, satisfied grin and Andrea turn to Megan as if to say she still didn't think it was such a good idea, whilst at the same time hoping that in her annoyance, she hadn't just cut her nose off to spite her face.

CHAPTER FORTY-ONE

ZOOT SUIT

Jonathan could, once again, feel the air of excitement in the marquee intensify as the event organiser took to the stage with his microphone and signalled to the DJ to cut the music. It seemed now it was time to reveal the winners of the various competition categories and fingers crossed, one of them was going to be him.

"Everybody ready," called out the organiser, in an attempt to further whip up the audience. "Then let the honours begin..."

As each announcement was made, Jonathan watched the victors then one by one, all force their way through the congratulatory crowd, enjoying both thunderous applause and rowdy cheers of recognition.

However, despite joining in with these celebratory efforts, he knew deep down the award everyone was *really* anticipating, was the proclamation of who would be crowned 'Best in Show'. That was the trophy every contestant in their heart of hearts truly coveted and surprising himself with just how much, Jonathan was compelled to acknowledge that he was greedy for it too.

As he nervously waited for the result, he reassured himself in the understanding that his Vespa was certainly of a high enough standard to take the title. Then again, although cool and classy in a traditional understated way, especially compared to many of the other entries, he was also forced to acknowledge that ultimately it would come down to what was and what wasn't currently in vogue. And considering he'd been away from the scene for as long as he had, he did have to admit that that was, in fact, something he knew absolutely nothing about...

Jesus, Jonathan, he suddenly self reprimanded. All at once realising he was starting to take all this a little too seriously. *Anyone would think it was your machine in the first place, the way you're going on.* Which meant any credit that might or might not be forthcoming, he reminded himself, did, in reality, belong to The Ace Face.

Although it would still be exciting to hear my name called out, he couldn't help but contradict, at the same time thinking back to the good old days, when on a couple of occasions he'd thought the title was his for the taking, only to then end up missing out. So with the organiser now coming to the last of his envelopes, Jonathan found himself, once again, caught up in the moment, thanks to his being only seconds away from finding out if he'd been pipped to the post once more.

"So here we are..." the organiser, at last, declared. "We've come to the final award of the evening. The one category everyone's been waiting for. Yes everybody, it's time to announce the 'Best in Show'."

Not that Jonathan gave a damn about such a preamble. He just wanted to know if he'd won or not.

"Now I think you'll all agree we've had some excellent entries this year," the organiser continued. "However, the judges have decided there was one machine in particular, that stood out just that tiny bit more than all the rest..."

"Get on with it..." Jonathan called out, by now really getting into the swing of things – much to the overall crowd's amusement.

"Okay, okay," the organiser replied, before clearing his throat in preparation. "And the winner is, as they say..."

Jonathan waited with bated breath.

"Swifty Parkes!"

"Yes!" shouted Jonathan in response, unable to quite believe it, as both he and Mickey P. automatically and rather animatedly began jumping up and down in celebration. Moreover, such was his exhilaration, he even found himself accepting a celebratory kiss from his new lady friend. However, as he then turned to The Ace Face to include him in the revelry, he was met with a distinct lack of merriment on his part.

"What's up with you?" he quickly asked.

Not that there was time to wait for an answer; as far as he was concerned, he did, after all, have more important considerations to think about – like basking in the rapturous glory of being crowned 'Best in Show'.

So, ready to accept the glory and with nothing but a dismissive shake of his head, he eagerly headed off into the masses to collect his prize. At the same time determined to show each and every single person there, that no matter what, he was still a winner.

CHAPTER FORTY-TWO

AND YOUR BIRD CAN SING

"Hang on a minute," said Pepper, wondering if he'd just heard right. "Did I really just hear the DJ call out the name 'Swifty Parkes'?"

"Now that would be way too easy," he scoffed, tempted to assume he must have simply got it wrong.

Nevertheless, he began forcing his way towards the stage in the hope of getting a closer look just in case, tingling with excitement in the hope that he hadn't. And, as he, at last, watched the victor climb the steps to collect his trophy, immediately recognising him in the process, it was all he could do to stop himself from jumping up and punching the air.

"I knew it!" he asserted, his police man's nose having said all along that his arch enemy was most definitely amongst this lot somewhere and despite having to acknowledge the fact that finding Mickey P. hadn't been quite as easy as first anticipated, he was just glad he'd maintained his resolve to stick with it.

However, he also knew the last thing he'd expected in all of this, was for good, old Jonathan to step into the breach and unwittingly lead him straight to his target.

Eager to make the most of this unexpected yet very much welcome surprise, he realised if he wanted to apprehend his prey, all he had to do now was trail at a safe distance until he finally had Mickey P. in his sights.

"Looks like I won't be going to Brighton, after all," he cheerfully congratulated, as he began covertly following in Jonathan's footsteps. What's more, in what felt like a little extra bonus, he was pleased to find it didn't take too long, before he spotted what he'd come for.

"Yes!" he said, as he, at last, espied his long standing rival. "Now I've got you!"

Except instead of racing in all guns blazing as planned, he found himself abruptly stopping in his tracks thanks to yet one more unforeseen development .

"Hang on a minute," he, once again, said. "Isn't that what's her face? What's she doing here?"

Confused, it seemed he hadn't only managed to find the illusive Mickey P., but Mickey P. in the company of Maximus' equally illusive girlfriend/daughter/second cousin three times removed. Not that he had any clue as to how the two of them would know each other.

"And not that I suppose that matters," he said.

He stood watching them for a moment, trying to weigh the situation up. Then, with a big, sly smile suddenly spreading across his face, he found himself coming to the conclusion that it might be an idea to delay the impending arrest, after all.

"Especially if that delay means I can have a bit of fun first," he told himself and with that, he slunk off back into the crowd, taking his wide grin with him.

CHAPTER FORTY-THREE

SHUT UP

"Have I still got it? Or what...?" asked Jonathan, having landed back with his prized trophy.

"Never doubted it for one minute, mate," laughed Mickey P. – and even though his new lady friend was also pleased for him, jumping up and down and squealing as she was, Jonathan thought it just a shame The Ace Face couldn't bring himself to show much interest; particularly as it was *his* scooter being recognised to begin with.

Then again, on second thoughts he did suppose that he, too, would be a bit pissed off under the circumstances, if someone had stolen an award from under his nose like that.

Well, it's not as if I've exactly stolen it as such, he corrected. *That would be Mickey P.'s job... No, I have to say it was, in effect, given to me.* And despite knowing that this was only as a result of mistaken identity, he reassured himself in the knowledge that that was hardly his fault.

Still, the trophy wasn't the only thing he'd brought back with him and he knew if anything was going to lift his old friend's spirits, it would be the arrival of his surprise guest.

"And look who I found along the way..." he said.

Jim from The Jim Jams stepped forward, but it seemed The Ace Face still couldn't bring himself to cheer up and, rather disappointingly for Jonathan, instead of showing any great joy, he seemed to find the whole situation somewhat awkward.

"Er, yeah, right. Hi ya, mate..." he said, ill at ease. "How's things?"

Jesus! Jonathan thought to himself in response. *What is your problem?* After all, to say the two of them were supposed to be 'like that', as far as he was concerned, The Ace Face certainly wasn't acting like it.

At least he wasn't until he suddenly stepped forward to embrace Jim in one of his bear hugs, Jonathan observed. In spite of it being a gesture that for some reason seemed forced, with both the giver and the receiver seemingly finding it equally as embarrassing.

However, Jonathan quickly appreciated The Ace Face's sulking was, in fact, the least of his worries – thanks to the unexpected interruption that came from a vaguely familiar voice.

"Good evening lads," it simply said and turning to find himself not just recognising a rather strangely dressed Pepper, but also The Scorpion Scooter Rebels, Jonathan realised when it came to degrees of simplicity, this situation was going to be anything but.

He looked to Mickey P., telling himself with regards to the stolen scooter, he should have known things wouldn't be quite as straightforward as his friend had made out. On the other hand and to be fair, Mickey P. did seem just as surprised by the new arrivals' presence. As did The Ace Face, he noted and as did his new lady friend – although in his book quite why she should be so dumbfounded, well that was anyone's guess.

One of the Scorpion Scooter Rebels all of a sudden stepped forward, a giant of a man whom Jonathan could only assume was the actual gang leader. Then, much to Jonathan's horror without even as much as a bye or leave, he proceeded to grab Mickey P. by the scruff of his neck, lifting him so far off the ground in the process that if he'd wanted to his poor mate could've actually counted the whiskers on his aggressor's face.

Jonathan turned to The Ace Face wondering what the hell was going on and despite the fact that he didn't see himself as a natural have-a-go hero, he silently questioned if they should between them, attempt some sort of rescue. However, in catching an eye-balled warning from his new lady friend, he realised she was counselling him to stay exactly where he was and although he felt bad about following her advice, he supposed at least it explained why, like him, she'd previously been somewhat taken aback.

Saying that, in her case it clearly wasn't so much Pepper's sudden arrival that had spooked her, he acknowledged, it was that of the gang leader.

The very same gang leader who for some inexplicable reason now found the need to growl menacingly in Mickey P.'s face; a growl that, understandably so in Jonathan's view, elicited a pathetic squeal in response from his victim. Not that Jonathan had a clue as to what either of them were actually saying, but whatever the conversation, he could see the giant of a man obviously needed clarification on the matter. Unfortunately with no thoughts of releasing his grip in any way, for some reason this responsibility fell to Pepper – something Jonathan knew wasn't exactly a good sign, especially when it came to a decision regarding Mickey P.'s fate.

"Yep, that's definitely him," confirmed Pepper, clearly looking forward to Mickey P. being taught a lesson or two.

However, whereas Jonathan had a very good idea as to what form these lessons were going to take, he still wasn't sure as to what lay behind them and it was only when his new lady friend chose to put herself in the firing line that things, at last, started to become clear.

"Sweetheart, Daddykins, Maximus" she began expertly placating. "This kind gentleman here wasn't messing with me. He was looking after me."

What? thought Jonathan, for the first time realising this altercation had absolutely nothing to do with stolen scooters at all, but was, in reality, because of some man on woman mis-deed that hadn't even taken place. Then it dawned on him that were it not for Pepper's vindictiveness towards Mickey P. in particular, it could just as easily have been himself stranded up in the air like that; leaving him now just hoping against hope that his new lady friend didn't see fit to point that out.

" There's only one culprit here," she said. "And that's...

Please don't say me, please don't say me, Jonathan prayed.

"Him!"

Thank God! he thought to himself, as she, instead indicated to Pepper.

"He's the one who really tried to take advantage of me."

Jonathan watched on as the gang leader suddenly released his grip, allowing Mickey P. to just drop to the floor in a heap. Moreover, as he then observed him turn his unwanted attentions towards Pepper, it was evident that whatever the man had been scheming, it had by now seriously backfired.

"Maximus... mate..." he begged.

With the rest of the Scorpion Scooter Rebels struggling to contain their excitement, Jonathan knew it didn't matter how much pleading Pepper did, the result still wasn't going to be pretty. On top of that, he felt himself cringe at the pain the gang leader's new victim must have experienced, when the first punch to his face landed so hard, his wig actually flew off high into the air – although for Jonathan why he'd chosen to wear a wig in the first place was still a bit of a conundrum.

Not that he was about to think too hard on the matter and as every other gang member took Maximus' blow as a cue for themselves to start throwing punches willy nilly, with a full scale brawl, western style developing around him, Jonathan's fight or flight instincts took priority.

Of course, he very quickly came to the conclusion that it was now time to leave and he was just glad to see his travel companions were of the same opinion, more than happy to follow his lead, as he fought his way out of the marquee in a distinct bid for freedom.

*

"What the bloody hell's he doing here, anyway?" asked Jonathan, as the three of them, at last, managed to break out into the fresh air.

As he led the race over towards their two scooters, he was pleasantly surprised to find himself still clutching his 'Best in Show' trophy, just as tightly as The Ace Face was hanging on to Malcolm's urn.

"You think I knew he was coming?" replied Mickey P., incredulous and out of breath. Not that there was time for a full and frank explanation regardless, Jonathan realised and he quickly tossed his award over to The Ace Face for safe keeping, before hastily jumping onto the Vespa and starting its engine.

"I haven't got room for that!" The Ace Face argued, already desperately struggling to pack Malcolm away.

"Well you'll have to make room," Jonathan ordered. "But for God's sake get a move on."

"Yoo hoo!" a female voice called out from behind. "Wait for me!"

Jonathan turned, somewhat surprised to see his new lady friend speedily tootling her way towards him. "What does she want?" he asked, thinking now was definitely not the time for a goodbye chit chat, let alone swapping contact details. "It's 'cos of her we're fucking in this mess!"

"Who cares..."" said Mickey P. jumping onto his Lambretta. "Let's just go."

"I'm coming with you," she called out, leaving Jonathan no time to protest as she picked up speed in her forward assault and literally threw herself onto the pillion seat behind him.

Jesus! he, once again, thought to himself. *This is all I need.*

"You can't," he insisted. "You haven't got a helmet."

However, as he hastily donned his own headgear and checked his scarf, the last thing he expected was for her to scan the neighbouring two wheeled machines and, spotting one hanging from a set of handle bars, just grab it.

"I do now," she said.

Feeling like they were wasting enough time as it was, Jonathan knew the real priority was to get their sorry asses out of there. So, with The Ace Face automatically leaping onto the Lambretta, he found himself with no choice but to speed off into the distance with his new lady friend in tow – whether he'd wanted to or not.

CHAPTER FORTY-FOUR

GHOST TOWN

"I thought these things were meant to be buzzing," said a disappointed Tracey, as she, Andrea and Megan stepped into the marquee. And she couldn't help but question if her travel companions had been exaggerating somewhat, when they'd said these rallies were electrifying, exciting events, held in giant tents crammed to the rafters with hip, like minded people.

Unfortunately, there was no live band present, happily pumping out Mod anthem after Mod anthem as described and even though she had to acknowledge there was, indeed, a DJ in the house, he wasn't exactly spinning the decks. Oh no, from what Tracey could see this venue certainly wasn't 'happening' in the way she'd been led to believe – a quick calculation telling her it had to be at least three quarters empty. In fact, to put it bluntly, with an atmosphere, if you could call it that, definitely lacking in the fun! fun! fun! stakes, she told herself, Malcolm's funeral had to have had more life to it than this.

"Because the way you two went on," she continued. "This is not what I was hoping for."

"And neither was I," said Megan, clearly unable to hide her own disappointment, as Tracey wondered if it might have been better to have taken Andrea's advice, after all, and just gone and found a room for the night.

"Well I suppose when it comes to a mix of party people, alcohol and loud music, some things just never change," Andrea joined in. "It's just a shame we missed out on all the action."

"What action?" asked Tracey, taking another look around their somewhat dismal surroundings. "What're you talking about?"

"The police vans we passed on the way over," Andrea explained. "A tenner says they'd just come from here."

However, watching some mass brawl play out in front of her very eyes certainly wasn't Tracey's idea of having a good time and if that was the kind of thing that went on, she realised in her condition, it was probably better that there wasn't any hustle and bustle for her to contend with.

"Well I suppose we should at least try and make the most of things, now that we're here," said the mother-to-be. "You two go and sit down and I'll get us a drink."

"Three orange juices," she said, as she approached the bar – noting that this was the first time in goodness knows how long, that she hadn't had to use her pregnancy to queue jump. Moreover, as she glanced about the place whilst she waited for the barman to get her order together, she found herself automatically and happily tapping her feet to the music, pleasantly surprised at how catchy these Mod tunes were. To the point that, had the dance floor not been so deserted, she did think she might even have been tempted to get out there and have a bit of a boogie herself.

Not that you have a dancing partner anyway, she supposed and after a quick glimpse over at her travel companions, she doubted very much that *they* were in any mood to step into the breach.

Yep, it looks like there's going to be no tripping of the light fantastic for you tonight, young lady, she told herself, dejectedly drumming her fingers on the counter.

She tried to recall the last time she'd been in a position to let her hair down and really enjoy herself for once, left saddened in the knowledge that it must have been so long ago, she couldn't actually remember.

Well it's no wonder your husband's buggered off like he has, then, is it? she scolded.

Then again, she counter-argued, life *had* become so consumed with getting pregnant, a task that should have been so easy, yet turned out to be anything but. So after months, more months and yet even more months of feeling like some sort of failure to womanhood, was it any wonder, she asked, there'd been a shortage of laughs along the way? In truth, was it any wonder, she further questioned, that she'd become, dare she say it, a little obsessive?

She couldn't help but start to feel as miserable as her environment, as she began to realise exactly what Jonathan had had to put up with. At the same time speculating over whether she should just forget the drinks altogether and tell the other two they were leaving. However, as she was making her mind up to do just that, she found herself catching the eye of a man so large, not only could the size of his belly have competed against the size of her own, with his shiny bald head and rather gigantic stature, he could only have been described as Buster Bloodvessel's identical twin.

Not exactly an attractive look as far as Tracey was concerned and under any other circumstances, she knew she would, by now, have been running for the hills.

However, it wasn't just his build that was huge, the same could be said for his smile and for some reason on this occasion, she was surprised to feel anything but threatened. What's more, when he then indicated to the dance floor in an open invitation for her to join him, she realised he was offering her just the tonic she needed.

Shall I? she asked, mischievous but still not sure.

Of course, what was good for the goose was good for the gander, she told herself. And just because the last few years had been difficult for Jonathan as well, that hadn't given him the right to take himself off for a bit of fun without a bye or leave, had it? Besides, wasn't it about time she enjoyed herself for a change, too? Which had, she acknowledged, been her intention when she'd made the decision to come here.

"Oh sod it," she said.

She graciously took 'Buster' up on his offer, telling herself to just forget her woes for now. It was, at any rate, only a dance and where was the harm in that?

CHAPTER FORTY-FIVE

THICK AS THIEVES

Jonathan watched on as The Ace Face, having elected himself Scout Leader, stood back to admire his own handiwork. However, it was only when he was satisfied that the tent had been expertly erected, its canvas and guide ropes sufficiently taut, that he began skilfully setting about making an open fire on which he could brew some coffee – at the same time making sure to maintain a safe distance, Jonathan noted, between their sleeping quarters and their cooking facilities.

It was all very painful viewing, especially for an observer who was somewhat less than keen on spending a night under the stars, in a random field and in the middle of nowhere. And Jonathan could've kicked himself, for not having had the foresight to double check their sleeping arrangements prior to actually leaving home. Instead, he'd regretfully operated under the erroneous assumption that they'd be booked into some sort of hostelry for the night. One that didn't just have a proper bed for him to climb into, but also a nice warm duvet and a couple of fluffy pillows – pillows upon which he could lay his, by now, rather weary, little head.

"If you wanted five star accommodations," said The Ace Face, once again, digging Malcolm out of his rucksack so he could join in with the rest of the group. "Then you shouldn't have left the travel arrangements to someone else." He turned to face Jonathan in order to emphasise his point. "Should you?" he said.

Jonathan felt suitably scolded.

Although to be fair and feeling somewhat indignant, it wasn't as if Jonathan had meant for his resentful sulk to be quite so obvious. On the other hand, after the day's events so far, he also couldn't help but think he was entitled to feel just that little bit sorry for himself. There had, after all, been one fiasco after another – from being scared witless even before that damn game of chicken, he recalled, to being forced back behind the wheels of a scooter. From coming face-to-face with Pepper at the rally, to their subsequent great escape. None of it, he noted, being any of his fault.

And now this, he further complained, as he looked about him. Three grown men stuck in a field with a casket of ashes and a young woman they didn't even know. All expected to cram themselves into a tent that was never going to be big enough for the original party number, let alone any extras.

So is it any wonder I might be feeling a bit aggrieved? he asked, sarcastic.

He watched The Ace Face as he prepared the coffee and in clocking that his mate no longer had enough plastic mugs to go round, it seemed one of them was going to have to go without a hot, bedtime drink.

Clearly your organisational skills don't extend to expecting the unexpected, Jonathan sneered.

Although at the same time it was a farce too many in his book and before he knew it, his misery was quickly replaced with a form of hysteria and he couldn't help but start to giggle.

"What?" asked The Ace Face, defensive.

"The cups..." chuckled Jonathan. "And the tent..." Moreover, he quickly realised the source of his amusement didn't just lie in the here and now and the more he thought about their roller coaster of a day, the more he began to titter.

"And Malcolm in the bushes..." he sniggered.

In turn, the more he began to snicker, the less able he was to get a hold of himself and his laughter didn't just become worse as a result, it became infectious. Therefore, before he knew it, it seemed Mickey P. was joining in with his giggles too.

"Don't forget the Scorpion Scooter Rebels..." his mate chortled.

"And her..." added Jonathan, pointing to his new lady friend.

"I do have a name, if you don't mind," she jumped in, slighted. "And 'Olivia' is so much nicer than 'her'... don't you think?"

Not that Jonathan was particularly listening. "Let's not forget Pepper," he said, still laughing. "And that bleeding wig..."

He recalled how the dodgy hairpiece had been sent flying off into the air the way it had and as a result, was immediately sent into an absolute fit of howling.

"You've got to give him his due," said Mickey P., trying to control himself. "The man's certainly determined."

"What do you mean?" asked Jonathan, wiping the tears from his eyes.

"Oh come on, you didn't think he was there just for the music, did you?"

On the contrary, that was exactly what Jonathan had thought. That it was a chance meeting with an off duty Police Officer, purely coincidental and as uncomplicated as that. "What're you talking about?" he asked, beginning to sober.

"So I missed a bail appointment," replied Mickey P. "What can I say?"

However, as he tried to get his head around what he was hearing, Jonathan struggled to see the situation as being quite so simple. In fact, as it dawned on him just how serious it was, he felt his good humour completely disappear.

"I wouldn't worry about it," said Mickey P. "He can chase me all he wants, I'll still only get a slap on the wrists, whatever stunt he tries to pull."

But as far as Jonathan was concerned, again, that wasn't the point.

"You're a fucking idiot," he said, unable to comprehend such a dismissive attitude. "You just don't give a shit about anything, do you?"

"And you're fucking over-reacting..."

Jonathan scoffed. "Over reacting... look at you, sat there like you haven't got a care in the world, whilst the rest of us have no choice but to just get on with it. Call yourself a man, I bet you've never done an honest day's work in your bloody life, have you?"

"Yeah, well that's where you're wrong," replied Mickey P. "I've had a couple of jobs over the years as it happens. It's just that when owt goes missing, guaranteed it's me that gets the blame. And I'm not working anywhere where I'm not trusted."

"Not trusted! And whose fault is that?" asked Jonathan, incredulous. "If you weren't such a fucking tea leaf..."

"Come on lads," The Ace Face cut in. "There's no need to get personal... Rational adults and all that..."

A look of disdain swept across Jonathan's face as he was, once again, unable to believe what he was hearing.

"And pray tell me," he said, all at once rounding on the interjector. "What would you know about anything? You're so far in fucking fantasy land, you couldn't spot rationality if it jumped up and bit you on the arse!"

He could see The Ace Face start to flush with embarrassment, but Jonathan still couldn't bring himself to care.

"All that crap about Perugia being in Greece..." he continued. "It's in fucking Italy, you tool!"

"That's a bit harsh, mate," said Mickey P., quick to defend. "None of this is his fault."

"Oh no," said Jonathan. "Well whose bloody idea was all this in the first place, then?" He waved his arms at their pathetic surroundings.

"Was it not his?" Olivia innocently dared to ask, at the same time pointing to Malcolm's urn.

However, despite the fact that technically it could be said she had a point, it wasn't a point Jonathan was about to concede and he huffed at the mere suggestion.

"And like you can talk anyway," protested The Ace Face. "Giving it the big 'I Am' when you were up on stage collecting *your* trophy! What's real about that, eh? In case you've forgotten, which you clearly have, it's not even your bleeding scooter, mate. It's bloody well mine!"

"You're just jealous," Jonathan hit back, not prepared to give credence to any such claim. "Always have been and always will!"

"Well rather that than selfish," retorted The Ace Face. "I mean, what's him and Pepper got to do with you anyway? He's the one running the risk of getting locked up...! Oh, I forgot, like everything else going on in the world, it's all about you, isn't it?"

Jonathan snorted, wondering where all this was going.

"The great Swifty Parkes. Swanning around on his scooter saying *look at me everyone, look at me...* patronizing the likes of anyone else, who didn't have the required rich parents to get them their own wheels. And heaven forbid the poor sods who couldn't even scrape together enough cash to build up the right record collection... For God's sake, even your own sister's death was about fucking you..."

Jonathan froze, The Ace Face's inclusion of Melanie in his little speech being a step too far.

"Look mate, I'm sorry. I shouldn't..."

But as far as any apology was concerned, it was too little too late and Jonathan angrily lunged forward in response, charging The Ace Face to the ground.

He began throwing punch after punch, each one landing harder and harder, as years of pent up frustration and rage were finally able to come to the fore. And adrenalin racing through his veins, his fury was such that he felt nothing of the right hooks and left uppercuts that reigned back at him, as The Ace Face desperately tried to regain some control. In fact, for Jonathan it was as if he wasn't even wrestling with The Ace Face anymore – his combatant suddenly becoming anyone and everyone.

Even when Mickey P. frantically intervened, Jonathan was more than ready for another bout, struggling to control every ounce of his emotions, as he huffed and puffed and glared at his target, determined to lunge for a second time.

Albeit, as the seconds passed, then so did the moment. Leaving Jonathan with a long, testosterone fuelled silence to contend with.

"You know, I might exaggerate about what is, or is not, going on in my life," The Ace Face eventually ventured, at the same time wiping blood from his lip. "But that doesn't mean I'm the only one running away from reality."

Jonathan looked down at his fists, his actions having shocked even himself.

Nevertheless, he was still in no mood for lectures, let alone in any frame of mind to listen to a bullshitter like this. And with the urge to fight having, at last, subsided to a weary nothingness, he simply and silently turned his back on the rest of the group.

More to the point, he turned his back on whatever it was they had to say, before grabbing his rucksack and heading for the tent.

CHAPTER FORTY-SIX

THE BITTEREST PILL

"Sod off!" ordered Jonathan, as the tent zip went up. Whatever it was Mickey P. or The Ace Face had to say to him, he most certainly didn't want to hear.

"Is that any way to talk to a lady?" said Olivia, letting herself in regardless.

Upon hearing a female voice, Jonathan suddenly sat bolt upright, wondering what on earth it was *she* could possibly want.

"You don't mind, do you?" she asked. – not that she bothered to wait for his response, Jonathan noted.

"I mean you can't expect a girl to sleep out in the cold, not when there's a nice warm bed in here she could be sharing..."

Much to Jonathan's *Oh my God please no, shock, horror,* she began to slowly unbutton her dress.

"What're you doing?" he asked, somewhat shaken and feeling the need to protect at least his own dignity, he found himself automatically pulling his sleeping bag right up to his chin.

"What does it look like...?" she replied, with a knowing smile. "Besides, it's not as if it's anything you haven't seen before."

Not sure quite how to respond to that, Jonathan was left lost for words.

Please stop, he nervously thought to himself. However, as much as he knew he should have actually been voicing this request, or at the very least diverting his eyes to give her some privacy, he couldn't actually bring himself to do either.

Not that Olivia seemed to mind his gaze, he realised. In fact, if anything, she was actively encouraging it. So much so, that with every item of clothing she removed, she seemed to become increasingly provocative in the way she went about it. And, unfortunately, for Jonathan the more he told himself this shouldn't, indeed, be happening, the more he secretly wanted it to continue.

He couldn't remember the last time a woman had made such a display especially for him and he was forced to acknowledge that not only was this kind of foreplay not in his wife's nature, but for a long time now, sex with Tracey had been all about hormone levels, temperature charts and accurate timings. It had become a means to an end, rather than the love making it was supposed to have been and as far as Jonathan was concerned, he was just the sperm donor, in what had come to feel like a mechanical process.

Here with Olivia, however, it didn't just seem to be all about pleasure, she seemed to be making it all about him. Consequently, it was as if he was back to being a real, blood running through his veins, man again – the definite stirring in his groin only serving to confirm this.

Not that a respectably married bloke should be comparing his wife's bedroom activities to those of another woman to start with, he reminded himself – and wasn't his marital status something he should be explaining anyway?

However, as thoughts of telling her to cease what she was doing, once again, began running through his head, unfortunately words, once again, failed him. Even more so when Olivia silently crawled into the sleeping bag with him, ensuring her soft, smooth skin rubbed against his.

Jesus, he thought to himself, his body all at once tensing.

Not that it stayed that way for long, it seemed. Moreover, as she began expertly caressing his neck with her lips, gradually working her mouth and tongue down to his chest and eventually his abdomen, Jonathan didn't just feel his body begin to melt, he realised his feeble yet internal arguments to resist had been completely and utterly futile.

Especially considering he hadn't wanted her to stop from the very beginning, he finally admitted. His having passed the point of no return, the second she'd stepped inside the tent.

CHAPTER FORTY-SEVEN

HAPPY DAYS TOY TOWN

"I don't know," teased Tracey, feeling ready to take on the world, as she happily tucked into her bowl of breakfast cereal. "Some people just can't take the pace."

She continued to observe Andrea and Megan, the pair of them still bleary eyed and yawning and she couldn't help but feel a little bit guilty, as she remembered her previous night's antics and the numerous times they'd both tried and failed to drag her out of the marquee.

However, in the same breath, she knew letting her hair down on the dance floor with the Buster Bloodvessel look-alike had been just the tonic she'd needed. And in the midst of having the first bit of fun in what had clearly been quite some time, as far as she was concerned, any fool could understand why she hadn't wanted to give it up all that easily.

In addition, it had obviously done her the power of good, she acknowledged; giving her the ability to wake up this morning with a fresh perspective on recent events, as it had. A perspective, she realised, that could only be beneficial in the long run.

For one, she was finally able to acknowledge that trying for a baby, had obviously taken its toll on Jonathan more than she'd previously wanted to recognise; which, in turn, she considered, might, in part, explain why he'd decided to run off to Brighton. After all, he'd suffered the trials and tribulations of their starting a family too and as such, he probably needed to have a good knees-up as much as she had.

Not that any of this explained why he'd kept the existence and not to put it too mildly, subsequent non-existence, of his sister to himself, she conceded. But that was something only he could account for. At least she now had the clarity of mind to know she should, at any rate, listen to what he had to say on the matter, before making a decision on whether or not to end their marriage. *Especially* in view of everything they'd been through, she told herself.

"Yeah well, it's easy for you to say," replied a groggy Megan. "You aren't the one who, on top of everything else, had to sleep in a bleeding camp bed, are you?"

"You can't blame me for the lack of rooms in this place," said Tracey, pouring herself another cup of tea.

"That's true," Andrea joined in. "But if you hadn't insisted on strutting your stuff for hours on end, we might've been able to find an establishment that did have enough proper beds to go around... "

"Mind you..." she continued, looking back on their evening's entertainment. "It was funny."

"I'm sure it was," agreed Tracey, not really wanting to dwell too much on what she and her dancing partner must've looked like, both their rather rotund bellies bouncing about here, there and everywhere, to a musical beat of their own, as they were.

"Well I slept absolutely wonderfully, thank you very much," she said, in a quick change of subject. "A couple of twinges from little Tuesday here, granted. But after all that jigging, I suppose that's only to be expected."

"Swifty'll have you on the back of his scooter in no time," laughed Andrea. "All you need is a little side car for the baby seat."

"I don't think so," said Tracey. "Enjoying the music is one thing... And besides, he doesn't even go near it himself."

Having suddenly reminded herself as to the reason why this was the case, the conversation no longer seemed so amusing.

"Anyway, me and Jonathan have a lot of sorting out to do before we can even begin to think about playing happy families," she asserted, determined not to feel sorry for herself over the whole issue.

In fact, taking this another step further, she decided that from now on, she was going to remain cool, calm and collected, whatever was thrown her way.

"Which reminds me," she said. "Shouldn't we be getting off by now?"

She downed what was left of her tea, but just as she was ready to get to her feet, it seemed Tuesday was still feeling restless and another pain suddenly began searing through her stomach, as a result.

"Oh no!" said Megan, all at once alert, as she remembered the previous day's trauma. "Don't you be starting with all that kafuffle again."

"Don't worry," replied Tracey, just glad to see her travel companion, at last, showing some signs of life. "I won't."

However, as she then rose to stand up, the undulating agony only seemed to get worse and she was forced to use the table to steady herself, until it eventually passed.

"That was a good one," she said, trying her utmost to make light of it. Then, as if to make matters worse, she felt something happening in her nether regions and was somewhat reluctantly forced to look down because of it.

"Oh dear," she said, nervously watching as a great, big puddle developed around her feet. "It looks like you're going to have to scrap that."

She looked from the floor, to Andrea and Megan and back again and knew this could only mean one thing.

"This time, I really do think I'm about to have a baby," she said.

CHAPTER FORTY-EIGHT

DON'T PUSH ME

What the hell were you thinking...? Jonathan cringed.

On top of the burdensome weight sitting in the pit of his stomach, he'd been awake for what seemed like hours and hours already, repeatedly going over the mess he'd gotten himself into. However, regardless of it being the morning after the night before, it wasn't as if he had the luxury of blaming a heavy duty, alcohol binge for the regret he was now feeling. Regret not least because of the young woman still sleeping soundly beside him.

But whereas one minute he was consoling himself in the certain knowledge that any normal, hot-blooded male would've found Olivia's obvious charms impossible to resist, she was, after all, an expert seducer, the next he was mocking himself for even coming up with a word like 'seduce' to begin with.

And talk about being a cliché, he scoffed – for the first time actually starting to identify with all those sad, middle-aged men out there; men who couldn't help but be flattered by the attentions of a younger woman and all because their wives didn't understand them.

Not that he, himself, had seen fit to mention the fact that he did, indeed, have a wife, Jonathan further considered. At the same time wondering if that made him better or worse than all those other philandering so and so's?

On the other hand and to be fair, he reassured himself, he hadn't gone as far as hiding his current marital status either. He hadn't taken his wedding ring off like some men in his situation might've done... and even though Olivia must've seen it at some stage, she was still more than happy to sleep with him.

Oh, who're you trying to kid? he admonished. *You're still a shit whatever you did or didn't own up to. Tracey's the real injured party in all of this.*

He couldn't help but sigh, with no choice but to take the view that what was done was done, whatever the whys and wherefores. That the most important thing for him now was to just get rid of the girl and forget the whole sorry event had ever happened. It was just a case of figuring out how best to do that.

He looked about himself, wondering how attached The Ace Face was to his tent, entertaining the notion of leaving Olivia exactly where she was, so that he and his two original travel companions could be long into the distance by the time she awoke. Deep down, however, he knew he was more of a gentleman than that, even if he didn't particularly feel like one at the moment. Still, as he then carefully crawled out of his sleeping bag, gathered up his clothes and let himself out into the open air, he thought it best to let her sleep a while longer anyway.

After all, he told himself, more men of the world than he'd ever be, The Ace Face and Mickey P. would know exactly what to do under the circumstances.

That's if they were talking to him now, of course, he was forced to acknowledge and thinking back to their row from the night before, he knew he had a lot of making up to do.

*

"Morning," he said, trying his utmost to sound cheerful, as he threw his clothes on and made his way over to them.

However, despite having crossed his fingers in the hope the two men would've calmed down by now, judging by the silent yet frosty reception he was met with, it seemed the previous evening's argument was still fresh in their minds.

"Come on lads," he coaxed. "Last night's history. We all said things we shouldn't have said, it was just heat of moment stuff, that's all."

"It's not what you said, Swifty," The Ace Face icily replied. "It's what you did."

"I know, I know," said Jonathan, genuinely apologetic, as he plonked himself down next to Malcolm's urn. "And I'm sorry. I should never have flown at you like that."

"What? You think this is about some pathetic fight?" Mickey P. joined in. "We're talking about what you did, with her..."

"Oh," said Jonathan, lowering his head in embarrassment. And although he'd been hoping for their assistance in the matter, he couldn't help but think it was one thing them having an idea as to what had taken place, but quite another for them to know full well.

"It's a bloody tent," explained Mickey P. "Not exactly known for their sound proofing, are they?"

Inwardly, Jonathan squirmed, the realisation that they must've heard every single pleasurable moan and groan hitting him smack, bang in the face.

"Look..." he excused, expecting at least a little bit of man-to-man empathy. "It didn't mean anything... I made a mistake."

"And that's what you're gonna tell Tracey, is it?" asked The Ace Face. "I mean did she even cross your mind last night? Or were you too busy swapping bodily fluids to give her a second thought?"

"What?" Jonathan asked, choosing to ignore the crassness of his comment. "I'm not telling Tracey anything!"

At first, he didn't really think they were expecting him to confess anyway, they were just sounding off. Except the disdain that swept across their faces in response to his refusal, quickly told him they were in fact serious.

"Oh, come on," he said to The Ace Face, unbelieving. "You of all people should understand?"

"Why?" he replied, clearly even more affronted. "Because Megan's only twenty-two? That means I should find you shitting on your wife and getting your rocks off with a complete stranger acceptable, does it?"

"Yes... I mean no..."

Jonathan turned to Mickey P., hoping at least he'd appreciate where he was coming from.

"You're not gonna get any sympathy from me, mate. I agree with him. We all know it's one thing to look, but you certainly don't touch. Speaking of which, I take it you did use a condom, didn't you?"

Jesus, Jonathan thought to himself. *Who are you? My bloody father?*

In fact, more than uncomfortable at being faced with his actions so directly, he couldn't help but start to feel somewhat defensive.

All this from a fucking lying bastard and an occupational thief...

"Yes, I've done something I shouldn't have," Jonathan admitted. "Slept with a girl half my age... but does that really make me the lowest of the low? Or do your reactions just make the two of you, down right hypocrites? 'Cos let's face it, neither of you are exactly angels, are you?"

Not that it mattered one way or the other, he supposed and not that all this arguing was getting him anywhere.

"Look, if you just help me get rid of her," he said, both hopeful and desperate at the same time. "We can pretend none of this ever happened."

But once again, he was met with a stony silence.

"I don't believe this," said Jonathan. "So what do you want to do now? Shoot me?"

"You didn't learn anything from a bloody word I said last night, did you?" asked The Ace Face.

Jonathan was at a loss. Half of him knew if he needed their help, he was obviously going to have to bloody well earn it, whereas the other half suggested he just fuck the lot of them off completely. Moreover, why stop there? he asked himself. Why not disappear altogether?

At least that way he wouldn't have to deal with Olivia, he acknowledged. Or face Tracey's wrath over his sudden disappearing act, for that matter. And she'd certainly never find out about last night's dalliance. Yes, it would mean he'd never properly know his unborn child, he accepted. But was that really a bad thing? The baby was probably better off without him anyway.

And then it struck him. If he did exactly what The Ace Face had accused him of always doing and ran away, he need never have to take responsibility...

CHAPTER FORTY-NINE

WALLS COME TUMBLING DOWN

(TAKE TWO)

"I want my husband...." wailed Tracey, any earlier determination to maintain a sense of dignity come what may, having completely deserted her the second she'd informed the other two that her waters had, indeed, broken.

Furthermore, she was, once again, forced to suffer the humiliation of having lost the use of her legs. Her feet scraping along the ground as, yet again, Andrea and Megan were forced to half drag and half carry her across the B&B car park.

"Why did he leave me...?" she bemoaned.

"He hasn't left you," replied a struggling and increasingly frustrated Megan. "He's gone away for the weekend, that's all."

"Not that you need to think about that now," panted Andrea, in an out of breath attempt at reassurance. "You just concentrate on your breathing."

In spite of it not being for the want of trying, the mother-to-be soon realised that that was a task easier said than done and not just because the pains in her belly were becoming increasingly overwhelming. In addition, her rather large frame was now being somewhat forcibly pushed and shoved into what was a very small space – an act that seemed to be becoming a bit of a habit.

"You did pay the bill this time, didn't you?" she desperately asked, as she was, at last, prized into the back seat.

However, in a continuing case of de ja vu Tracey found herself subjected to yet another repeat performance, when, without a bye or leave, Andrea suddenly began racing back towards the B&B – obviously to settle up.

"I know, I know," pre-empted Megan, hastily jumping behind the steering wheel. "I don't want you to give birth inside this car either."

Then, much to Tracey's relief, she hastily started up the engine and hit the accelerator, only to screech to a halt just seconds later, outside the hostelry's entrance.

"Go! Go! Go!" Andrea screamed, suddenly re-appearing and by now seemingly an expert at throwing herself into passenger seats.

However, as the mini, at last, zoomed out onto the main road and with another contraction looming, a contraction, she had to acknowledge, far worse than any she'd experienced only the day before, Tracey couldn't help but question whether or not on this occasion, they *really, really* were going to make it to the hospital in time.

CHAPTER FIFTY

TIME FOR TRUTH

Pepper didn't just feel a bit battered and bruised, he sported the biggest shiner of a black eye he knew many of his co-detainees from the rally would've been proud of.

But that's undercover work for you, he couldn't help but gloat. Then again, it wasn't as if he, himself, had had to remain a detainee for very long.

Not once he'd been able to show his warrant card to the arresting officer and explain all about his covert operation to catch Mickey P., he acknowledged – only the number one most prolific felon in the North West. And even though he had to confess some might argue this was something of an overstatement, thanks to a bit of cross county force co-operation, he had managed to get himself out of a rather tricky position. The reason why, instead of having to spend the night in a dank, dark police cell thanks to the Scorpion Scooter Rebels, he was able to congratulate himself on spending the night in a nice, warm, cosy bed, courtesy of The Rising Sun.

Nevertheless, after everything he'd been through the previous night regardless, as he now heartily tucked into a well earned Full English breakfast, he did think a good morning meal was the very least he deserved.

He looked about the room, hardly surprised to find himself the only overnight guest. After all, in the cold light of day, his surroundings were pretty dismal. Furthermore, with clientele like Maximus and his cronies frequenting the place, in his opinion any other decent potential customers, were probably scared off the second they popped their heads round the door. Observations that didn't even take into account the Landlady's obvious sexual advances...

Still, Pepper was pleased to admit, not all citizens were gifted with his degree of courage and staying power, or, indeed, his people skills.

"It's been a long time since I've cooked a man breakfast," said the Landlady, making her entrance with both a suggestive smile, as well as a hot pot of coffee.

Needless to say, Pepper was more than happy to accept the hot drink, but as far as her disclosure was concerned, she could bloody well keep it.

Does she ever let up? he groaned, thinking it had been bad enough already, thanks to his having to sleep with one eye open, just in case she'd decided to pay him an unwanted night time visit. Now, on top of that, having to cope with such innuendo and double entendre at this time of the morning, well it was almost enough to put him off his food.

Then again, he did suppose dealing with a sex charged, red head was nothing when compared to the kinds of villains he'd had to sort out over the years. Speaking of which, he was happily reminded, one of whom was about to get the comeuppance he so rightly deserved. Yes, Mickey P. might have escaped his clutches at yesterday's rally, Pepper admitted. However, he wasn't about to let that happen for a second time. No siree, he affirmed. Today, he was definitely going to bag his man.

"So, you managed to get all your business stuff sorted out, then?" probed the Landlady.

However, the last thing Pepper wanted was to partake in general chit chat with a wanton sex addict, let alone disclose sensitive information.

"Not quite," he replied. "But there's time yet."

He wished she'd just stop hovering and leave him to get on with his breakfast in peace. But as she then went on to take a seat at his table, clearly keen to talk some more, he realised that that wasn't about to happen any time soon. Moreover, unaccustomed as he was to having a female in such close proximity, especially one who seemed to be watching his every single move, he began to feel more and more self conscious with each and every mouthful.

"So go on then," she said. "What business is it you're in? Why are you really here? 'Cos even you've got to admit you don't exactly look the scootering type?"

"Excuse me?" he said, refusing to admit to anything of the sort. In fact, in his view and thanks to the fancy dress shop, he did actually think he'd blended in with the two wheeled fanatics quite well.

However, despite disagreeing with her on that score, Pepper also had to give the Landlady her due. At any rate, she'd been astute enough to pick up on the fact that he was there under false pretences, leaving him wondering if there was more going on in this woman's head than he'd originally given her credit for.

"If you must know," he said, deciding she was worth confiding in, after all. "I'm here as an Officer of the Law."

"Really?" she asked, incredulous.

This was clearly the last thing she'd expected to hear and her surprise only reinforced Pepper's confidence in just how good his undercover skills had been.

"So what brings you down to us?" she asked.

Pepper looked about the empty room, making sure to lower his voice as he leaned forward. "If I tell you," he began. "You can't repeat it... not to anyone."

Thankfully, the Landlady did, indeed, seem to recognize his need for secrecy. "You can trust me," she said, swiftly making a sign of the cross over her heart.

"Well there's this bloke..." he explained. "On the run..."

Much to his delight, he could see the woman before him was suitably impressed, her eyes widening half frightened, half excited, in eager anticipation of what was to come.

"What did he do?" she asked, in as equally hushed tones. "Did he kidnap someone? Is he a murderer?"

"Some might say worse," said Pepper, glad of an appreciative audience for once. "He steals things... I mean we're not talking about a bank robber or owt like that. This chap's not that clever."

"You're talking about a shoplifter, then?" she asked, her voice now back to a more audible level. "You came all this way chasing after a shoplifter?"

"Yep!" Pepper proudly confirmed.

"Although he has moved on to nicking scooters as well now," he added.

Bewilderment seemed to sweep across the Landlady's face, as she threw herself back in her chair.

"But don't you think that's a bit obsessive?" she asked, dumbstruck. "Or I take it there's not really a lot of criminal activity up where you come from? Either that, and unlike everywhere else, your Police Force is made of money?"

"Oh no, no" Pepper felt the need to defend. "The job's not paying me. I'm doing this on my own time."

Unfortunately for him, however, instead of clarifying the Landlady's confusion, for some reason, his confession only seemed to make her somewhat more dismayed.

He watched her silently get to her feet, pick up his empty plate and with a shake of her head decide to just leave him to it and Pepper could only assume that like most people, she just didn't appreciate his high level of conscientiousness. However, it wasn't as if this was the first time his dedication to the role of upholding the law had been misunderstood, he acknowledged. At the same time hazarding a pretty good guess, that it probably wouldn't be the last.

"If you knew this man," he called after her. "You'd understand..."

Having got her attention once more, he watched the Landlady, all at once, stop in her tracks, before slowly turning to face him.

"With an increase in gun crime, in a country that's rife with drugs and God knows what else," she said. "All I can say is, you must be wrong in your bloody head!"

Obviously this wasn't really what Pepper had hoped to hear, but he supposed on a more positive note, at least she'd finally left him in peace.

And with nothing else for it he simply picked up his cup and began slurping on his morning coffee.

Civilians, he thought to himself, dismissive. *They'll never understand.*

CHAPTER FIFTY-ONE

THE YOUNG AND THE OLD

As he and Mickey P. sat waiting for The Ace Face to bring over their coffees, Jonathan couldn't help but think about how easy it had been to re-accustom himself with riding a scooter again.

Maybe it was because he'd been forced to confront his fears head on thanks to circumstance, he surmised. Or maybe it came down to something as simple as like riding a push bike, on account of it being something you just never forgot. But to go from feelings of near panic attack only yesterday morning, to taking the helm down the M1 today, well it was something of a triumph. And although aware he should probably be thanking the Scorpion Scooter Rebels for forcing his hand, he knew if it weren't for his two travel companions insisting he come on this trip in the first place, it would never have happened at all.

Not that he felt able to voice the gratitude he now felt as a result, especially as relations between the three of them were still somewhat strained.

Besides, he reasoned. *I suppose there is another more important problem that needs to be dealt with before anything else.*

As Jonathan looked through to the shop area in search of the source of his dilemma, despite it still being early, he was surprised at just how busy the service station seemed. However, that still didn't stop him immediately spotting Olivia through the throng, he resentfully noted. No doubt, because she was the only one *not* dressed for travelling.

Instead of sporting a comfy pair of jeans and a casual jacket for her journey like everyone else in the vicinity, she unfortunately appeared more than happy to browse the shelves and rails whilst still dressed in last night's evening wear. One of the reasons why, as he continued to watch her,

Jonathan was forced to wonder if the girl had any shame at all. The absurdity of his situation beginning to get him down, even more than it had already.

"You know how we all agreed to carry on this journey, regardless? Keep our word to Malc's mum?" asked Mickey P.

"Yep," said Jonathan, alas knowing full well where this line of questioning was going.

"Well you did realise we were only talking about the three of us, didn't you?"

"Of course I did," he glumly replied. "And I tried telling *her* that as well. But everything I said just seemed to go in one ear and then straight out the other."

"You could always try mentioning the fact that you're married," suggested The Ace Face, finally landing back at the table with the drinks.

However, the last thing Jonathan needed was another holier than thou lecture on the sins of the flesh and although, deep down, he knew The Ace Face was right, he should be informing her of his marital status, he doubted very much, it would make any difference to Olivia anyway.

As far as he was concerned, she'd already proven herself either so determinedly thick skinned, she only heard what she wanted to hear; or, to put it bluntly, so brain dense, she wouldn't have understood anything of what he was saying, however simply he tried to phrase things. Not that it really mattered which of the two it was, he just knew that no matter what, the message simply wasn't getting through.

He looked over to the shop area once more, only to be met with a returning little wave from the object of his frustrations and now feeling completely at a loss, he was finally able to admit this sticky predicament was all of his own making.

He buried his head in his hands, full of despair.

She obviously thinks this is the start of something beautiful, he said, shuddering at the thought.

But then again, he asked. *Why wouldn't she think that, considering I bloody well slept with her?*

"How could I have been so stupid?" he lamented, lifting his head back up.

"Come on lads," he pleaded. "I need your help here. What am I going to do?"

CHAPTER FIFTY-TWO

MOVE ON UP

Why does everyone insist on lying to me? whimpered Tracey, feeling very sorry for herself, indeed.

Yes, Jonathan might've still been in first place when it came to her list of fibbing offenders, she had to admit. However, thanks to the degree of pain she was experiencing and it only getting worse by the minute, it was fair to say the other women who'd attended her pre-natal classes back up North, were definitely coming in an exceptionally close second.

This is nothing like shelling peas... she moaned, remembering their reassuring claims. In fact, as Megan's mini, at last, screeched to a halt outside the hospital for the second time in as many days, she wanted nothing more than to give each and every single one of them, a very large piece of her mind.

If only they were there at that precise moment, she considered, wishful thinking – to witness the reality of her anguish. That way she could point out their blatant dishonesty right to their faces and she couldn't help but imagine herself doing so, in the most colourful language possible.

Not that this meant she was going to let Jonathan off the hook for his role in this, she reminded herself, at the same time envisaging giving him a lively telling off as well. And not just for the emotional ups and downs he'd forced her to endure over the last couple of days either, she asserted. After all, were it not for him and his blasted sperm, she wouldn't have been in this physically agonizing position to begin with.

In reality, as far as Tracey was now concerned, it was no longer of any consequence at all, that she, herself, had been the driving force behind their decision to get pregnant in the first place; that she, herself, was the one who'd insisted they keep trying at all cost. Oh no, now was definitely not the time to be thinking rationally about any of it and her husband was to blame for everything.

"This is all Jonathan's fault," she re-iterated, as Andrea and Megan jumped out of the vehicle, threw their seats forward and began attempting to haul her out from the back. "Just wait until I get my hands on him."

"You can think about who is and isn't responsible, once we get you inside the hospital," said Megan, through gritted teeth as she heaved and ho-ed.

"Well that's easy for you to say," the mother-to-be grumbled.

"Yes, but she's right," Andrea placated. "We just need to concentrate on you and the baby for now."

Such words of comfort, however, only fell on deaf ears, as the enormity of her situation suddenly hit the mother-to-be straight in the face.

This isn't right, she thought to herself. *This isn't supposed to be happening.*

She thought back to the hours she'd spent meticulously working out her birthing plan, how she'd built up a relationship with her Midwife, who she now trusted not just with her own life, but with that of her baby too and it bothered her to think someone who she'd never even met before, would now be delivering her child. The last thing she wanted was to spend what should have been one of the happiest days of her life surrounded by complete strangers, which, to some extent, also included Andrea and Megan. But with not even her own husband there to hold her hand and see her through it, what choice did she have?

No, this most certainly wasn't how she'd imagined any aspect of Tuesday's birth in her mind's eye over the last eight and a half months and she found herself feeling very, very lonely and very scared, as a result.

Suddenly, she decided she'd be damned if she wasn't going down without a fight.

"What do you mean? We?" she asked. "There's no 'we' about it!"

Furthermore, she, all at once, found both the energy and the necessary agility to lug her own body out of the car – an act that seemed to surprise both her travel companions in the process.

"You're not coming in with me!" she declared, finally on her feet. "You two still have a job to do."

Megan didn't seem to need much convincing on the matter, Tracey somewhat begrudgingly noted, relief exuding from her every pore as it now was. Then again, as she recalled the trauma of yesterday's escapade for herself, she couldn't exactly blame her either and was able to admit she'd probably be doing the exact same thing if she was in her shoes.

Andrea, on the other hand, appeared more than hesitant, clearly unhappy about her choice to go it alone.

Tracey very much appreciated the sentiment, but she still wasn't having any of it. "Don't worry," she confidently and adamantly asserted. "I'm telling you, this baby's staying right where it is until the two of you get back with Jonathan."

Even so, as she watched Megan more than willing to take her at her word, already getting her overnight bag out of the car boot on her behalf, it seemed Andrea still wasn't convinced. In fact, if anything, she seemed just as determined to stay right where she was.

"Come on then!" Megan called out, hastily jumping behind the steering wheel and starting up the mini's engine. "What're we waiting for?"

"Go on..." urged Tracey. "I'll be fine. I promise."

"Well only if you're sure," said Andrea, genuinely worried.

"I'm sure. Now go." However, as Andrea then reluctantly did as she was told and climbed back into the car, Tracey could feel her fears and loneliness starting to return.

In an attempt to prevent her bravery beating a hasty retreat, she took a deep breath accordingly.

"Right Tuesday," she said, once again taking charge. "I need you to stay just where you are until Mummy says otherwise..."

She looked down at her stomach.

"Do you think you could do that for me?" she asked.

She picked up her travel bag, having felt like she'd gotten just the answer she needed and began her solitary, yet purposeful, march towards the hospital doors.

CHAPTER FIFTY-THREE

ONE'S SECOND THOUGHTLESSNESS

"Jesus Christ!" said Jonathan, all at once horrified. Except he had to admit it wasn't so much Olivia's approach that he found all that surprising, after all, from the minute she'd clapped eyes on him she'd made it quite clear she wasn't actually going anywhere; rather, it was more her sudden change of attire.

"Bloody hell," said The Ace Face, following his gaze.

"So what do you think?" she asked, giving a twirl to show off her new outfit in all its glory.

"You look like you've been tango-ed," remarked a tactless Mickey P.

"Well it's certainly colourful..." said Jonathan, opting to be a bit more diplomatic than his clumsy mate, whilst at the same time not quite sure how else to best describe the bright orange fleece and matching coloured waterproof trousers she now wore. "I'll give you that."

"Well better bright than freezing to death on the back of a scooter," said Olivia, with a cheerful smile.

She went on to squeeze herself into the seat next to him, regardless of there being plenty of room elsewhere around the table and such was Jonathan's irritation as a result, he began to wish he'd taken a leaf out of Mickey P.'s book and chosen to be a bit less charitable.

"Ooh, is that for me?" she asked, also helping herself to his coffee.

Of course, he couldn't *really* complain about her invading his personal space like that, Jonathan realised. However much he wanted to. Not when they'd certainly gotten a lot closer only the night before.

However, that still didn't stop him feeling a little bit grudging about it, he acknowledged; or indeed, a bit resentful towards Mickey P. and The Ace Face, for not saying something on his behalf.

He thought back to when the three of them were young lads. A time when they were so close, they'd have had each other's backs whatever the situation, when they'd have helped each other out no matter what.

But not anymore it seems, Jonathan sadly observed and he found himself contemplating what a motley crew of travellers they'd turned out to be.

The Ace Face, a man so keen on giving Malcolm a good send off, he'd yet again given a dead man's urn pride of place in the centre of the table – and proudly so, at that. Mickey P., a colourful character who couldn't keep his hands off other people's possessions, yet at the same time had managed to keep hold of his childhood sweetheart. And not forgetting himself in all of this, a run-a-way father- to-be, who having slept with the young woman at his side only a few hours ago, was now so uncomfortable in her presence, that he wished she'd just bugger off, never to be seen again.

Not that you should've slept with her to begin with? he part stated, part scolded.

He wondered if it had been some sort of sub-conscious ploy to prevent himself from focusing on what really mattered. After all, when it had first been suggested, this trip had seemed like an opportunity for him to finally get to grips with past events; a chance to not just scatter Malcolm's ashes, but finally lay Melanie's ghost to rest too. His dalliance with Olivia, however, had created a convenient diversion to stop him from doing that; leaving Jonathan unable to help but question, whether or not this had been his subliminal intention all along.

On the other hand, Jonathan knew he'd never been all that comfortable with deep and meaningful psycho babble and he quickly found himself dismissing such thoughts as pointless internal ramblings that had no place taking up space in his head.

Moreover, he, once again, turned his attention to the woman sat next to him, speculating why *she* would choose to run off with three strange men in the first place; three men probably twice her age.

"So, Olivia..." he ventured, clearing his mind of everything else. "What's the story behind your great escape?"

CHAPTER FIFTY-FOUR

SOLE SALVATION

Despite the prospect of having to tackle the motorway and its chaos, Pepper was just glad to be back on the road and away from The Rising Sun. Its Landlady's somewhat blunt cynicism in relation to his dedication to the job, having for reasons he couldn't quite fathom, hit a bit of a nerve.

Certainly, it wasn't exactly the first time he'd attracted such criticism, he was forced to admit. *Haven't you got anything better to do?* and *Why don't you go and do some proper police work?* being firm favourites when it came to him carrying out his duties. And even though that was just from his colleagues, he knew if he'd had a pound for every time he'd heard such jibes, he'd probably be a very rich man by now.

However, it was precisely because all this claptrap *had* previously been levelled at him, that he knew it wasn't so much the Landlady's condemnation of his work fervour that was the problem, as something else. Subsequently, he was now having a hard time trying to actually figure out, just what that 'something else' was.

And anyway, he grumbled. *I can't help it if the law's the law, can I?*

Therefore, if an individual chose to not wear his or her seatbelt whilst driving, or, indeed, to use their mobile phone whilst in transit, as far as he was concerned, what was so wrong in them then having to pay the price? Besides, it wasn't as if there were many Police Officers out there who could boast they earned the equivalent of their wages in fines every month, was it? A record that in his book, if anything, was worth celebrating.

"But as usual, everyone's a critic," he told himself. "Ready to condemn my work ethic, when they don't even know what one is."

But as for getting flak for trying to catch what some people chose to call a 'real' criminal, well that was definitely a new one on him and he wasn't quite sure how to take that either. "And she dared to call me obsessive because of it," he scoffed, full of indignation.

"I mean everybody knows Mickey P. is a thieving so and so!" he maintained. "And is it my fault he's decided to take his unlawful activities to the seaside...?"

He fell silent for a moment, once again, trying to get his head around things.

Whereas he'd gotten used to people simply mocking his level of enthusiasm for his profession, he realised the Landlady had been different in that she'd seemed so offended by it. Especially the bit when he'd gone on to explain he was carrying out a work related operation on his own time, he further acknowledged. It all of a sudden dawning on him, that that was why her response wasn't sitting quite so well.

Then again, so what if he was taking a Busman's holiday? he defended. It wasn't exactly uncommon these days, was it? Builder blokes were always taking themselves off to foreign lands to build schools and what not; doctors voluntarily went off to Africa to heal the sick all the time. In fact, helping to develop a better community in some far off village or other was quite the in vogue thing to do as far as Pepper could tell. So, in getting Mickey P. banged up in prison, wasn't he only following their lead in trying to make his 'village' a better place for his community?

Fair enough, he had to admit that Burnley could never be described as some sort of war torn nation – no matter how often it felt like one. But surely the principles behind what the builders, the doctors and what he, himself, were all doing, were simply one and the same thing. He, himself, just didn't have to use as many air miles as all the others, he considered, in order to make his difference to the world.

Not that Pepper was particularly happy about feeling the need to defend his actions; especially as he didn't think he'd done anything wrong. In his opinion he'd always been conscientious to a fault and when push came to shove, was that really a quality others should be criticizing to begin with?

CHAPTER FIFTY-FIVE

ENJOY YOURSELF

"So," said Jonathan, as they all de-helmeted and disembarked the two scooters. "Here we are."

He took a deep breath as he looked along the seafront.

"Yep," said The Ace Face, already retrieving the deceased Malcolm from his rucksack. "We've finally made it."

However, as Olivia commenced squealing her particular delight at their arrival, for Jonathan it was more of a bittersweet moment and as such, he struggled to share in the enthusiasm.

He told himself it was because unlike her, he hadn't come to Brighton to have fun in the first place; that he'd come to help scatter a friend's ashes and, dare he say it, to honour *all* those no longer earthbound. Something of a contradiction, he was forced to admit, especially considering he was also doing his level best *not* to think about the last time he was here, as well as who he'd been here with.

Then again, as memories of Melanie started to press their way forward regardless, it seemed he wasn't succeeding much at that either. Memories that up until now he'd been managing to suppress and he couldn't help but wonder if his earlier thoughts hadn't been such psycho babble, after all.

Nevertheless, it was now clear Olivia had been the perfect ruse to stop him focusing on the enormity of what this trip had meant to stand for and it was also fair to say she was no longer doing it for him. So with recollections of his sister fast pervading his mind, not just as a body lying contorted and lifeless on the side of the road, but as the living, breathing, joyful, young girl that she, in fact, was, it was now more than obvious to Jonathan that side stepping what really mattered, was no longer going to be an option.

"You okay, Swifty?" asked Mickey P.

It was a simple enough question and Jonathan really, really appreciated the sensibility. "Yeah, I'm fine," he replied. "I think I just need a minute, mate."

He spotted an empty bench over to his left and headed straight for it. Moreover, as he took a seat and gazed out across the channel, watching the endless ebb and flow of its waves, it finally dawned on him just how much he'd failed his sister. After all, not only was she dead because of him, but in his self-loathing guilt, he hadn't just denied her very existence, but also her right to be remembered.

"What must you think of me?" he asked, more than regretful and finally able to acknowledge that The Ace Face had been right all along to call him selfish, that he had turned Melanie's death into being about himself instead of her, he suddenly felt very much ashamed for it.

The irony amidst all of this, he mused, was in the fact he knew Melanie of all people would've been the first in line to tell him he had nothing to blame himself for. That freak accidents by their very nature can happen to anyone – not just to her and Malcolm, but to him too.

And let's face it, he conceded. *She'd only have to highlight yesterday's near miss collision with the Scorpion Scooter Rebels to prove her point.*

He found himself almost laughing, as he imagined her telling him to get up off his backside and stop wallowing. In her own indomitable way, ordering him to not just start celebrating her short years and everything the two of them had been lucky enough to share in between, but also commence enjoying his own life too – past, present and future.

However, in reluctantly admitting that she would probably be right, he still wasn't sure if he could take her advice. It was as if he'd been stuck in that self-pitying rut of his for so long now, that he didn't even know where to begin with regards to climbing out.

Although there's no time like the present to start trying, he told himself, for both their sakes, knowing he did, at least, have to give it a go.

"You alright now, Swifty?" asked Mickey P., interrupting Jonathan's thoughts, as he, The Ace Face and Olivia joined him on the bench.

"I'm good thanks," Jonathan replied and, for once, he actually felt like he meant it. "Just thinking about stuff, you know?"

"So what happened to him, then?" blurted Olivia. "To your mate in the jar?"

With thoughts of untimely demises still running through his head, Jonathan couldn't help but feel a little offended by the matter of fact tone she'd chosen to employ. Fair enough, Olivia had never had the pleasure of meeting Malcolm, he acknowledged. But that didn't mean she couldn't show a little bit of respect for him, did it?

Then again, he did suppose when someone asked a question they had to be prepared for the answer. What's more, once she'd had hers, once she'd heard the awful tragedy of what had happened to Malc, he doubted Olivia would ever be quite so blasé about death from then on.

CHAPTER FIFTY-SIX

LEAP BEFORE YOU LOOK

"I've told you," insisted Andrea, frustrated. "If we don't go that way, we won't have any chance of getting Swifty back in time for the birth."

"And I've told you," counter-insisted Megan. "I don't do motorways."

However, despite their circular argument, Andrea was resolute and against her better judgement having already been forced to leave Tracey to her own devices at the hospital, there was no way she was about to let the mother-to-be down now when it came to this.

As far as she was concerned, anyone with any sense knew the motorway afforded them both the quickest and the most direct route to Brighton. Therefore, from hereon in, that was the only way forward. What's more, as her driver's continual refusal to leave the 'A' roads had wasted them so much time already, she doubted a few more minutes was going to make much difference. So round and round this latest roundabout they would go, she determinedly maintained, until Megan came round to her way of thinking.

"You're being very unfair about this," said Megan. "You know I'm not used to driving in heavy traffic."

"You think?" asked Andrea, yet again preventing her driver from steering off onto her preferred route. "And what would you know?"

"But I'm more than happy to enlighten you, if you like?" she continued. "About what is fair and what isn't..."

"Now let's see... A woman having to shoulder all things responsible, when there's a perfectly capable partner on the scene as well, well that's unfair. A woman forced to give birth on her own because the same said partner is off doing his own thing... Believe me and, once again, that's unfair. Having to drive on a road that happens to have more than one lane to think about, however. Well that's not something you can really complain about in comparison, now, is it?"

"And feel free to call me cynical if you must," she somewhat sarcastically finished. "But these are just some of the facts of life that I've absolutely no doubt, you'll more than come to appreciate over time."

With the board sign for the M1, yet again, coming into view and despite her words of wisdom, Megan still refusing to show any sign of relenting, Andrea couldn't help but start to reach the end of her tether. And, unfortunately, it now seemed that the only way this issue was ever going to be resolved, was if she were to take some sort of decisive action – and fast.

She hastily scanned their surroundings to make sure they were out of harm's reach with regards to any other traffic and in opting for the element of surprise, she suddenly grabbed at the car's steering wheel and yanked their vehicle over to the left, before Megan even got the chance to do anything about it.

"Nooooo!" her driver shrieked.

"I'm afraid it's a case of needs must," Andrea called out, as she watched Megan cringe in absolute fear, having realised not only what her front passenger had just done, but that they were now on what she obviously considered to be the wrong slip road.

"Although you might want to open your eyes just a tad bit more before we join the masses," Andrea then suggested, not feeling even the slightest bit of guilt at forcing her driver's hand. After all, drastic times did call for drastic measures and in her book, having been in Tracey's shoes herself, this was one hell of an emergency.

"And whilst you're at it," she further instructed. "Now's probably a good time to be putting your foot down as well."

CHAPTER FIFTY-SEVEN

ANYWAY, ANYHOW, ANYWHERE

As they all sat staring out to sea, Jonathan heard The Ace Face clear his throat in preparation of answering Olivia's question. At the same time, just glad he, himself, wasn't the one having to do the explaining.

"Well as you've probably gathered," his mate began, obviously setting the scene of the final Act in his deceased friend's life. "Malcolm was a Mod. He loved everything about it... the music, the clothes... Just everything."

"And ever since he was old enough to ride one, not a day went by when he wasn't out and about on his scooter," he added.

"Enjoying the feel of the wind in his face, his scarf blowing in the breeze behind him," interrupted Mickey P. and even Jonathan, who hadn't seen Malcolm in years, couldn't help but smile as he pictured the sight.

"But not just any old scarf though," carried on The Ace Face. "One knitted with love and devotion... by his very own mum, would you believe?"

"Shit!" said Jonathan, his smile immediately replaced with down right disbelief. "I didn't know that!"

"Well you do now," confirmed The Ace Face. "I know. It's sad, isn't it?"

"That poor woman," Jonathan replied, in whole hearted agreement. "No wonder she couldn't control herself at the funeral."

"Anyway," said Mickey P., with a sigh. "When Malcolm pulled up at some traffic lights and the wind dropped... then so did his scarf."

"Which was when it got caught up in his wheel," The Ace Face explained. "And when the lights changed and he set off again..."

"No...!" said Olivia, aghast.

"Yep... I'm afraid so," said The Ace Face.

"He was garrotted," explained Mickey P.

"By his very own neckwear," finished The Ace Face.

Jonathan caught sight of Olivia bringing a hand up to her throat, in his view, understandably stunned by what she'd just heard. It was, after all, a terrible end to any man's life.

But his own thoughts, however, were still just as much with Mrs. Riley – he of all people knowing full well what she must be going through. And as he, once again, recalled her rather dramatic behaviour at the funeral, he realised she'd obviously been demonstrating her guilt. Although rightly so, he granted , in the end it not doing anybody any good to bottle things up – yet something else he had to admit he knew all about.

Life totally stinks at times, he said to himself. *It's just so unfair.*

Well no more of it, he went on to insist, asserting that if he'd learnt nothing else over these last couple of days, he'd certainly come to appreciate life was definitely too short.

Furthermore, he'd wasted so much energy already wallowing in his own misery, at the same time trying to balance that with pretending all was well, so he decided in honour of both Malcolm *and* his sister, Melanie, he was finally going to sort his shit out and actually start living again, once and for all.

"So where to first?" asked Olivia, interrupting his determined contemplation. "What shall we do now?"

And in answer to her question, Jonathan knew exactly what he wanted to do.

CHAPTER FIFTY-EIGHT

ALL OUT TO GET YOU

Pepper had gone from feeling infuriated and misunderstood, to bloody well miserable.

In fact, to say only yesterday when he locked his front door behind him he'd had such high hopes, it seemed his journey to capture the absconded Mickey P. wasn't turning out to be anywhere near as enjoyable as he'd originally anticipated. Then again, as he began listing all the events that had happened to him since leaving home, he couldn't help but think it no wonder.

One! he said to himself. *I've encountered a motorway tailback;*

Two! I've been forced to take out temporary membership in a violent scooter gang;

Three! I've gotten arrested as a result of that membership;

Four! Only to be then, thank goodness, de-arrested;

And finally number five and for all my troubles! I then had to endure a lecture on the rights and wrongs... of my own personal style of policing.

"And even that, I have to say, seemed to highlight more wrongs than rights," he resentfully corrected.

To top it all, as he'd never actually been to Brighton before, he was now having to try and control a moving vehicle and map read – both at the same time. "Which is so bleeding annoying," he said to himself, as he attempted to locate the exact page he needed.

Irritated, he wondered why his Police Advanced Driver Training course hadn't included the basics of driving with only one eye on the road; especially seeing as back then satellite navigation systems hadn't even been invented. "Not that I'd have used one anyway," he remarked, on account of his view that they only made people lazy. But, as if to make matters worse, his rather cumbersome atlas then decided now would be a good time to jump off of the passenger seat and down into the passenger foot well – which, rather exasperatingly, meant Pepper had to test his driving skills all the more.

"You should've just arrested him when you had the chance," he grumbled to himself, now forced to take both eyes off the road as he reached over and down in an attempt to pick it back up. "Instead of thinking you were bloody well clever."

"Beep! Beep! Beep!" a hollow car horn suddenly rang out from behind.

Pepper jolted back upright in response, unfortunately to find his own vehicle fast veering into the next lane and he only just managed to correct its course, before some maniac driving a Union Jack roofed mini got the chance to plough straight into him.

"Bloody idiots!" he yelled, his heart racing as the mini zoomed past. However, as he began rapidly flashing his headlights to further demonstrate his fury, with the little car already fast disappearing into the distance, he realised he was actually venting his frustrations on each and every other motorist instead.

"You shouldn't be allowed on the bloody road!" he called after them, regardless.

He took a few seconds to try and calm his beating heart and pull himself together. At the same time attempting to console himself in the knowledge that Mickey P. wouldn't just soon be in his sights, but safe and sound in his handcuffs as well.

Even so, whereas thoughts of bagging his man usually provided him with the perfect tonic whatever his situation, rather disappointingly on this occasion, they seemed to be doing absolutely nothing when it came to lifting his mood.

"And I have a pretty good idea exactly who's fault that is," he said, knowingly. "It's all thanks to that damned interfering Landlady!"

CHAPTER FIFTY-NINE

SUBSTITUTE

Jonathan was now glad Mickey P. and The Ace Face had refused to help him out with regards to Olivia. It was, after all, his problem. And thanks to his new invigorated outlook, he'd realised it was only right he should be the one to man up and sort it.

Furthermore, he might not have been used to sleeping with women and then dumping them, but he didn't see the point in prolonging the agony either. So despite not exactly looking forward to hurting a woman's feelings in the process, he told himself the quicker he did the deed, the quicker he could start to honour his sister's memory. Moreover, the quicker he could begin getting his life back on track.

"Can you give us a minute, lads?" he asked, rising to his feet ready to take Olivia off to one side. However, feeling nervous enough over what he was about to say already, he then found her eagerness to actually hear it only making him feel worse.

He waited until the other two were out of earshot before stopping to speak. "Look, Olivia," he awkwardly began. "You're a lovely girl and last night... well last night was great..."

"I know I am. And I know it was," she both unexpectedly and bluntly interrupted. "But do we really need to waste time making half baked speeches about it?"

"Oh," said Jonathan, somewhat surprised by her honesty. "If that's how you feel."

In addition, having wrongly anticipated some sort of drama or at the very least a few tears over their parting, he had to admit he was just relieved to hear she was as happy as he was, to make their final goodbye all the more swift.

"Now if we wait until they're not looking," she continued, at the same time checking out their surroundings. "We can be across the road and round that corner before they've even noticed we've gone."

Jonathan found himself confused. "What?" he asked, suddenly perplexed. "What're you talking about?"

However, as he followed her gaze over his shoulder towards Mickey P. and The Ace Face, it suddenly dawned on him. It seemed Olivia's distinct lack of theatricals hadn't, in fact, been because she, too, saw no future in their relationship, but because she was under the misguided impression he was about to ditch his mates, as opposed to ditching her.

Jonathan could've kicked himself for thinking he was ever going to get off so lightly in the first place.

"That's not what I meant," he said, unfortunately only to find the tables now turned, with him causing her some confusion.

"Well what did you mean, then?" she asked, genuinely bemused, whilst leaving Jonathan more and more frustrated by the second because of it.

Jesus! he thought to himself, wondering if a girl could really be that stupid. *Does she really think I'm going to run off into the sunset with her...?*

Of course she does, he conceded. After all, she was young and naive and no doubt out for a bit of fun and adventure. Not that she was going to get them from him, Jonathan re-affirmed. Although after their previous night's shenanigans, he did have to accept it was hardly surprising she'd think otherwise.

He looked from his friends to Olivia and back again, suddenly feeling the pressure from both sides – from Olivia because she was ready to start traffic dodging the very second he gave her the word and from his friends because they were now indicating to their watches, whilst signalling for him to get a move on.

However, whereas in that moment he could've quite easily told them all to bugger off, as tempting as it may have been, he realised that that was the old Jonathan speaking. The new Jonathan took responsibility for his actions – whether he wanted to or not.

"Look, Olivia," he repeated, polite yet adamant. "I appreciate how it got into your head, but this running away business, it isn't going to work."

"Oh," she replied, at least some sort of penny finally dropping. "I get it."

Jonathan dared to be hopeful. "You do?" he asked.

"Of course..." Olivia laughed.

"I mean it's only right you'd want to say your goodbyes before we go," she continued, the fact that she most definitely didn't 'get it' leaving Jonathan, once again, at something of a loss. "So you go ahead, I'll wait here for you."

He took a deep breath and sighed. He had hoped he could be gentlemanly about the whole thing, to let her down nicely, but with Olivia refusing to get the message, that was becoming increasingly difficult.

"You do know I'm married, don't you?" he suddenly blurted out. "I mean you have seen this wedding ring, the ring that tells you that?"

"Yes, but..."

"To a woman I have no intentions of leaving, Olivia," he insisted. "To a woman who's carrying my child."

However, as soon as the words were out, Jonathan immediately regretted his sharpness, especially as the poor girl now looked like she'd been slapped in the face.

But whether that was because she wasn't used to men giving her the boot, after all, she had been making rather a lot of assumptions about where the two of them were heading; or whether it was because she wasn't quite the sassy individual she liked to portray... Either way, in the end Jonathan didn't suppose it mattered. Tracey was the woman he'd really let down in this scenario – and she most certainly hadn't deserved it.

"But what about last night?" asked Olivia. "Didn't it mean anything?"

"Of course it did," he replied. "Just not in the same way as you thought."

An awkward silence developed as Jonathan pondered over his next move. It didn't seem right to just walk off, but having made his position clear the last thing he wanted was to say something that might muddy the waters all over again.

"I think it's time you went home," he eventually suggested, planting a farewell kiss on her cheek. "That's what I'm going to do."

As if deserting women was becoming a bit of a habit, he turned to re-join Mickey P. and The Ace Face, leaving Olivia just standing there watching after him, like some abandoned little puppy.

Still, at least they could now focus on what they'd come here to do, Jonathan told himself. With no more interruptions.

CHAPTER SIXTY

JACKPOT

"Ha!" said Pepper, his spirits suddenly lifted. "You're not so clever now, are you?"

He began to sail passed the Union Jack roofed mini, now sat on the hard shoulder thanks to it having been pulled up by the Police.

"That's what you get for driving like a maniac!" he called out, unable to help but gloat. In fact, it was all he could do to stop himself honking on his horn, in much the same way had been done to him.

After the misery he'd been experiencing all morning, he was surprised at how good it felt to know the mini driver was, at last, getting his or her comeuppance.

"And what a comeuppance it's going to be," he asserted, knowing full well that back in Lancashire, Traffic Officers didn't have a bit of a reputation for nothing. And despite crossing his fingers just in case, he told himself he most certainly couldn't imagine it being any different here. After all, why should it?

"Gutter rats, that's what they call them," he said, gleeful.

Not a particularly celebrated title for such a conscientious group of professionals, he was forced to acknowledge, however. Especially considering the kinds of jobs they were forced to deal with in their line of duty.

Still, he of all people knew the flak an individual could get, simply for being by the book and even though he was trying *not* to think of all the jocular criticism he, himself, had been on the receiving end of over the years, he did suppose all the crap was worth it in the end.

"Especially when morons like that," he said of the mini driver. "Finally get what's coming to them."

"And he or she isn't going to be the only one getting their just desserts today," he declared, for some reason feeling his morale, all at once, start to wane.

"Except in Mickey P.'s case," he continued regardless. "It's more than a £60 fine, three points on his licence and the prospect of a dangerous driving course that he has to look forward to..."

But alas, no matter how much he tried to force it, it seemed his humour had gone for good. Leaving him staring out at the road ahead, whilst unable to help but let out a despondent sigh.

"So why, oh why?" he asked himself. "Are you not excited?"

CHAPTER SIXTY-ONE

YESTERDAY'S MEN

"Well Malc," said The Ace Face. "I don't suppose you'll be seeing this again anytime soon."

They'd decided to give their deceased friend one last treat before his final send off, but being back in the infamous Quadrophenia alleyway only left Jonathan with mixed feelings.

He thought back to his last visit all those years ago, recalling how he'd stood in awe at the signature ridden walls. For many a young Mod, it had been the backdrop for one of the most seminal moments in the film...

And in more ways than one, he laughed to himself.

Moreover, as he remembered his amazement at the legions of fans who'd flocked from all over the world just to stand where he'd stood, each and every one of them having borne testament to their fanaticism just by leaving their mark, he thought it no wonder it only seemed right that he and the rest of the gang added their names to the countless other scribbles as well.

Including his sister, Melanie and Jonathan couldn't help but smile, as he remembered her making such an excitable *Hoo! Ha!* over what she should write.

Something meaningful and creative, she'd said at the time. Merely to then settle with just her name and the year, having come to the conclusion that *simple and to the point* was actually more her style. Of course, as big brothers do, Jonathan had ribbed her for it, saying she only put that because she didn't have the required imagination to come up with something more profound.

Melanie Parkes, 1985, he wistfully reminisced and in that moment, he would've loved nothing more than to find her moniker, just to see it one more time.

Unfortunately and much to his regret, however, just like her, it seemed his sister's contribution to the devotional graffiti had long since gone. *No doubt, painted over time and time again,* he resentfully acknowledged, telling himself that as far as he was concerned, an autographic mural beat the current putrid, French mustard coloured walls more than hands down.

Nonetheless, as he, once again, took in his surroundings, at least there were a couple of more recent signatures to break up the bareness, he noted. Just begging for additions to come and join them.

"Not exactly the Mod Mecca of the world it once was, is it?" he said. In fact, the only thing that did appear to stand out these days, he noticed, was the CCTV camera pointing directly at them from the far corner, something that definitely hadn't been there during his last visit.

Still, he of all people knew that no matter how many times these walls were painted over, white washing, or in this case condiment washing, just didn't work. Those signatures would still be there underneath the layers somewhere, he told himself. As would the people who wrote them. And as notions go, he had to admit that he found this one quite reassuring.

"Twenty-five years," he said. "Can you believe it?" Two and a half decades later, yet it felt like only yesterday.

"We did have a laugh back then though, didn't we?" said The Ace Face. "Until..." he trailed off.

"It's alright," said Jonathan. "You're allowed to mention her name. And I promise not to bite your head off for it this time as well."

He realised he was opening the flood gates. But up until now Melanie had been a white elephant hovering between them and if Jonathan was serious about changing his ways, however difficult it might be, he knew it was only right they got the chance to clear the air too.

"It was hard on all of us, you know," ventured Mickey P.

"I know," replied Jonathan.

"And we did try and be there for you," said The Ace Face.

"I know that too."

"So then why? Why shut us out like that? We were supposed to be friends..."

Jonathan thought for a moment.

"Because I didn't want to hear it," he started to explain. "I didn't want you telling me over and over again that it wasn't my fault, when it was. And although that might seem daft to the both of you, it's how I felt."

"But how can you say that?" insisted Mickey P. "That car came from nowhere, there was nothing anybody could've done."

"Yeah, well, that's easy for you to say. You weren't the one supposed to be looking out for her... I was. Isn't that what big brothers are for? And if I'd have been riding that bit slower, seen it sooner or swerved a bit earlier, not hit the brakes quite as hard even... oh I don't know... it might have made a difference..."

"And if you'd not been giving her a lift in the first place...," added Mickey P. "Swifty we can all live in the 'what ifs' but in the end what happened, happened. If onlys don't change anything. It's how we deal with them that counts."

"Speaking from experience are you?" asked Jonathan.

"Maybe... but we're not talking about me, are we?"

"No, we're talking about me. About how I lived and how she died. It's alright you lot saying none of it was my bleedin' fault, that there was nothing I could've done. But you didn't see her flying through the air like some sort of rag doll... You didn't see the look in mum and dad's eyes afterwards... it wasn't just me blaming me, you know. The two of them blamed me as well."

"Yeah well, even if that's true, which I very much doubt, for what it's worth, we didn't," said The Ace Face.

Jonathan appreciated the sentiment and in seeing the sincerity now written all over the both of their faces, even though one of them might be a bull shitter and the other a thief, he couldn't help but acknowledge that they were still good lads underneath it all. For the first time since meeting up at the funeral, able to remember just why they'd become such good friends to begin with, all those years ago.

"Isn't it time we got going?" he asked, ready for a change of subject, as well as a change of scenery.

"Probably," said The Ace Face, as they all took one last look around for old time's sake.

"Here, look at this!" he then suddenly and animatedly called out, indicating to one of the more recent scribblings. "M 4 L 4 Ever... you think it could be Malc and Louise?"

"Nah," replied Jonathan. "Surely only a kid would put something like that?"

"I suppose..." replied The Ace Face, clearly disappointed.

"I wonder why he didn't just up sticks and move down here," wondered Mickey P. "If his girlfriend lives in Brighton? And from what Mrs. Riley said, the two of them were pretty tight."

"Mmm," replied Jonathan, coming over all pensive. "'Cos if he had, he might still be alive."

He clocked Mickey P. raising a disapproving eyebrow and realised he'd just done what he always did. He'd thought about the 'what if', instead of the reality.

"Sorry, mate," he said. "Old habits die hard and all that."

Of course, he knew Mickey P. was right to correct him and he, once again, re-iterated that it didn't do *anybody* any good to wallow in the things they couldn't change. That from now on, there would be no more of it and instead of focusing on the 'what could've beens', he was, instead, going to do what he was now sure *both* Melanie and Malcolm would have wanted.

Which was to start learning not just from their missed opportunities, but to learn from his own as well. After all, how else was he going to give his family the positive future they deserved, if he didn't?

CHAPTER SIXTY-TWO

IS IT IN MY HEAD

"Oh, come on...?" moaned a weary Tracey and as she threw herself back into her pillow, exhausted, she was forced to wonder how much more of this she could take.

Her contractions were giving her pain like she'd never experienced in her life and just managing them seemed to be zapping every ounce of energy she possessed. So much so, that she wasn't sure she was going to have the required oomph left in her body, when the time to push finally came around.

"Your baby will come when it's good and ready, Mrs. Parkes," replied the Midwife – and as far as Tracey was concerned, a bit too officiously, at that.

"In the meantime," she continued. "It might be an idea to try and relax."

Relax! thought the mother-to-be. *Relax! Is this woman for real?*

"I wasn't talking about the arrival of my baby," she sarcastically explained. "I was talking about the arrival of my child's father. Who I think you'll agree, should be here holding my hand right now, instead of being God knows where, doing God knows what!"

Not that the Midwife was prepared to offer a response, Tracey was quick to note. Moreover, rather than give her patient the attention she deserved, it seemed she preferred to unnecessarily busy herself with some sort of medical contraption.

Either that, or she's just trying to hide the fact that she finds my predicament somewhat amusing, Tracey thought to herself, convinced she'd just spotted a little smile on the woman's face.

Well it's alright for you, isn't it? she silently fumed. *You aren't the one with a weak husband.*

Yes, weak, Tracey re-iterated. *A husband who seems to have spent his whole life shying away from all the important stuff that crops up, all the decision making that goes on. And now, it seems, even the birth of his own child.*

And you think that's funny, do you? Well you want to try living with it, Missie.

She sighed, asking herself just where it all went wrong.

"I know, I know," she said, appreciating at least some of her Midwife's apparent lack of understanding. "You've heard it all before. Lots of women slagging their partners off whilst in the throes of labour..."

"But I assure you, my situation's different," she insisted. "Unlike them, I'm not angry *just* because of the physical pain I happen to be in, although granted, it's not exactly helping any... I'm angry because of the emotional crap he's putting me through on top of everything else."

"I see..." said the Midwife, although in the mother-to-be's eyes she obviously didn't.

"And I think you'll find that my bitterness," Tracey continued regardless. "Is going to continue long after Tuesday has made his or her appearance. And that whatever the size of *my* newborn's fingers and toes, when it comes to Jonathan at least, all will *not* suddenly be well with the world."

She paused at the onset of another contraction, clutching her belly as she waited for the agony to pass.

"Sorry about that," she eventually said, at last, ready to carry on with her onslaught. "Now where was I?"

"Oh yes, we were talking about my pathetic other half and how nothing would give me more pleasure than to, well you know...?"

"Mrs. Parkes," interrupted the Midwife. "Are you sure I can't give you something for the pain?"

Tracey threw her head back, frustrated.

Is this woman ever going to understand where I'm coming from? she asked herself.

"Well that depends," she replied, lifting her head up again. "If you're talking about the physical suffering I'm going through at the moment, then the answer, I'm afraid, is still a definite 'no'. Like I said, I want to enjoy every single blissful moment of this birth... not that I think 'blissful' is quite the right description for what I'm currently experiencing. But hey, what's in a word?"

"However, if you're offering to give me something to take away the emotional suffering that I'm going through right now," she continued. "Then the answer would be a distinct 'yes'. And whatever it is you've got, I'll take it."

The Midwife shook her head, bemused.

"Well it looks like we're still waiting on Jonathan then, doesn't it?" the mother-to-be finished.

CHAPTER SIXTY-THREE

LIP UP FATTY

"Thank goodness for that," said Megan, relieved.

However, as Andrea looked through her wing mirror to also see their tailing Police car finally disappear up the passing slip road, she, in fact, felt anything but.

Please come back! she willed, nervously cringing at the thought of what was to come.

She knew she'd been the one to insist Megan drive somewhat faster in the first place and she couldn't help but now wish she hadn't – especially as her driver's foot was already twitching on the accelerator, she clocked, ready to push down once the coast was definitely clear, just so its owner could re-start having the most fun she'd had since leaving home.

Of course, it was never Andrea's intention to create some sort of speed freak, but in her determination to make sure they got Jonathan back to the hospital in time, much to her regret, she was forced to acknowledge that's exactly what she'd done. And to say Megan had originally been so averse to both motorways and such fast moving traffic, as the car once again began picking up velocity, Andrea couldn't help but note how very quickly her driver had gotten into the swing of things.

"I thought you didn't like going too fast?" she said, automatically gripping her seat, as she nervously watched the needle on the vehicle's speedometer steadily begin to rise.

"I didn't," replied an enthusiastic Megan. "But that was before I realised how much fun it can be."

As far as Andrea was concerned, such an opinion wasn't just subjective, it was very much dependent on where a person was sitting – 'fun' not being quite the word she would have used to describe the way their little car now seemed to be flitting from lane to lane and back again; all the while coming perilously close to every other vehicle it happened across in the process.

"You do know if we get stopped again," she desperately warned. "You might not be so lucky next time?" But, unfortunately and much to her consternation, it seemed even the subject of punishment wasn't going to be enough to curb Megan's erratic driving.

"Oh don't be such a killjoy..." she dismissed, leaving Andrea even more shook up thanks to what appeared to be yet another dangerous manoeuvre. "What's the worst they can do? Give me a bit of a fine and a couple of points on my licence?"

I was thinking more of a prison sentence, Andrea considered, her anxiety by now really starting to get the better of her. *A prison sentence for death by reckless driving... And by that, I mean mine.*

"Besides," Megan continued. "Do you really want to have to go back to the hospital without Jonathan? Because I know I don't."

Andrea didn't quite know how to answer that question; particularly when it felt like she was both risking her life if she did and risking her life if she didn't. However, she did suppose that the better option was to simply carry on as they were and not just because she didn't want to have to face Tracey's wrath either.

After all, she knew from experience that giving birth wasn't always one of the most fulfilling, womanly events, as portrayed in many a women's magazine and on telly. That it could be scary and daunting at the best of times, even when things were running smoothly and a woman's partner was actually in the room to support her.

Needless to say, that was nothing compared to having to go through it alone, with no-one but a midwife to hold the mother-to-be's hand – which was something else Andrea had to admit she knew all about. A predicament she wouldn't have wished on her own worst enemy, she acknowledged. Let alone a first time mum. Furthermore, as she continued to fretfully grip her seat as if for dear life, she fast came to the conclusion that her own current discomfort was, in fact, a small price to pay. Particularly if that meant first time mum, Tracey Parkes, didn't have to go through what she, herself, had previously been through.

"I suppose you're right," she reluctantly conceded.

Although as the car then began to shake, rattle and roll as if ready to fall apart at any given moment, Andrea still couldn't help but cross her fingers and silently pray to the heavens – all in the hope that she'd come to the right decision.

After all, at this rate of speed the question of whether they'd make it to their destination on time may have been answered. But nevertheless, there was still the not so little question of whether they'd make their destination at all.

CHAPTER SIXTY-FOUR

WATCH OUT I'M BACK

As he followed the main road into Brighton, Pepper found himself questioning whether or not he was doing the right thing. On top of that, having never before felt quite so unsure of himself, he had to admit it was a somewhat alien and scratchy experience. Especially when all his uncertainty surrounded his decision to come chasing after Mickey P. – their cat and mouse games having been a way of life for years.

Whereas on the one hand he knew Mickey P. deserved everything he had coming to him, he was, after all, a criminal, on the other, a niggling, little voice was insisting this vendetta of his had gone on long enough. Not that he found it all that easy to admit to holding some sort of vengeful grudge, he acknowledged; particularly when he'd spent years telling himself he was only acting in accordance with his professional duty. A position he wished he still felt able to maintain at that moment, but for some reason couldn't.

"I mean, does it really matter who picked on who when we were kids?" he asked himself, scoffing at the very idea of it. "Does it really matter who got the girl, when the girl is clearly more than happy with her choice?"

Of course, the very fact that he'd felt the need to ask such questions in the first place, was enough to tell him it did. Although as he began to think about all the time and energy he'd spent trying to get back at Mickey P. over the years, he found it hard to get his head round who he'd managed to hurt the most – his arch enemy or, indeed, himself.

It was uncomfortable contemplation and as he dropped down onto the sea front, he hoped that at least finding a parking space would be straight forward enough. Sadly, he soon realised that even that was just wishful thinking, considering it wasn't just a Saturday lunchtime, but a Saturday lunchtime when every man and his dog seemed to have hit the streets.

"Here we go," he said, relieved to spot a 'car park' sign, as he turned right at a set of traffic lights.

However, things only went from bad to worse when he then hit a long queue of other vehicles; vehicles whose drivers had clearly thought the same thing. And once in line, just like them, he found there was no turning back.

"Bugger!" he seethed.

He looked about for an escape route, but it appeared he really was committed to staying exactly where he was – thanks to a rather cunning local council, he noted. An authority who'd seen fit to provide the rather narrow 'in' lane with a raised divider, thus, preventing any form of subsequent U-turn

"Well that's just bloody fantastic," he said, wondering if anything about this trip was going to run smoothly and he couldn't help but begin to toy with the idea of just sacking the whole damn thing off, in favour of joining the rest of the throng for a spot of seaside shopping, instead.

"No," he asserted. "That wouldn't be right. And let's face it, you're still a professional, whether you like it or not."

So in telling himself he'd never been a man to give up on anything to begin with, he decided that having come this far, he should at least try and finish what he'd started.

Then again, as he checked his dashboard clock to see it was already nearing noon as it was and counted the number of non-moving cars ahead of him, he realised the chances of his ever managing to catch his man anyway, were becoming increasingly slim by the minute.

CHAPTER SIXTY-FIVE

THINGS ARE GOING TO GET BETTER

As he, Mickey P. and The Ace Face made their way along the pier towards Malcolm's final resting place, Jonathan couldn't help but feel a bit distracted. In fact, what with all the exciting chaos going on around them, trying to maintain a respectful silence wasn't exactly the easiest of tasks; their somewhat sombre death march, he acknowledged, certainly standing out amongst all the other pier users.

Mostly tourists, student types and romantic couples, Jonathan observed. All of them more than happy to admire the pavilion's glitter ball, try their hand at Hook a Duck and bump and grind on the Dodgems. Furthermore, as they passed through the hordes of people he found himself anticipating having to refuse a request from The Ace Face; hoping he wasn't really about to suggest they join in the fun and take Malc on the thrilling yet nauseating Waltzers – all in the name of Malc's send off, of course.

Oh no, this certainly wasn't the most conducive environment in which he and his travel companions could prepare to scatter their deceased mate's ashes, he was forced to repeat. Not that those lining up for their Halal lunch, Japanese noodles or good old Fish and Chips seemed to care.

I'm friggin' starving, he thought to himself, taking in just how varied the array of available take-away cuisine was and he felt his belly begin to rumble somewhat, as a result.

He couldn't help but think the aromas emanating from each and every one of the food stalls did smell bloody good and although as a rule he knew he wouldn't have hesitated in joining the queues with them, under the circumstances, he had no choice but to tell his tummy it was just going to have to wait.

Maybe I'll get something when we're done, he comforted, putting all thoughts of food and his stomach to one side for now, with a view to concentrating on Malcolm.

He began to contemplate the seriousness of what they were about to do, wondering if there was some sort of protocol they needed to follow; or whether there was some special prayer that had to be said. However, having never been involved in this kind of act before, he had to confess he was damned if he knew, but with a bit of luck, that was where The Ace Face and Mickey P. stepped in.

"Is there a procedure to this?" he asked them. "To scattering ashes?"

Not, it seemed, that they had any idea either.

"I wouldn't have thought so," replied The Ace Face, with a shrug. "I think we just say a few words and then send him on his way."

"Well if there is," joined in Mickey P. "It sounds like poor Malc's knackered."

Still, as they passed the Merry-go-Round and neared the end of the pier, the last thing Jonathan wanted was to let his friend down on the final leg of his journey and as such, he told himself there was yet one more person with whom he could consult, who just might have a clue as to what they were talking about.

"Well maybe this Louise woman will know," he hopefully suggested, but having now reached their final destination, as he went on to scan his surroundings in the hope of spotting her, alas, there wasn't a mournful looking female in sight.

On the other hand, he did espy a rather sad looking Mod in the vicinity, nervously holding a big bunch of deep, red roses and momentarily distracted by the sight, he couldn't help but think a bouquet like that, must have cost the man a packet. Even so, judging by their owner's forlorn expression, he could only assume his intended date had stood him up.

Or maybe they're for his girlfriend after an argument? Jonathan further pondered. *And the flowers are just his way of saying sorry.*

Either way, it was clear the poor chap had wasted his money, because whoever she was, she clearly wasn't turning up. And knowing that he, himself, was going to have to do some serious begging for forgiveness of his own in the not too distant future, Jonathan could only cross his fingers in the hope that when it came to Tracey, his apology was going to have a more positive outcome.

His staring caught the Mod's eye and for a second there, it did look as if he was going to actually say something. In then spotting the urn, however, it was no wonder he went on to change his mind again, thought Jonathan, opting for a more cautious nod of the head, instead. After all, three men and a casket of ashes, on what was to all intents and purposes a floating fairground, wasn't something you see every day of the week and understandably so, was enough to put anyone off striking up a conversation. Therefore, Jonathan returned the gesture with a nod of his own, before returning his attention back to the others.

"I would've thought she'd be here by now," he said, once again, looking around for Louise. "Maybe we should just get on with it."

As he went on to lead the way, Jonathan did have to wonder if getting to the actual pier's end was, in fact, allowed. After all, the authorities hadn't exactly made it easy, he noted. What with their having to dodge the frighteningly close, death defying swing of the strangely named 'Booster' ride, before negotiating a precarious aluminium staircase. Moreover, even if Jonathan hadn't been able to control his trembling nerves at this point, he realised no-one would've heard any escaping whimpers anyway – thanks to the Bon Jovi rock classic that conveniently blasted out from the strategically placed, industrial sized speakers.

It suddenly dawned on him just how apt their surroundings were. The whole weekend had, after all, been something of a fairground roller coaster from start to finish. What with the ups when it came to taking the helm of a scooter again, the buzz of the rally and, dare he say it, the sex with Olivia. Then the downs of being forced off the road by a gang of two-wheeled thugs, the in-fighting and for different reasons, again, the sex with Olivia.

However, his one night stand was best forgotten either way, as were all the negatives, a determined Jonathan told himself. Although at the same time he was saddened by the fact that yet someone else had to die, just so he could reach this more positive state of mind.

Not that the weight he'd been carrying around all these years had vanished completely, he admitted. And in being honest, he doubted it ever would. However, with a little help from his friends at least he was now taking steps to off load some of the burden and in time, he asked, who knew how he was going to feel?

In that moment what he did know, however, was that his two travel companions did, indeed, deserve an apology. Because without them, he wouldn't have even come this far.

"About what I said last night," he ventured.

"Ah, don't worry about it," replied The Ace Face, unconcerned. "I think we all said things we didn't really mean."

"But that's the point," Jonathan persisted. "At the time, we did mean it. Every bloody word."

"Yeah well, we're friends, aren't we?" said Mickey P. "Friends can be honest with each other."

All at once, Jonathan felt very lucky, indeed, and in an attempt to show his appreciation, he didn't just surprise his two old mates when he suddenly gave them an impromptu hug of gratitude, he also surprised himself. Then again, realising where he came from this kind of behaviour might be alright at the end of a drunken night out on the town, it definitely wasn't what a rufty tufty Northern male like himself did, in the broad daylight of a Saturday afternoon.

"Must be all this sea air," he said, stepping back in inflated masculinity.

"Too right," agreed The Ace Face.

"Yep," said Mickey P. "No male bonding fest going on here."

Jonathan checked about himself to make sure no-one had seen and although he did have an idea his friends had valued the gesture just as much as he had, he was relieved to find everyone else in the area still having too much fun to even notice what the three of them were up to.

Everyone, he noted, except the unfortunate Mod with the flowers.

CHAPTER SIXTY-SIX

BATMAN

"Finally, we're here," said a relieved Andrea, as she and her driver, at last, reached their destination.

Megan prepared to hastily reverse into a parking space, but as far as Andrea was concerned, just going forward had been bad enough. So much so, she knew there was no way her stomach could handle a manoeuvre that involved going backwards.

"Just let me out," she said., already grabbing at the door handle. "I need some air."

As she disembarked, she couldn't help but tell herself that, rather than the simple drive from A to B it should've been, this last couple of hours had fallen somewhere between an exaggerated hazard perception test and a Formula 1 race. What's more, whereas Megan as the driver seemed to have handled it well, she couldn't say the same for herself as the passenger and unfortunately far from feeling like some caped crusader, Batman style, on an emergency mission, Andrea just felt sick. Nausea like she'd never experienced before, not even when she, herself, had been pregnant.

She waited for both Megan to finish up and for some semblance of colour to return to her cheeks, able to see there was still some distance between where she now stood and the actual pier's end. Thus, with time already moving on, she realised this wasn't just another hurdle for her to overcome, it was probably the worst obstacle she'd had to face in the whole of this sorry journey so far.

"I don't believe it," she said. "After everything I've been through to get here already... Now I have to take part in some bloody speed race?"

"Right," said Megan, jumping out of the car. "We're going to have to leg it!"

"Can't we just walk fast, instead?" Andrea asked and by now feeling somewhat desperate, she had to acknowledge the fact that she didn't just hate running, she found it nigh on impossible.

In addition, with the humiliation of many a school sports event still haunting her to this day, she could only imagine the sniggers she was going to no doubt attract, were she to demonstrate her rather 'special' and 'unique' style of sped up jog to Brighton's all and sundry. Not only that, she hadn't exercised in what was probably years; the nearest she'd come to picking up any sort of speed being when she ran around the house doing housework or when she was chasing after the kids.

"Come on," insisted Megan, already darting ahead. "We haven't got time to dawdle."

"Alright, alright," she half heartedly replied, grudgingly ordering herself to treat this as some sort of aversion therapy, as she reluctantly followed suit. Moreover, in realising under the circumstances she didn't really have any choice *but* to show herself up, she decided to ignore the obvious amusement from passers by, in favour of doing what she was good at – which was just getting on with it, whatever the cost to her dignity.

"The things I do for other people," she complained, once again, forced to acknowledge her responsibility in getting Jonathan to his child's birth on time.

Although in the same breath, she just had to hope that he, as the proud father-to-be, was going to appreciate the full embarrassing extent of her efforts.

"And if you're not there at the pier's end to thank me personally," she insisted. "When I do get hold of you Swifty, don't be surprised if I wring you're bloody neck!"

CHAPTER SIXTY-SEVEN

THE DOORS OF YOUR HEART

Jonathan felt very privileged to be a part of the scattering of his old friend's ashes, even though he still wasn't sure how the three of them should be going about it. Nevertheless, it didn't feel right to just un-ceremoniously tip Malcolm's remains out of their casket and straight into the water, not without at least some sort of acknowledgement first. But devoid of knowing the correct etiquette for this kind of act, he did suppose a few words about the dearly departed's life, would at least give proceedings the respect such an undertaking deserved.

On the other hand, for a man who hadn't seen his deceased mate in years, Jonathan didn't view himself as the right guy to take the bull by the horns and get things started either. That, coupled with the fact that he'd already let his manly guard down once that day and despite knowing his spontaneous group hug had felt pretty darn good at the time, almost liberating in some soft shite way, that didn't necessarily mean he was ready for a repeat performance.

"Maybe you should say a few words," he said, pushing the responsibility onto The Ace Face.

Much to his surprise, it was clear The Ace Face, in turn, felt as awkward about doing so as he, himself, did. Leaving Jonathan no choice but to then look to Mickey P, wondering if he would be prepared to do the honours, instead.

"Don't look at me," said Mickey P. in response. "Out of all of us, he was the one Mrs. Riley chose to organise all this."

Which wasn't quite the rejoinder Jonathan had been hoping for.

However, with nothing else for it, he decided that as someone was going to have to say something and soon whether they liked it or not, that that 'someone' may as well be him. Even more so, as he recalled the way things had panned out the last time he'd actually seen Malcolm face to face, when he'd basically screamed at him to eff off.

You do owe the man something of an apology he silently admitted. Telling himself there was no time like the present, even if his mate wasn't physically there to hear it.

"Alright, give him here then," he said. "I'll do it."

He took Malcolm's urn and he cleared his throat in preparation, feeling somewhat self-conscious as he tried to gather his thoughts.

"You were a good friend Malc," he began, somewhat ill at ease. "And although it's been a while, I just wanted you to know that."

"Not that I can say the same about me," he nervously quipped. "I mean I didn't treat you very well the last time we saw each other, did I?"

He paused to collect himself, finding this much harder than he'd originally anticipated.

"Anyway, I hope deep down," he was finally able to continue. "You know I was just sounding off... reeling after what had happened to Melanie... and to me as well, I suppose. But I do understand that you were only trying to help, to be there for me. And instead of accepting your support like I should've done, the support of all my friends, I just threw it back in your faces. And for that, I truly am sorry..."

He turned to his travel companions.

"To all of you..."

He felt grateful for their returning appreciative and understanding smiles, slightly embarrassed by them even.

"Anyway," he said, suddenly pulling himself together. "I think that's probably enough from me, don't you?"

He passed the urn over to Mickey P., encouraging him to now take the mantle and say a few words – public speaking clearly not this man's particular forte either.

"Well Malc, I hope you enjoyed your send off," he said. "'Cos I know we've all found it eventful... haven't we lads?

And I know you're sat up there on your cloud, watching us, looking after us. So cheers."

Then, much to Jonathan's surprise, it seemed he was done.

"It's what Andrea said to the kids," he explained, at the same time passing the urn over to The Ace Face. "You know, when the goldfish died."

"Ah," Jonathan replied, telling himself that when it came to some people, maybe short and sweet was probably best.

"And we're all sorry we didn't get to meet the lovely Louise," took up The Ace Face.

"Although I think you'll agree it's probably for the best that she isn't here," he continued. "And that she didn't come to the funeral... I mean at least this way she can remember you exactly as you was... Still in once piece, that is."

"Excuse me?" said Jonathan, unable to quite believe what he was hearing.

"What?" asked The Ace Face. "It's true, isn't it? Would you want to remember your boyfriend as a pile of dust in a box?"

"No, I suppose not," he replied. "Not when you put it like that."

Although as far as last images went, compared to how he'd had to remember his sister all these years, he did have to admit a casket of ashes was definitely preferable. Not that he felt able to say that.

"You're right." he added. "I'm sorry."

"That's your third apology today, mate," whispered Mickey P.

"And probably not my last," replied Jonathan, all at once thinking of Tracey.

In fact, knowing that she could be less forgiving than most, especially when it came to something that mattered, he realised 'sorry' was a word he was going to have to get used to articulating, on a somewhat regular basis. He just hoped against hope that by the time he got back to Lancashire, she was going to be around to hear him say it.

CHAPTER SIXTY-EIGHT

LONG HOT SUMMER

Pepper had always prided himself on keeping fit, but as he fast made his way along the pier he didn't just begin to slow down regardless, he felt like he'd lost his sense of purpose.

More to the point, he couldn't help but ask himself why he wasn't enjoying life like everyone else seemed to be, comparing himself to all the other pier users as he made his way through the Arcade and towards the Pavilion. Not that slot machines were particularly his thing, he admitted. But then again, what exactly was?

All he ever did was work, he reluctantly acknowledged. As well as look after Harry, of course. However, as rewarding as that could be, he did have to confess it didn't really take much time and effort on his part. It was just a case of keeping him fed and watered and making sure his cage was nice and clean. Not exactly a challenge, he told himself, beginning to wonder if when he got back to Lancashire, it might be an idea for him to take up some kind of hobby.

A hobby like hamster breeding, maybe? he thoughtfully considered. That way he could utilize the experience he'd already garnered and, thanks to all the love and affection he'd poured on the hamster he'd got already, it wasn't as if he didn't have a head start on the male of the species reproductive front.

Then again, he reasoned, that wasn't exactly expanding his horizons, was it? Furthermore, in realising there was no point in trying to organise his pet rodent's love life when he couldn't even organise one of his own, he was forced to concede it wasn't really the kind of leisurely activity he should be thinking about anyway.

Not that that meant he was all set to give up on the hobby idea altogether, of course. He would just find something else to do – something more social; like dancing, or an art class, or a Genealogy group where he could both learn something and meet other people at the same time...

At last, feeling the spring in his step beginning to return at the prospect of trying something new, Pepper decided to think about the exact ins and outs of his down time pursuits later, once he'd gotten the task at hand out of the way.

However, as he got to the end of the pier, with his target now in sight, unfortunately it was clear Malcolm's ashes hadn't actually been scattered yet. And no matter how much he just wanted to get this arrest over and done with, as he slowed to a complete standstill, it just didn't seem right to interrupt such an event half way through.

"Must be nice to have mates like that," said an unknown voice.

Sure it was talking to him, Pepper swung round to see who it belonged to.

"Yeah, it must be," he replied, finding himself face to face with a bloke he'd never met before – a Mod with a bunch of wilting red roses, he noted, who looked just as out of place as he did, amongst the throng of happy fun fair goers.

He continued to stand there, silently watching on as Jonathan, Mickey P. and The Ace Face began pouring Malcolm's remains out into the vast waters beneath. Not that he could actually hear any of what they were saying – thanks to the ear splitting, eighties rock music that came from a set of massive speakers. Still, it was a moving experience all the same and he decided to give everyone concerned, a respectful moment's contemplation after the fact, before eventually making his move.

"Right," he said to the Mod, as he stepped forward. "Time for me to get this over with, I think."

The trouble was, Pepper knew his heart was no longer in it. Probably thanks to all the brooding deliberation he'd had to do since leaving home, he reflected. In fact, to say this lock up had been his sole aim throughout the majority of this trip, as Mickey P. caught sight of him in return, Pepper found himself reluctantly having to admit that the prospect of finally making his arrest didn't feel anywhere near as rewarding as it should have done.

CHAPTER SIXTY-NINE

MAYBE TOMORROW

"I hope to God we've not missed them," prayed a breathless Andrea. Moreover, as she made her way along the pier, it really did feel as if her legs were moving quicker than they could actually carry her.

"Well if we have," replied an equally out of breath Megan. "No-one can say it's because we didn't do our best."

And whilst Andrea realised this little fact probably wasn't going to be much comfort to Tracey if they, indeed, had failed in their mission, she did have to agree that at least the two of them had tried.

She squinted in the hope of being able to single Jonathan, Mickey P. and The Ace Face out from amongst the crowds, however, it wasn't easy considering the numerous pier's end gatherings. Then again, thankfully the nearer she got, the easier it became and she was finally able to bring the three of them into focus.

"Thank you Lord," she said, all at once relieved.

With her prayers, at last, answered, she realised all she had to wish for now, was that the mother-to-be had managed to keep her legs tightly shut thus far and would continue to do so, for the duration of the up and coming return journey back to the hospital.

"Hang on a minute," she said, suddenly stopping in her tracks. "Who the hell's that?"

Despite knowing all along that a fourth member would be joining the travelling trio here in Brighton, instead of finding this person to be a female who went by the name of Louise as expected, she was surprised to find herself looking at, not a woman, but rather a man – a man who, unfortunately for her, went by the name of Pepper.

"What's he doing here?" she asked, momentarily confused.

Then it dawned on her that this unwarranted imposter had done exactly what she'd hoped he wouldn't and come chasing after her other half, hell bent on making an arrest.

Why can't he just leave us alone? she fumed and although she knew she'd be the first to admit Mickey P. was no angel, she was also of the opinion that he didn't deserve this kind of stalking.

Yes, stalking! she insisted. Something Pepper seemed to have been doing for years now and as far as she was concerned, enough was most definitely enough.

In fact, she continued, somewhat re-assessing the situation to include her other half's role in the two men's antics. *I'd say the two of you are actually as bad as each other.*

But whilst Mickey P. seemed more than happy to join in with Pepper's perpetual game of cat and mouse, she was forced to admit it just wasn't funny anymore.

No, she told herself. *This needs sorting. Once and for all.*

With her anger now fuelling a second wind, she suddenly picked up pace, setting off on a very determined march towards them – more than ready to give both Pepper *and* Mickey P. a very large piece of her mind.

CHAPTER SEVENTY

A MESSAGE TO YOU RUDY

"What the..." said Jonathan, wondering if it was just his imagination, or did the woman making an indomitable beeline straight towards him and his friends, really look the spit of Andrea?

Then, as he saw yet another woman bringing up the rear, this one baring more than a striking resemblance to The Ace Face's girlfriend, Megan, he realised it wasn't his mind playing tricks at all. In fact, all he needed now was to spot Tracey in order to get the hat trick, but as he looked around and beyond, his heart lifting in the hope of seeing her somewhere in the distance, much to his ensuing disappointment she wasn't anywhere in sight.

Of course she's not going to be here, he told himself, ridiculing his own optimism. After all, Tracey wasn't one to go chasing after anyone. *Mickey P.'s the one with following, you fool. Not bloody you."*

In spite of not being able to hazard a guess as to why Andrea and Megan should turn up in the first place, he did have an idea that they probably weren't the bearers of glad tidings. Most certainly not if Andrea's rather furious expression was anything to go by and he watched on as the forerunner barged straight passed the Mod, nearly knocking him over in the process. Then, as if the poor guy's day hadn't been bad enough, Megan stop to catch her breath, at the same time inadvertently using the unsuspecting man's shoulder as some sort of resting post.

"Andrea?" said Mickey P., making it clear he hadn't anticipated their arrival either.

However, even Jonathan could see Andrea's mood was more about expecting an explanation rather than giving one.

"Megan?" said The Ace Face, apparently equally as bemused and upon seeing the young woman's eyes light up by way of a reaction, Jonathan realised that whatever the problem here was, it obviously didn't have anything to do with this particular duo.

"Ace..." squealed Megan, in response, all at once finding the energy to race forward and throw herself into her other half's welcoming arms.

"Could someone please tell me what he's doing here," ordered Andrea, unmistakably referring to Pepper.

"Like I don't know already..." she immediately added.

Jonathan was left with no choice but to just stand there observing his friends; one of the couples using their lips to seemingly suck the life out of each other, whilst the other used theirs to start warming up for what was, without hesitation, going to be one hell of a row.

Either way, that must be really liberating..." he thought to himself. *Being able to openly show feelings like that.* At the same time recognising that ever since Melanie's accident, that was something he'd refused to allow himself to do.

Not that he and Tracey didn't show their emotions at all, he acknowledged. Covering both ends of the emotional spectrum, there was often a little touch of the hand here or a stern, yet controlled, word there. Even so, it wouldn't hurt for the two of them to be a bit more demonstrative, he supposed – especially on his part, he further considered. At any rate, he *was* the one with years of holding back to make up for.

"Never mind him, Andrea," said Mickey P. "What are you doing here?"

It was a question that Jonathan was also curious to know the answer to. But thanks to her wrath, her reasons had obviously paled in significance, to the point that they were no longer important.

"Anyone else and this would be classed as harassment," she formidably replied, completely ignoring the question. "And just because he wears a bloody uniform, it doesn't mean he can get away with it..."

Jonathan began to think that maybe being passionate in public wasn't all it was cracked up to be, after all. This kind of arguing in the street couldn't be good for anyone, as evidenced by the amount of amused and somewhat embarrassing attention they were now starting to receive.

"Why this couldn't wait until he got back home," she continued regardless. "I don't know..."

And although *she* might have been oblivious to her surroundings, Jonathan most certainly wasn't.

"Yeah... yeah... yeah..." she carried on, this time reeling on Pepper, at the same time making sure he couldn't get a word in edgeways. "You're only doing your job... Now tell me something I don't know..."

Jonathan watched Mickey P. step forward in an attempt to calm her down. A brave move in anyone's book, he decided, doubting if he, himself, would ever have the courage to interrupt a woman in the middle of such a heavy duty rant.

"Come on love," he said. "I've got to face the music sometime. And we've done what we came here to do, so it may as well be now."

"Don't you *'love'* me," she insisted. "As far as I'm concerned, the pair of you really are as bad as each other."

"And you're right to think that, 'cos we probably are," Mickey P. continued. "But come on, the man *is* only doing his job. So if you've got to blame someone, it's only right you blame me."

Wow! thought Jonathan, surprised to hear his old mate finally taking responsibility for his actions. *Good on you.*

However, he could see his own astonishment was nothing compared to what Andrea must've been thinking, her other half's admission having shocked her into a stunned silence on the whole matter.

This is better than television, he considered, as Mickey P. went on to place both his hands behind his back, ready for the handcuffs to be donned.

But what was even more of a shocker, was the fact that it seemed even Pepper was a changed man.

"I don't think that's necessary on this occasion, do you?" he said.

As the others began gradually making their way off the pier, Jonathan hung back for a moment, wondering just how long this truce, in reality, was going to last.

Nevertheless, he was just glad to see he wasn't the only one willing to change the error of his ways and he found himself questioning whether both Malcolm and Melanie had had more of a hand in this than he'd originally thought.

"Now you're just being daft," he told himself, thinking back to The Ace Face's comments only the night before. However, his dismissal still wasn't enough to prevent him looking back to where he and his friends had stood scattering Malc's ashes only moments before – just in case.

"What's he doing?" he asked, suddenly bemused as he spotted the Mod making his way up the rickety, aluminium staircase, only to then start gently dropping his roses, one by one, onto the water's surface.

He presumed such a gesture was simply a better means of discarding them. After all, being so expensive, he wasn't sure if he, himself, could've just dumped them in a rubbish bin. Then, for the first time noticing the artwork on the back of the Mod's parka and reading the name 'Lewis' boldly emblazoned around an emblematic target design, he couldn't help but reconsider.

"Louise... Lewis. Louise... Lewis," he repeated.

He looked over towards his friend's in the hope of getting their opinion. However, in continuing their stroll off the pier, they were too wrapped up in each other as couples to have eyes for anyone else.

CHAPTER SEVENTY-ONE

ANGEL

"It's a bit windy up here," said the Mod. "Gets in your eyes."

Jonathan could see he was just making excuses in an attempt to hide his tears. However, rather than embarrass the man completely, he simply followed his gaze down to all the individual roses, now floating on the water's surface alongside Malcolm's ashes.

"Why didn't you say something?" he eventually asked, saddened by the fact that the Mod really shouldn't have had to. "Or you know, come and joined us or something? You were more than welcome."

"You didn't ask me to," the Mod merely replied, leaving Jonathan unable to help but let out a bit of a laugh in response.

"Yeah well," he said. "That's because we were expecting to meet up with a Louise as opposed to a Lewis. But I suppose that's The Ace Face for you. He can be more of a talker than a listener when he wants to be, if you know what I mean."

"Don't worry about it," said the Mod. "It's an easy mistake to make."

Not that Jonathan necessarily agreed.

"Well I think you're being a bit generous there under the circumstances, mate... but honestly, if we'd known who you were..."

"It's fine," the Mod reassured. "Besides, at least this way I get to say my own, personal goodbye."

A personal goodbye that Jonathan suddenly realised he'd had no right to interrupt and he suddenly felt a bit awkward as a result.

"Anyway," he said, self consciously telling himself he'd intruded long enough already. "I better get off, the others'll be waiting."

He held out his arm to shake the Mod's hand.

"I'm Jonathan by the way," he said. "And if you ever find yourself up North...?"

"I'll be sure to call..."

Jonathan paused, all at once pulling the man into a surprise bear hug.

Then, without another word he set off back down the rickety staircase to catch up with his friends, just glad he'd got the chance to meet Malcolm's partner before doing so.

CHAPTER SEVENTY-TWO

BANKROBBER

By the time they all stepped off the pier, Jonathan could see Andrea had gone from feeling extremely angry to being very upset.

What's more, with Mickey P. and Pepper set to go left, whilst he and the rest of the crew went right, it was one of those awkward moments where someone had to decide which party was going to be the one who walked away first.

He looked to Pepper indicating that it might be an idea to give the separating couple a minute together, before anyone went anywhere. And much to his surprise, Pepper actually agreed, even taking it upon himself to instruct everyone else to step to one side.

Well, will wonders ever cease...? Jonathan asked himself.

Not that the two of them had this tender moment completely to themselves, he soon realised and overhearing them say their goodbyes was as equally touching as it was embarrassing and both at the same time.

"Once this is sorted," said Mickey P. "Things'll be different. I promise you..."

Thanks to Andrea's apparent self-consciousness, it was obvious to Jonathan that such loving exchanges must be a rarity between the two of them and that Andrea was more used to being on the receiving end of jovial banter, than she was any heartfelt declarations.

"Now when've I heard that before," she quipped.

"Yeah, well... this time I actually mean it," Mickey P. replied. "I'm telling you, you deserve better."

Of course, Jonathan didn't doubt that Andrea had, indeed, heard such assertions countless times previously, but he could see for himself the genuine sincerity written all over his friend's face.

"Right," Mickey P. continued, giving Andrea one last kiss. "I suppose it's time I was off..."

Jonathan couldn't believe how matter-of-fact he now sounded; especially for a man facing the possibility of a prison sentence and with tears springing into Andrea's eyes as her other half went on to make his departure, even Jonathan couldn't help but feel worried about what was to come.

He wondered if he should try and take advantage of Pepper's new and more understanding disposition. Whether he should go after them to discuss the possibility of Mickey P. surrendering himself in to the Police Station, preferably on Monday morning, rather than him having to go right now? However, with Mickey P. having recently gained a record for absconding on top of everything else – which, in part, was what got him into this mess in the first place, Jonathan did have to acknowledge that this would probably be pushing his luck a bit too much.

Besides, he reminded himself. *Haven't you got enough of your own problems to think about?*

Speaking of which... Although he didn't yet quite know how he was going to sort things out with Tracey, he did know that when she wanted to, she could be something of an enforcement officer, herself. And with that in mind, he just hoped the punishment she was going to dish out as a result of his own runaway misdemeanours, wasn't about to be anywhere near as severe as Mickey P.'s.

He placed a comforting arm around Andrea's shoulders. "It'll all turn out right in the end," he said, in an attempt to reassure not just her, but himself as well. "You'll see."

"Mmmm," she replied, not quite convinced. "I suppose only time will tell..."

The two of them watched on, with Mickey P. and Pepper fast heading off into the distance... and it was only after a few moments contemplation, that Jonathan remembered he still didn't know why the two women had turned up to begin with.

"Can I just ask," he said, his curiosity finally getting the better of him. "What're you doing here anyway?"

"Shit!" she said, in response. "I can't believe I forgot!"

"Forgot what?" he asked, finding her sudden freaking out almost amusing.

"About Tracey... your wife..." she said. "God Jonathan, I'm so sorry."

A terrifying panic gripped him. "What are you talking?" he said. "What's happened to her?"

"She's having the baby..." Andrea frantically explained. "No, I mean she's having it right now... as we speak!"

CHAPTER SEVENTY-THREE

THE SUN AND THE RAIN

For Jonathan, the race back to the hospital felt like some kind of surreal triathlon.

First came the swim. However, instead of confidently diving into the water like some impressive, powerful athlete, upon hearing about Tracey's labour he felt the searing sting of one hell of a belly flop, only to then experience the suffocating sensation of drowning. And even though he knew he had to get himself together somehow, he was only able to recover sufficiently enough, to symbolically yet frantically doggy paddle his way back to The Ace Face's scooter.

Then there was the cycle leg for him to overcome. Of course, Jonathan was fortunate in that his two wheels were, indeed, motorised and he didn't have to rely on pedal power to get himself from A to B. Nevertheless, the road ahead still seemed endless. In fact, even being on the motorway where he could get more speed up didn't seem to help any and passing junction after junction, by now he was convinced he was never going to get there.

And finally, there was the foot race. But as he zoomed into the hospital car park, dumped his scooter and like all good athletes found the surge of energy needed for the final sprint, instead of tearing towards the hospital doors and charging straight through them, he found himself coming to a complete standstill – even before he'd actually gotten to the entrance.

"What are you doing?" asked Andrea, having told Megan to just let her out of the mini so she could, at last, catch him up. "What have you stopped for?"

"I just can't do it," said Jonathan, all his earlier assertions about dealing with things head on suddenly deserting him, as much as he'd deserted his wife.

"What are you talking about?" she impatiently replied. "You can't do what?"

"I mean..." he forcefully re-iterated. "That I can't go in there... in the hospital."

"But what if Tracey hasn't had the baby yet?" said Andrea, seemingly at a loss as to what she should do. "You could still be there. To see her through it..."

Jonathan suddenly dropped to his knees and put his head in his hands.

"But what if she doesn't want to see me?" he asked. "What if she tells me to get lost and never come back?" Although under the circumstances he wouldn't have blamed her if she did. In spite of it being the last thing he wanted to hear.

"What's going on?" The Ace Face called out, as he and Megan finally approached to join them.

Andrea shrugged. "He says he doesn't want to go in."

"Come on mate," said The Ace Face. "You can't sit here, not when you have a baby to say hello to."

Jonathan didn't agree. "They're probably better off without me anyway," he replied, still not moving.

"Why don't you girls go and see what gift you can come up with for the baby?" suggested The Ace Face, indicating they give him a few minutes, as he dug out his wallet.

"Don't mind if we do," replied Andrea, happily taking the cash.

As the two women headed off, Jonathan felt his friend crouch down next to him.

"You don't mean that," said The Ace Face. "Not really. You're probably just having a bit of a wobble, like most new dads do."

"Yeah?" scoffed Jonathan. "And what would you know."

"Enough to appreciate you shouldn't be out here when you have a wife and kid in there to think about," The Ace Face replied.

"Yeah well, I haven't been doing a very good job of that up to now, have I?" Jonathan admitted. "Bloody running off to Brighton when I should have been here... well, not here exactly, but you know what I mean."

"And now's your chance to make up for that, isn't it?"

Jonathan knew he was right. He finally rose to his feet.

"But what if I can't do it?" he said. "It's not as if I've been a brilliant husband, so who's to say I'm gonna make a good dad?"

"I suppose it's like anything," said The Ace Face. "You just do what you can."

"And like everything in life," he continued. "There'll be times when you get it right. And times when you get it wrong... And then there'll be the times when you haven't got a clue what on earth you should be doing. But that's when you just have to put a brave face on things, pretend you're in control and simply hope for the best."

"Like you do, you mean?" Jonathan quipped.

"Yep," said The Ace Face. "Like I do."

Jonathan led the way as they began the walk to the hospital doors.

"You know, you were right about what you said," The Ace Face piped up. "About me giving it the big 'I Am', when underneath it all I'm still just good, old Roger Pickup."

"There's nothing wrong with that, mate," said Jonathan.

"No, I agree. But I'd still prefer it if you call me The Ace."

Jonathan couldn't help but smile.

"And there's nowt wrong with you being scared at being a dad either," The Ace Face added.

Jonathan paused before going inside. "I just don't want to get it wrong," he said. "I don't want to let Tracey down again."

"Look," said his old friend. "You either go in there, determined to be the man you want to be? Or you turn around and walk? Either way, you'll never let your wife or your child down again. And even though I know what I'd do in your shoes, it's not my choice to make, is it? It's yours."

CHAPTER SEVENTY-FOUR

MUSIC MUST CHANGE

"What is it about a baby's teeny, weeny fingers and toes?" Tracey asked, feeling a real sense of astonishment, as she looked down at Tuesday, now safe and sound in her arms.

She couldn't believe she and Jonathan could produce a little human being so beautiful and breathtaking. And fascinated by the masses of thick, black hair on her baby's head and the clear blue eyes already staring back at her, she did have to admit that although not one hundred per cent perfect thanks to Jonathan still being AWOL, maybe the world now wasn't such a bad place to be, after all.

What's more, in acknowledging that the midwife had probably been right all along not to listen to her embarrassing 'in the throes of labour' rantings, she couldn't help but cringe at how badly she'd behaved.

"Poor daddy," she said, remembering all the venom she'd spat his way.

She realised the excruciating agony was probably what really lay behind most of her fervour and even if Jonathan had been in the labour room with her, she wouldn't have managed to maintain a sense of dignity anyway. She'd have only found other excuses with which to blame him for her suffering, she conceded; admitting her pain threshold had never been one she could be proud of to begin with.

"Although Mummy didn't do too badly, now, did she?" said Tracey, pleased she hadn't had to resort to any form of medical intervention, no matter how much it had hurt at the time.

"But it was all worth it in the end, wasn't it?" she said, suddenly thinking about *everything* she'd been through on her long journey towards motherhood. "Otherwise I wouldn't have you, now... would I?"

Tracey's thoughts were interrupted by a little knock on the door and she looked up to see one of the nurses cheerfully bobbing her head into the room.

"You have a visitor," she said, smiling as she stepped to one side to let the caller in.

However, when Jonathan then showed himself, sheepishly hovering in the doorway as if waiting for his wife to actually invite him in, Tracey could see this wasn't the kind of coming together that the young woman had been anticipating – the nurse's smile beginning to fade somewhat as a result.

"I'll leave you to it then, shall I?" said the nurse, before awkwardly disappearing off again.

Left with just Jonathan standing there, all forlorn and pitiful as he was, Tracey wasn't sure if she should seize the opportunity to let rip for all the crap he subjected her to, or simply cry with relief that he had, at last, made an appearance.

"Better late than never, eh?" she said, not really all that amused.

Part of her wanted him to rush over and hug the hell out of both her and their new baby, with nothing but a mouth full of promises that everything was going to be alright.

It was pretty evident by now, however, that that wasn't, in fact, part of her husband's plan; that without her explicit permission, he'd already ventured as far into the room as he dared go. As a result, another part of Tracey was left saying he didn't deserve to play happy families anyway and that all he was really worthy of, was her punishment.

And what better way to get back at him, she thought to herself. *Than not letting him anywhere near.*

"Tracey, I'm sorry," said Jonathan, finally finding his voice.

Nevertheless, Tracey was determined it was going to take a lot more than 'sorry' to make up for what he'd done.

"For what?" she asked. "For choosing people you haven't seen in years over your own wife? Or for leaving me nothing but a note, instead of telling me to my face where you were off to?"

"Or..." she continued. "Could it be that you're sorry for leaving me to give birth on my own. And all because you thought it was more important to have a good catch up with your long, lost mates?"

She could see Jonathan was squirming, that he was genuinely upset over what he'd put her through and even more so, that he wasn't quite sure if he was really meant to be answering these questions.

The trouble was, she wasn't sure if she, herself, wanted a response either; if this was still just her hormones venting, or the distress of the last few days finally catching up with her, once and for all?

Albeit, as she looked down at her innocent newborn, what she did know was that her baby deserved more than this. That she shouldn't be quibbling over what was, to all intents and purposes, nothingness, at least compared to the more crucial issues at play here. Moreover, if she and Jonathan were ever going to provide a proper, loving family life for Tuesday at all, there were other more important questions that needed to be asked... and other more important answers that needed to be given.

"Then again," she gently said, turning a now more tender gaze on her husband. "It could also be because you have a sister who you chose not to say anything about..."

CHAPTER SEVENTY-FIVE

ENGLISH ROSE

Tracey had often seen her husband with a moving, far away look in his eye, but she'd never seen him appear *so* sad and dejected before. It was heart breaking stuff and almost feeling a bit guilty, she couldn't stand it any longer.

"Aren't you going to come and say hello?" she said, by way of an olive branch.

However, it wasn't until he self-consciously accepted it, anxiously approaching to take a seat next to her, that she could see just how positively worried he was.

And not just because of how things were between the two of them, she realised.

Seeing his awkward unease as she carefully handed their baby over to him, it was almost as if he didn't think he should be holding his own child at all. Or that if he wasn't ultra careful enough, he was somehow really going to break this tiny little person before him. Hence, there he sat as a result, frozen stiff, whilst holding Tuesday with the utmost of delicateness, seemingly too scared to move just in case.

Not that she didn't appreciate her husband's fears. Although, she doubted very much he'd be looking quite so scared, had he been there to witness the robustness with which their baby had tackled the birth canal; or, indeed, the strength and power, with which Tuesday had flown out of her nether regions.

On the other hand, now probably wasn't the time to be giving him a blow by blow account of her birthing experience, she told herself and quietly watching Jonathan bond with his first born, she knew it was far too special a moment to spoil with all the nitty gritty.

"She's beautiful..." he finally whispered, his eyes full of awe as he, at last, looked from the baby in his arms, to Tracey. "Just like you."

In that one, near perfect instant, Tracey found herself unable to help but hold his gaze... before the spell was finally broken.

"It was Andrea who told me," she said. "About Melanie..."

Despite the sadness returning to his eyes, she knew this was something they really needed to talk about.

"I guessed as much," he replied.

"But I don't understand," she continued. "Why keep something like your sister to yourself? Why Brighton? Why put us through all this?"

She could see this was difficult for him, but on what was supposed to be one of the happiest days of her life, it was hard for her too. Furthermore, under the circumstances these were fair enough questions, she had to tell herself, tears springing into her eyes as she waited for Jonathan to speak.

"It's hard to explain," he said. "But the last thing I wanted was to let you down..."

Be that as it may, it wasn't as if this told Tracey what had been going on in his head. Then again, she realised, how did he sum up not just his behaviour this weekend, but his silence throughout all these years?

"But don't you see..." said Tracey. "In buggering off to the seaside the way you did, in keeping your sister a secret, that's exactly what you've done. And I don't even know the reasons behind any of it."

She paused in an attempt to gather herself.

"Am I that hard to talk to, Jonathan?" she asked.

"None of this is because of you," he replied. "It's just that when Melanie died I thought it was my fault. Because I didn't protect her enough. And I didn't want you to know that about me... I didn't want you thinking I was some kind of failure, who couldn't even look after his own sister let alone you, as my wife. And then when we got pregnant, I was so scared of not being able to look after you *and* the baby, of something happening to you both... that it sort of took over. And it was easier to pretend none of this was happening..."

"I don't suppose any of this is making sense," he continued. "But it's how I was feeling and then Brighton came up. The last place me and Melanie had been to before the accident and I just thought by going, I might be able to sort my head out. Come to terms with things, you know... and you'd already said you didn't want me to and although I understood why, it was like I had to go anyway..."

"Hence, the note?" said Tracey.

"But don't you see, if I'd have told you I was gonna make this trip no matter what you thought, I'd have had to tell you everything. And I wasn't ready for that. Not then."

"And was it the right thing to do? Did going to Brighton help? Or are you telling me all this now, simply because I already know some of it from Andrea? Or because it's a good way of excusing the fact that you missed our child's birth?"

She knew that last question would sting, but she still needed an answer, regardless.

"Tracey, I'm sorry I wasn't here. I'm sorry for everything. But yes, it was the right thing to do, I just need you to let me prove it. Prove that I can finally be a good husband now everything's out in the open. Prove I can be a good dad and that I can take care of you both."

Tracey felt saddened by all the emotional turmoil he'd been going through all these years; by the fact that he hadn't felt able to share it with her.

"So what now?" he asked, desperately hopeful.

"I suppose we try and work through it," she replied. "Not just for our sakes, but for Tuesday's as well."

She could see her husband's relief was immeasurable, placing a reassuring hand on his arm.

"I do love you," she said. "I just wish you could've talked to me."

Another knock at the door interrupted them and Tracey looked up to see a giant teddy bear bobbing its head into the room and she couldn't help but let out a little laugh. "Can we come in?" said a voice, one that sounded remarkably similar to Andrea's.

"Of course you can," replied Tracey, glad of the light relief that Andrea, Megan and The Ace Face had brought with them.

"Everything okay?" she asked, cautiously stepping forward.

Tracey looked at Jonathan. "Everything's fine," she gently replied.

Then, as she looked back to her visitors, she suddenly realised they were an individual down.

"Where's Mickey P.?" she asked, curious.

"You don't want to know," laughed Megan.

"Let's just say you're not the only one to have an eventful morning," added Andrea, deciding it was now her turn to hold the baby.

Bemused, Tracey looked to her husband for an explanation. "Sounds ominous," she said.

"I'll tell you later," he replied.

"So..." said Andrea. "Having never been any good at guessing games, am I holding a beautiful baby boy? Or the prettiest of baby girls?"

EPILOGUE

THE COMMUNICATOR

"Go on then..." urged Tracey.

In contrast to her husband, she was more than happy for him to hand their baby over to the Vicar. Not that she couldn't understand Jonathan's reluctance, she also had to admit; especially considering the guy's somewhat nerve racking performance at Malcolm's funeral.

However, she did suppose the last thing *anyone* wanted was for him to accidentally drop Tuesday, head first, into the font. Although to be fair, with all traces of the Clergyman's stutter now replaced with an appearance of organised control, she couldn't really foresee anything like that happening anyway. Unlike her husband, it seemed, but if they wanted to see this christening through to its conclusion, what choice did her other half have?

She couldn't help but smile as he finally did as he was told – even if he did then go on to tensely anticipate the Vicar's every move, ready to jump forward for the save should the worst, indeed, happen. But knowing that she was one of the lucky ones when it came to joint child rearing, she couldn't help but feel proud at how seriously he did take his parental responsibilities.

After all, there was no way *he* was ever going to shy away from changing messy nappies like some dads did, she acknowledged. Or complain about helping out with the night feeds when she was tired. Moreover, he always made sure he was around at bath time, racing home from work of an evening, now simply a part of his daily routine...

Content, she returned her attention to the Vicar.

"Baby Ruby Melanie," he began, preparing to pour his first scoop of water over the top of Tuesday's head. "I baptise you in the name of the Father..."

Tracey looked to the Godparents whilst he got on with it and it seemed they, too, were equally as nervous as Jonathan. However, right from the start they'd made it clear they understood their role was a serious undertaking as well – particularly The Ace Face and Megan, she noted; who'd been plying Tuesday with the most outrageous and unnecessary gifts from day one.

Although what on earth she'd want with a push bike at her tender age, even with the stabilizers, thought Tracey, to this day not quite able to get her head round their thinking on that one. *Still, it is the thought that counts... and he has agreed to Tuesday calling him Uncle Roger rather than Uncle Ace, or Uncle Face,* she conceded.

"And of the son..." continued the Vicar, thankfully and once again, successfully pouring his second lot of holy water over her baby's head.

She felt a nudge from an excited Andrea, who Tracey had to admit looked very much the part not just in her brand spanking new dress, but in her brand spanking new dress that Mickey P. had actually paid good money for. His now 'legal' outlook on life being something that the both of them were very, very much proud of.

In fact, ever since he was released from his short prison sentence and from what Tracey had heard it was only short thanks to Pepper all of a sudden going soft in the head, Mickey P. had proved himself a changed man. The very reason Tracey had agreed to Jonathan's request for him to be a God Father in the first place. That, and the fact that it was another way of saying thanks to Andrea who, by all accounts, had also been put through the mill on the day Tuesday was born.

"And of the Holy Spirit..." said the Vicar, finishing with his third and final scoop of water.

But instead of feeling the need to join in with the collective sigh of relief now that part of the service had concluded without infant injury, Tracey was just happy to carry on contemplating everything that had happened since Malcolm's funeral.

She looked around at all her guests as a result, satisfied with how things had turned out in the end.

And where one life has ended, she couldn't help but think to herself, not just taking into account physical issues of existence and bereavement, but also new beginnings. *Another life has just begun.*

CPSIA information can be obtained at www.ICGtesting.com
Printed in the USA
LVOW131405031111

253399LV00001B/27/P